Death
Crashes
the Party

WITHDRAWN

Death
Crashes
the Party

Vickie Fee

KENSINGTON PUBLISHING CORP.
http://www.kensingtonbooks.com

KENSINGTON BOOKS are published by

Kensington Publishing Corp.
119 West 40th Street
New York, NY 10018

All Kensington Titles, Imprints, and Distributed Lines are available at special quantity discounts for bulk purchases for sales promotions, premiums, fund-raising, and educational or institutional use. Special book excerpts or customized printings can also be created to fit specific needs. For details, write or phone the office of the Kensington special sales manager: Kensington Publishing Corp., 119 West 40th Street, New York, NY 10018, attn: Special Sales Department, Phone: 1-800-221-2647.

Kensington and the K logo Reg. U.S. Pat & TM Off.

ISBN-13: 978-1-4967-0062-9
ISBN-10: 1-4967-0062-7
First Kensington Mass Market Edition: January 2016

eISBN-13: 978-1-4967-0063-6
eISBN-10: 1-4967-0063-5
First Kensington Electronic Edition: January 2016

10 9 8 7 6 5 4 3 2 1

Printed in the United States of America

For John, who always believed

Acknowledgments

I offer my heartfelt thanks to the Lord for his goodness, to my husband and first reader for his unflagging support, to my family for their love, to Melissa and Patty for their contagious enthusiasm, and to my agent, Jessica Faust, for bringing a dream to reality.

Chapter 1

Monday was a scorching August day that had turned into hell for me when the Farrell brothers crashed a party that already had disaster written all over it.

I was repeating the dreadful details for the umpteenth time to Sheriff Eulyse "Dave" Davidson.

At 10:00 a.m. I met yet again with the Erdmans to continue negotiations for their fortieth-anniversary party. Making all Mrs. Erdman's peculiar dreams come true, while still pacifying her husband, was a complicated balancing act—like spinning plates on poles. This is a skill every good party planner must learn.

Mrs. Erdman, her red hair sticking out in barbed curls, sat on a chintz sofa in the couple's expansive living room. We discussed every tedious detail of a moonshine- and magnolias-themed party. Mr. Erdman sat in a recliner, paying scant attention to anything that didn't require personal effort on his part.

In a nutshell—the Erdmans being the nuts—she

wanted an elegant party with frills, fancy foods, and elaborate decorations. Mr. Erdman wanted to wear comfortable clothes and drink lots of liquor. So he and his buddies would sample generous servings of different whiskeys, including moonshine from his cousin Vern's still. The ladies would dress as Southern belles, sip mint juleps, and listen to a Dixieland band on the veranda. The men, at the insistence of Mr. Erdman, would be dressed as bootleggers. Picture *O Brother, Where Art Thou?* We finally ironed out a major wrinkle when Mr. Erdman acquiesced to one dance with his wife. Hopefully, the other husbands would follow suit.

Mrs. Erdman's most recent vision for the party—and she'd had many—included ice sculptures. She wanted a giant forty perched atop a 1973 Plymouth Barracuda carved in ice, which would be displayed on the buffet table, with icy bare-butted cherubs to either side. The Barracuda was the car they took on their honeymoon. Not sure about the cherubs, but ours is not to reason why. After consulting with the ice sculptor, I now had to figure out how to store 250 pounds of ice—in August—so it wouldn't melt before the party. Although the Erdmans had two refrigerators with freezers in their kitchen, they were nowhere near large enough to accommodate the sculptures.

Mrs. Erdman offered that they had a deep freezer in the garage, which stored her husband's bounty of venison and catfish from his hunting and fishing exploits. She assured me that any game left in the freezer could be given away to friends and neighbors to make way for the sculptures. Mr. Erdman didn't dispute her assertion. I followed them into the garage, with tape measure in hand, to make sure the freezer could contain the ice sculptures.

"And . . . well, you know what happened next."

"Humor me," Dave said, with absolutely no sympathy for the day I was having. So I went through it—again.

I opened the freezer to measure the interior. Unfortunately, what we beheld was the frosty remains of Darrell Farrell, staring up at us like a fresh-caught walleye.

Mrs. Erdman screamed and ran back into the house. Her rotund husband stood for a moment, stunned. I backed away from the freezer, looking at a still slack-jawed Walter Erdman, trying to think of something to say. Instead, I tripped, knocking over a big green garbage can, and found myself sprawled on top of Darrell's very dead brother, Duane, who had toppled out with the trash. He was wearing what for the life of me looked like a Confederate uniform.

Walter Erdman screamed like a young girl and ran across the three-car garage and back into the house. I'd never seen anyone haul that much ass in one load. The Erdmans, who had the nerve of a bad tooth, had left me to deal with the problem at hand, despite the fact that it was not my house and it was definitely not my party. I dialed 911.

After phoning the police, I went into the house to let my clients know the sheriff was on his way. I found Mr. Erdman in his study, stretched out on a leather sofa, staring at the ceiling and clutching a bottle of Scotch. Sobs from the hallway indicated Mrs. Erdman had locked herself in the powder room.

"I went to the entry hall and sat on the stairs, waiting to open the door when you arrived."

The only fortunate aspect of this tiresome inquisition was that Sheriff Dave was conducting it in the air-conditioned comfort of the Erdmans' roomy kitchen, appointed with gleaming commercial-grade appliances and marble countertops. I helped myself to a Diet Coke from the under-counter fridge stocked with bottled water and soft drinks.

"Dave, you want something to drink?"

No, ma'am. I'm good."

Presumably to emphasize that this was official business, Dave made a point of calling me "Mrs. McKay" and "ma'am," instead of "Liv," despite the fact that we'd long been on a first-name basis. Tall, lean, and not bad looking, our normally genial sheriff could, nonetheless, present an imposing demeanor when he had a mind to.

"I know you didn't ask me, Sheriff Davidson," I said, following his cue on formality, "but, despite the fact the bodies were found at their house, which would naturally make them prime suspects, I can honestly testify that the Erdmans were both completely shocked by the discovery."

"Can't rule anything or anyone out at this juncture, but I take your point," he said.

After he finally stopped probing my brain for details, I had to ask, "Dave, do you have any idea why Duane was wearing a Confederate uniform?"

"He and his brother were both involved with one of those Civil War reenactment units," he said. "As to why he was dressed out in uniform, I can't say. They've got some big reenactment event coming up in a few weeks." He went on. "Now, let me ask you a question, Ms. McKay. You seem to keep your ear to the ground. Do you have any idea who might have had a reason to kill the Farrell boys?"

"Seems obvious to me, Sheriff," I said. "It must have been some damn Yankee."

Dave did not seem at all amused.

Chapter 2

After Dave finally allowed me to leave the crime scene, I went to my office. Not that I felt like working and not that anybody would let me get any work done. My phone rang all afternoon, and I contended with questions from inquiring minds. Apparently, everyone in the miniscule town of Dixie, Tennessee, had heard about the murders. And most of the nubs on the grapevine knew as much about the case as I did.

Liv 4 Fun, the party-planning business of which I am the owner and only full-time employee, is operated from a second-floor office above Sweet Deal Realty on Town Square. Our motto is "We plan so you can party." I rent the space from Nathan Sweet, who owns the real estate business, as well as the building. Liv 4 Fun has a separate entrance. My street frontage is literally the width of the plate-glass door, which opens to a steep staircase leading to my modest office.

After fielding phone calls for as long as I could bear, I switched on the answering machine, locked the front door, and went into the real estate office, which is both downstairs and next door, depending on how you look at it. Since there isn't a restroom in the upstairs space, my rent includes access to the facilities in my landlord's business for me and my clients. Such is life in a small town.

Winette King, the only agent besides Nathan Sweet who works at Sweet Deal Realty, gave me a sympathetic look as I collapsed into a chair facing her desk.

"Girl, I hear you had quite the morning."

Mr. Sweet wandered out of his back office, which is crammed so full of files and signs and other miscellanies that it looks more like a storage room. He sat down at the desk next to Winette's and launched into a story of how he once discovered a body while giving a house tour to prospective buyers.

"Not murder, like you came across this morning. Turned out to be natural causes," he said, stroking the stubble on his chinless jaw and gazing up at the acoustical tile ceiling. "Still, the sight of Mrs. Woods in the bathtub, gray and bloated as a beached whale, nixed what had seemed like a sure sale. Mind you, the sight of Mrs. Woods naked would have frightened away the buyers even if she hadn't been dead."

Mr. Sweet got up from his chair. The bell rang as he opened the front door, and he ambled across the street, where he joined a group of old men chatting in front of the barbershop.

"Is that man for real?" Winette asked rhetorically after he had gone. "Sometimes I think I'm working in a nuthouse. And I don't know what you're even doing here, Liv. You know anybody who sees you is just going to pump you for information about those poor dead boys. Speaking of which, if your clients, the whatsits . . . ?"

"The Erdmans," I said.

"Yeah, the Erdmans. If they didn't kill those young men, it seems to me someone who really hated the Erdmans must have killed them. Why else would someone leave bodies in *their* garage, instead of dumping them in the river?"

"I had the same thought. But Dave said it was actually a pretty handy spot to stash a body. You know what that neighborhood's like—a big cul-de-sac of McMansions. I'd never thought about it, but it has a service road running behind the properties that's used by lawn maintenance, landscapers, pool cleaners, and such. Apparently, workers are coming and going all the time. Dave says anyone with a work truck who looked like they knew what they were doing could have plopped a dead body in a wheelbarrow, thrown a tarp and a bag of fertilizer on top of it, and rolled it right up to the garage without anyone taking notice."

"I'll keep that in mind if I ever have a body to get rid of." Winette took a mirrored compact from her desk drawer and carefully painted on a fresh layer of violet lipstick, a shade that nicely complemented her creamy caramel complexion. She tidied her desk, scooping papers into her briefcase and dropping her cell phone and reading glasses into her purse. "I'm going to get my nails done. I got a date tonight. And you should go home."

"You're probably right," I said, rising from the chair and following her out the front door. She flipped the sign on the door to CLOSED.

I watched as Winette walked away confidently in heels higher than I'd dare to wear, her ample hips accentuated by a snugly fitting skirt. Mr. Sweet and the other men evidently had retreated into the air-conditioned barbershop.

I got into my car and backed away from the curb. But I didn't go home.

Chapter 3

After arriving at Di's trailer, I sat in a pink and green lawn chair on the deck that serves as her front porch, a small green awning providing a patch of shade. I had a key Di had given me in case she ever locked herself out. Truth was, I hadn't even checked to see if the door was locked. I would have felt kinda funny about going in without at least calling first, even though Diane Souther and I had been best friends for years.

I watched as a steady stream of Di's neighbors in Sunrise Mobile Village arrived home from work. Weary office types and blue-collar workers emerged from cars, many with young children in tow, presumably just collected from day care. I could hear the squeals and laughter of youngsters playing by the duck pond, which was obscured from my sight by a towering privet hedge badly in need of a trim. A chubby-faced girl wearing a pink gingham sundress hurried toward the entrance to the pond, trailed by an elderly woman toting a Wonder Bread bag, no doubt containing scraps of stale white bread to feed the ducks. Another young girl, who looked to be four or five, skipped past Di's place, pausing just long enough to give me a shy little wave.

Di swung her big old Buick onto the gravel parking pad she shares with her neighbor, Jake Robbins. She juggled a couple of grocery bags, flinging her strawberry-blond hair over her shoulder, as she stepped out of the car. We're both blondes, of sorts. Hers is of the strawberry variety, while mine is more a dishwater shade—or what my mama refers to as cocker spaniel blond.

"If you're trying to evade the police, you'd be safer sitting inside. Although I think even the cops would be smart enough to look for you here."

She handed me one of the bags and twisted a key in the lock. I followed Di, who stands several inches taller and weighs at least several pounds less than I do, into the open kitchen/dining/living area.

"I hope there's liquor in one of those bags," I said, dropping the bag on the counter and plopping myself into a faux-suede recliner. "This day's been one long turd."

"There's some rum in the cabinet and a bag of strawberries in the freezer," Di said. "If you want, I'll whip up some daiquiris in the blender."

This was by far the best offer I'd had all day. Di stood on tiptoe to reach the cabinet over the refrigerator. I wondered why people keep their liquor on a high shelf. Maybe the logic is if it's a little harder to reach, they'll drink less, although personally the extra effort just makes me thirstier.

The blender noisily mangling ice was a soothing sound.

Di, still in her mail carrier uniform, handed me a

frozen concoction, then stretched out on the couch, her taut and tanned legs extending from Bermuda shorts, and took a sip of her own beverage.

"I heard that the Erdmans' house was infested with dead people."

"Yeah. As if the Erdmans weren't already spooky enough. Di, you know I rarely complain about paying clients. Ninety-nine percent of the time, I love my job, but . . . ," I said, my voice trailing off.

"Some clients are just going to be a horse's patootie, no matter what you do," she said.

"Usually even picky clients don't bother me. I know I'm helping them plan an occasion that's really important to them and they just want it to be right. I guess the thing is, I can almost always exceed even the most difficult clients' expectations. I take pride in that. The chances of my exceeding Mrs. Erdman's expectations are basically diddly-squat."

Di related how it had taken forever to finish her mail route, what with every busybody along the way talking about the murders.

"Are they positive it was murder?" she asked.

"Seems unlikely Darrell Farrell would just crawl inside a deep freezer and die."

"It has been awful hot," Di posited.

I explained how his brother, Duane, had been stuffed inside a big trash can and filled her in on other unpleasant details, including the barrage of phone calls at the office, Mr. Sweet once finding a dead woman in a bathtub, and Sheriff Dave questioning me for what seemed like hours on end.

Di perked up at the mention of Dave's name, then tried to shrug it off. She and the local lawman had been doing an awkward mating dance for the past year or so. If they'd actually consummated their obvious attraction, both had done a good job of keeping it mum.

"Somebody told me one of those Farrell boys worked at McKay Trucking. I suppose the sheriff questioned Larry Joe and your father-in-law about their dead employee?"

"He's probably already talked to Daddy Wayne, but Larry Joe's at a sales conference in Little Rock until tomorrow. I called to let him know what had happened as soon as Dave let me go. I knew Darrell Farrell worked at McKay's as a mechanic, but Larry Joe told me the younger brother, Duane, had also worked there in maintenance for like a year."

"I sure feel sorry for their mama," Di said. "Can't imagine what it's like to lose both your kids like that."

"Do you know her?"

"Just to speak to. Her name's Tonya. She works as a waitress at that place up on the highway, Rascal's Bar and Grill, which is more bar than grill."

Di and I drained the remains of our daiquiris with a noisy and nearly simultaneous slurp. I picked up the empty glasses and walked to the blender for refills.

"Oh, Lord," Di said. "I just remembered. Donna at the Quick Stop was telling me that Tonya Farrell won big just a couple days ago down in Tunica. Won something like ten or fifteen thousand dollars at one of the casinos. What a turn of luck she's had, huh?"

"Yeah. I guess she'll probably have to use her winnings for funeral expenses now."

After we had finished off a couple of blenders' worth of daiquiris liberally laced with rum, I decided to accept Di's offer to sleep on her sofa instead of driving home. Larry Joe was out of town until tomorrow, anyway.

I dreamed that I opened a deep freezer and hundreds of rats came scrambling out of it. I tried to run, but there was a huge gray snake wrapped around my legs, making it impossible to move. And the snake was whistling "Dixie."

I woke up with a cotton mouth and a throbbing head. Di had left me half a pot of coffee and a note saying to help myself to toast or cereal. After sucking down enough coffee to clear the cobwebs, I drove home and took two aspirin and a long hot shower.

I made it to my office a few minutes after nine and returned a couple of phone calls on my answering machine. Some fool had left a message asking if I knew of a deep freezer he could buy cheap.

I called back one of the guests for the Erdmans' party about scheduling a fitting for their costumes, which the Erdmans were picking up the tab for. Most of the women were renting Southern belle dresses and parasols and such. Although, one lady was planning to wear the bridesmaid's dress she had worn for the Erdmans' wedding forty years ago. I surmised she wanted to flaunt the fact that she could still fit into it. And some of the men were actually renting hillbilly outfits, instead of just buying a pair of overalls at the Tractor Supply Company, which seemed more practical to me. But, come to think of it, if the Erdmans' friends were anything like Mrs. Erdman, practicality wouldn't be a likely trait.

As a professional party planner, it's my job to indulge fantasies—to a point. I once backed out of a job that involved planning a bacchanalian orgy because the hosts wanted to get a little too literal with the theme for my comfort.

After checking with the shopkeeper, I gave a call back to Mrs. Lockhart and offered a choice of three different times for fittings with the costume shop in Memphis. Most of the guests lived in the Memphis area, about forty-five miles from Dixie. But I also had to arrange for costumes and fittings for one couple in Little Rock and one in Nashville at costume shops close to them.

Mrs. Lockhart expressed concern that the Erdmans might want to cancel or postpone the party on account of their "recent troubles." I knew there was no way Mrs. Erdman was going to nix the party. I assured Mrs. Lockhart that the Erdmans wouldn't want to disappoint their guests and that, since the party was still three weeks away, all the unpleasantness should be cleared up by then. I think I convinced her, but I was having trouble convincing myself.

I thought about phoning Mrs. Erdman but couldn't quite muster the courage. I had a feeling that she was still popping Valium at this point and that it might be wise to wait another day or two before risking a conversation.

I tried to concentrate on work, but nothing could take my mind off the horrifying images of the Farrell brothers lying dead in the Erdmans' garage. A little before noon, I finally decided to drive over to McKay Trucking and talk to Ralph Harvey. Maybe he could tell me something about them. After all, I was the one who had had the gruesome pleasure of discovering the bodies—and I figured that at least entitled me to a few answers. Besides, maybe there was something we could do to help their mom.

I don't know what his title is exactly, but basically Ralph Harvey oversees the diesel truck mechanics, along with the maintenance and janitorial staff. My father-in-law manages administrative, freight, and shipping matters. And Larry Joe, who co-owns the company with his dad, mostly handles sales and deals with clients.

About a half mile out of town the pavement devolves into a minefield of potholes. I pulled up the gravel driveway, heading through the open gate in the chain-link fence and past the whitewashed concrete-block building that contains my husband's and father-in-law's offices. After circling around to the back, I parked beside the gray metal buildings that house the garage and warehouse.

Ralph's office is upstairs, along one side of the hangar-like building, with a wall of glass and a bird's-eye view of everything going on down below. The din of motors and clanging wrenches, punctuated by staccato bursts of compressed air, was muffled as he closed the door behind us. Ralph Harvey is a barrel-chested man with a face as red as what little hair he has left on top of his head. I accepted Ralph's offer to sit down but declined his offer of coffee after observing a pot that had probably never been washed.

"I hate to bother you when I know you're short-handed. But with Larry Joe out of town, I just wanted to stop by and see how everyone's holding up after yesterday's tragedy. How are the guys in the shop taking it?"

"It was a shock, ma'am, sure enough. Darrell had worked his way up to lead B mechanic in just a couple of years. The younger one wasn't quite right, you know, a little slow. But he did good work. He was only twenty. . . ." Ralph's voice trailed off.

"It's hard enough to imagine one of them getting murdered, but why in the world would someone kill both of them?"

"All I can say is where one of 'em was, the other one went along. They worked together and shared an apartment. And it seems they got killed together, too."

We both sat there for a moment, sharing an awkward silence.

"Ralph, I know it's none of my business, but had they gotten into any kind of trouble? You know, with drugs or some girl who had a protective daddy?"

"No, ma'am. They never had any run-ins with the law that I know of. I'm pretty sure they smoked some weed. Most of the young guys here do. But it never interfered with their work, which is all I care about."

I was a bit taken aback by Ralph's lax attitude toward drug use. It was not what I would have expected from him.

"I thought random drug screenings were performed on the employees?"

"Just the drivers," he said. "If they all had to pass drug screens, especially the casual labor, I'd never be able to find enough hands to load the trucks."

"Well, I won't keep you," I said, grabbing my purse and rising from the chair. "Is there anything we can do for Mrs. Farrell? I don't ever remember hearing of a Mr. Farrell."

"Their daddy died in the Iraq War, when they were just little kids. But if you don't mind, you could do me a favor. I had Charlene cash out Darrell's and Duane's last checks. If you wouldn't mind taking the envelope by to their mama. I figure she can use the money and . . . ," Ralph said, stammering a bit. "Well, you could talk to her better, you being a lady."

Ralph obviously didn't want to get stuck with Mrs. Farrell crying on his shoulder. But at least it gave me a legitimate reason to go by and talk to her.

"Sure, Ralph. I'd be glad to."

"Thank you, ma'am. Her address is on the envelope. And Mr. Wayne called the funeral director and told him if Mrs. Farrell needs help with expenses to let him know. He also said we could give the employees time off for the funeral, once the arrangements are made."

Larry Joe's dad is a piece of work. But deep down he's just an old softy.

I headed out to see Tonya Farrell. I continued along a pothole-studded road for a bit before leaving the semi-paved roads of civilization and making a right turn onto a gravel road. I plunged into the recesses of Delbert County, where a soul can drive for miles without seeing a house or another car. Miles of woods and fields and ancient twisted oaks. And the occasional stray dog or chickens in the road.

Spying a mailbox up ahead, I slowed down until I spotted a dirt driveway leading to the Farrell house. The old farmhouse had a broad porch fronted with a tangle of camellia bushes, which were badly in need of pruning. It could use a coat of paint, but the house looked sturdy.

Tonya Farrell appeared on the porch as soon as I stepped out of the car. Whatever I had expected her to look like, she didn't. She was tall, with shoulder-length bleached hair, and a sleeveless T-shirt revealed athletic arms.

Before I could introduce myself, she said, "You're Liv McKay, aren't you?"

"Yes," I stammered, a little surprised. "Did Ralph Harvey call to tell you I was coming?"

"Naw. I've seen your pictures in the paper. You have that party-planning business, right? I figured you must be related to the McKays at the trucking company. Come on in," she said, propping open the screen door with her back and motioning for me to go through.

At her invitation, I took a seat on a floral sofa that looked almost as old as the house. Tonya sat down in a chair across from me. An air conditioner rattled and hissed from a window on the far side of the room. I scanned the walls and mantel, looking for childhood photos of her sons. But there were none.

"I'm so very sorry for your loss."

"Thank you. I thought maybe my luck had turned. I won a few dollars down at the casino recently. Just goes to show, I guess."

"I can't imagine how difficult this must be for you."

"It's hard, of course, losing both my boys. But I tell myself Duane—that's my youngest—would've been lost without Darrell. Duane was a sweet boy, but even I knew he wasn't the brightest bulb on the porch. Darrell always looked out for him. . . ." Her voice trailed off.

"It's nice when brothers are close like that," I said. "I understand, in addition to working together, they were both involved in those Civil War reenactments."

"Lord, yes. They'd been playing soldier since they were old enough to walk. Mind you, that wasn't my doing. After their dad died in the Iraq War, I didn't want to think about anything like that. But their pawpaw, my granddaddy, told them all these stories about the Civil War and took them on trips to Shiloh, helped them stage battles with toy soldiers.

"Duane wasn't as athletic as his brother, but he liked to draw and write stuff. My grandma gave Duane the journal of a Civil War soldier, which, she said, had belonged to her grandfather. Duane was fascinated with it and started keeping a journal of his own, still does, er . . . did, anyway."

I noticed she was fidgeting with a teardrop diamond necklace. The sunlight reflecting off it confirmed it was the real thing, not cubic zirconia. I conjectured that it might have been a gift to herself from her casino winnings.

After a pause, she looked at me and said, "I heard you're the one that found them."

I didn't quite know how to respond to that, so I finally just said, "Yes."

She stood and continued talking with her back to me. "I guess I wish you could tell me that they looked peaceful or that they didn't suffer, but . . . maybe the medical examiner can say when he's done."

I laid the envelope on the coffee table and told her it contained her sons' pay.

"We all get what's coming to us, one way or another," she said. "I plan to move away after all this is settled. There's not much keeping me here now."

"Ralph Harvey tells me your boys were well liked at McKay's. Please call us if you need any help with the arrangements."

As I stood to leave, my cell phone rang. Caller ID popped up on the screen, indicating it was Larry Joe.

"I should take this," I said apologetically. I stepped out onto the front porch as I answered. I heard some static before the phone went dead.

"That's odd," I said.

"Cell phone reception is pretty spotty out here," Tonya said, standing in the doorway behind me. "You might try calling back once you get over that big hill up on the main road."

On the drive home, I couldn't help thinking about the fact there were no family photos in Tonya's living room. I reasoned that she could have slipped pictures of her sons into a drawer after learning about their deaths. Maybe it was just too painful to look at them. *Besides*, I thought, *I still have a box full of honeymoon photos in the closet I've been meaning to frame for years*.

I walked into the kitchen from the garage to find Larry Joe twisting the cap off a beer bottle. He hopped on his soapbox without even bothering to say hello.

"I've been home an hour, and I already know you've been snooping around at the company garage, asking questions about the Farrells. And I know you didn't come home last night but slipped in this morning, looking like something the cat dragged in."

"That's because Mrs. Cleats across the street is a dang busybody who thinks it's her calling to keep her neighbors under surveillance. And Ralph Harvey has a big mouth."

"It's because we live in a small town," Larry Joe said as he sidled up to me and wrapped his arms around my waist. "Why don't you just tell me what's going on, Liv? You know I'm bound to hear about it, anyway."

I looked up at my husband's cleft chin, dimples, and smiling brown eyes and fought the urge to kiss him. He's not quite George Clooney handsome, but he'll do.

"So are you worried about where I spent the night?" I said, breaking free from his embrace. I backed up to the counter and hoisted myself onto the granite top. From this vantage point, I could look Larry Joe squarely in the eye.

"Not particularly. I told Mrs. Cleats you spent the night at your mama's house after all the excitement yesterday."

"Well, you lied," I said, stretching out the word *lied* as if it had three or four *i*'s. "I spent the night at Di's place after I got stinking drunk and passed out on her sofa."

"See there," he said with a wicked grin. "Doesn't being honest make you feel better?" He walked to the counter, positioned himself between my dangling legs, and began taking liberties—which was exactly what I wanted him to do.

I had planned to cook supper, but after we got

sidetracked for a while, we just called and had pizza delivered. Unlikely as it may sound, pizza is actually a romantic meal for us. We had it on our wedding night. A pizza parlor that delivered was the only place we could find open after we stopped for the night outside Hattiesburg on our way to New Orleans.

Larry Joe was already gone by the time I woke up on Wednesday. He and his dad were meeting with Ralph first thing this morning to address the sudden staff shortage and to make sure freight would get out on time.

I was ravenous and decided cereal just wouldn't cut it. So I dressed and drove to Town Square Diner for a ham-and-eggs-and-biscuits breakfast. Just as I finished giving the waitress my order, Sheriff Dave slid into the booth across from me and said, "I'll have the same."

"So you're having a bit of a late breakfast this morning, too," I said. The clock on the wall indicated it was 8:45 a.m.

"I don't know if this is breakfast or lunch. I've been at it since before five this morning," he said, taking off his hat and raking his fingers through a crop of dark, wavy hair.

"If you're going to ask me to go through the whole discovering-the-bodies story again, you'll have to wait until I've had something to eat. I just don't have the energy for it."

"We can skip that for now. I'm more interested in the fact that you seem to be trailing along behind me, talking to witnesses, and yakking to just about everybody else in town on the phone."

"I haven't followed you anywhere, Sheriff Davidson," I said, feeling pretty put out by his insinuation, especially after the grilling he had put me through on Monday at the Erdmans'. "I went by to see Mrs. Farrell to give her Darrell's and Duane's last paychecks, which I picked up from Ralph Harvey. And I haven't called anyone in the past two days, except Larry Joe. My phone's been ringing off the hook."

"That so?" Dave said, his scowl softening into a smile around the edges.

"Yeah, that's so. A double murder is pretty big excitement for a small town. I can't believe you're surprised it's got everybody talking."

"I just wish all the gabbing I've listened to added up to one solid lead on this case," Dave said, rubbing his eyes. He looked as wrung out as a dishrag. As sheriff of Delbert County, he was responsible for all the unincorporated areas of the county, along with contract coverage of the municipalities that were too small to have their own police department. Since there are only three towns in the county, and Hartville is the only one with its own police force, Dave and his small band of deputies have a lot of ground to cover.

The waitress brought our orders, and we both nearly cleaned our plates before another word was spoken.

I brushed a napkin across my lips. "Dave, the only thing I've heard about the Farrell boys that might have something to do with their deaths is that they apparently liked to smoke marijuana. Maybe they got on the wrong side of their dealer."

"Naw, I'm afraid that's a dead end. The Farrells bought their weed from a kid at the high school who I've had a 'Come to Jesus' talk with on more than one occasion. And I'm pretty sure his grandma is growing the stuff he sells," he sighed and shook his head. "They're a family of morons, but they're not dangerous."

Dave grabbed the check the waitress had left on the table. "I'll take care of this," he said, scooting out of the booth. "You can feel obligated to pass on to me any tidbits of information you pick up that might be pertinent."

I left a couple of dollars on the table, not knowing how much of a tip Dave had included with the bill. I spoke to my mom's next-door neighbor, Bubba Rowland, who was sitting at the counter, then walked across the street and past the courthouse to my office on the other side of the square.

Dixie has a town square like the ones that were once pretty typical in small towns, with a courthouse in the middle, surrounded by businesses and one-way streets on three sides. Our square has fared better than many since the sprawl of suburbia and the advent of big-box stores. We have only one vacant building at the moment. Of course, the theater next door to Sweet Deal Realty used to be a grand movie palace once upon a time. These days its grandeur is a little shabby around the edges, and it's used by the town's community theater group and for local dance recitals and gospel singings. But at least it hasn't been torn down.

What was formerly a good-sized furniture center on the other side of the square is now a storefront church, and the fancy hat shop I remember from my childhood is now a thrift shop. But we still have a diner and a bakery and a drugstore and a beauty salon and other businesses that keep our little downtown area teeming with people during the day, until they roll up the sidewalks at about 6:00 p.m.

I went upstairs and sat down at my desk in the 1950s-era building, with its green-tiled floor and paneled walls, which are painted white. After going over my notes for the Erdmans' party, I phoned the band and the caterer to confirm the date and time and to go over details.

As a party planner, I absolutely depend on a cadre of professionals, from caterers to musicians, from florists to magicians. And I depend just as much on my part-time, as-needed employees, who help me pull it all together, especially Holly Renfrew, assistant extraordinaire.

Wilson Washington, manager and trombonist with the Dixieland band I had hired for the Erdmans' party, confirmed the details and asked me to e-mail him a map to the Erdmans' house.

"The van's got GPS, but I don't trust it. Sometimes it acts crazy, you know?"

"Yes, I've had that experience on occasion, where the GPS voice keeps saying, 'Recalculating,' over and over. And if you do have any problems, you have my cell number. Feel free to call me anytime," I said.

Hiring Washington's Ragtime Band for the party was a real coup. They're top-notch and get booked months in advance. Before Hurricane Katrina, the band was based in New Orleans. They moved to Memphis after the devastating storm and eventually decided to stay.

I finally broke down and phoned Mrs. Erdman. I

was starting to get worried that she had gone so long without calling me. I was surprised when she picked up on the first ring.

"Rose, is that you?"

"Uh, n-no, ma'am," I stuttered. "This is Liv McKay."

"Oh, Liv, I'm sorry. I'm expecting a call from my sister. Why are you calling?"

"I just wanted to touch base. I haven't talked to you since . . ." I paused before adding, "Monday."

"Yes, that was quite a shock," she said. "And what a strange coincidence that both those young men worked for your husband. Don't you think?"

I wasn't sure what she was trying to imply.

"It's been quite a shock for Larry Joe and his dad, that's for certain," I said.

"Yes, I'm sure. Well, hopefully, the sheriff will arrest someone soon, so we can all move on with our lives," she said.

"One of your guests called about a costume fitting. I told her I was certain you would go ahead with the party, not wanting to disappoint your friends. You do want to proceed with the party?"

"Why, yes, of course," she said, sounding put out. "Those unfortunate boys have nothing to do with us. I can't imagine why anyone would leave them in our garage, can you?"

Again, I wasn't sure just what she was implying, but I could feel the hair on the back of my neck stand up.

"No, Mrs. Erdman. I really can't imagine."

"Well, I really can't talk right now, Liv. I'll call you if I think of anything," she said before hanging up abruptly. It chafed me that Mrs. Erdman seemed to imply that my family could have somehow been involved in the murders. But this is a small town, and I knew the dead men's connection to McKay Trucking was bound to fuel gossip.

My nerves were feeling a little frayed, so I decided to give up on work for the day. I'd go home and work on painting my living room ceiling. The never-ending chore of painting our fixer-upper house had become a kind of therapy for me.

Chapter 4

I had the presence of mind to stick my cell phone in my pocket before I climbed up to slather another coat of paint on the ceiling. I didn't, however, have the presence of mind to stick a cloth in my other pocket to clean the paint off my hands. This thought occurred to me as my ringtone started playing. I knew from the tune that it was Larry Joe. I wiped my hands on my T-shirt and answered the phone.

"I heard you had breakfast with another man this morning," Larry Joe said from the other end of the line.

"Don't you have anything better to do than track my every move?" I said, feeling a bit peeved.

"Oh, Dad and I just met a client for lunch at the diner, and Margie mentioned seeing you this morning, that's all."

"Are you jealous?"

"Not really. I figure the sheriff is just zeroing in on you as his prime suspect."

"Unfortunately, I don't think Dave actually has any suspects at this point."

"I'm sure he has his hands full with this one. So do we," he said. "Rumors are starting to circulate that we aren't going to be able to keep up with orders. That's why I'm calling, to tell you not to expect me for supper. Dad wants me to go to the Jaycees dinner and meeting tonight to do some glad-handing and rumor quashing. He's going to his Elks Lodge meeting tonight to do the same."

After he hung up, I tried to remember if Margie was the short, plump waitress or the one with the beehive kind of hair thing going on. If she was the beehive, I regretted leaving her the extra tip.

I heard a knock on the front door, followed by a "Hey, it's me."

"Come on in," I called out.

I heard Di's voice from below as I continued painting the ceiling of my living room a very calming shade of periwinkle. I was at that moment perched on tiptoe on a dining chair that was sitting atop the dining room table, both of which were covered with a painter's drop cloth and a fair amount of paint spatter.

"They've invented these nifty things called ladders that let you reach high places without having to climb on top of a pile of furniture. I like that color, though."

"Thanks. I think I've earned a break," I said, descending from my aerie with as much dignity as I could muster. Judging from Di's suppressed giggles, it wasn't much. I didn't tell Di, but Larry Joe had a ladder up on the second floor. I was just too lazy to haul it down the stairs.

Di followed me into the kitchen, where we popped open a couple of cold ones—Diet Cokes, that is.

"Liv, why the heck are you swinging from a chandelier with a paintbrush, anyway? You really should make Larry Joe do the painting, at least the ceilings."

I knew if I waited for Larry Joe to get around to painting the living room, the walls would be covered with moss. Not that it could be any uglier than the wedding mint-green shade on them already. "I just couldn't stand looking at these walls any longer. Besides, Larry Joe is still busy ripping holes in the upstairs bathroom." I really wanted him to focus on the upstairs bathroom. I was getting tired of having to trek downstairs to take a shower.

"At least the kitchen's beautiful," Di said.

"Yeah." I exhaled a sigh and admired my granite countertops.

It's become a running joke about how nice the kitchen looks. When we bought the rambling Victorian almost two years ago, the previous owners had completely ripped out the kitchen as the first step of a never completed remodel. Not wanting to live in the house without at least some semblance of a kitchen, Larry Joe agreed to hire professionals to do the work. It's likely the only room in the house that will ever be finished. The house was built in 1900, a garage was added in the early 1940s, and an enclosed ramp connecting the garage and the house was added in the 1950s.

The ongoing construction site status of the house

is one of the reasons I keep an office downtown instead of conducting business out of my home. My mother likes to refer to our house as "the nightmare on Elm Street." Okay, so we do live on Elm Street. But I see our somewhat ramshackle painted lady as an unpolished—and badly in need of painting—gem.

Di left to run some errands, and with Larry Joe out of the picture for supper, we agreed to meet for dinner at Taco Belles at a little after 6:30 p.m. After I rinsed the paint off the paintbrush and scrubbed the paint off the rest of me in the downstairs shower, the only working shower in the house, I dressed and headed to the restaurant.

Arriving at the restaurant before Di, I got us a table and ordered a couple of jumbo margaritas. A squashed mosquito adorned the wall next to the booth, its remains plastered beneath an oversize sombrero.

Owned by sisters Maybelle and Annabelle Wythe, probably now in their seventies, Taco Belles doesn't come close to approximating authentic Mexican cuisine. Still, the catfish tacos aren't bad.

"Sorry I'm late," Di said as she slung her purse and then her backside onto the bench seat.

I could tell from her leotard and pajama-style pants that she'd just come from her weekly yoga class. Di walks what must be miles a day on her mail route, so she doesn't really need the additional exercise. But she says pounding the pavement every day does a number on her joints and muscles, and the stretching and toning she gets from yoga is therapeutic, as well as relaxing.

"I haven't been here long. I went ahead and ordered us a couple of margaritas."

"That sounds good. As long as we eat some real food along with our liquor," Di said. "I had a headache yesterday that just wouldn't go away. I think the fact that we consumed huge quantities of daiquiris the other night with only a handful of nibbles probably instigated that headache."

A perky young waitress sat two fishbowl margaritas down in front of us, and we both ordered without bothering to peruse the familiar menu.

"Here's to the hair of the dog that bit you," I said, lifting my oversize glass with both hands.

"You'll never guess who's joined my yoga class."

"Mr. Sweet?" I said facetiously.

"No, but I'd pay to see that."

We both grinned at the thought of my spindly landlord twisting and lunging into some awkward yoga pose.

"Who, then?"

"Deputy Ted Horton."

"Oh, my," I said. "Why would he take up yoga, do you think? Is he keeping an eye on you dangerous subversives?"

"I think he's keeping an eye on us, or at least some of us, all right. I think it's probably a desperate attempt to meet women."

Poor Ted, I thought. He's a thoroughly nice guy. Unfortunately, a picture of him could serve as an apt illustration next to the definition of *pencil-necked geek*.

We had drained about half our fishbowls before the waitress returned with our catfish tacos and a squeeze bottle of chipotle tartar sauce.

I told Di how I'd ended up having breakfast with Sheriff Dave and how a lack of progress in the double-murder case seemed to be weighing pretty heavily on him.

"Oh," Di said, raising her fork to indicate she had more to say as soon as she had swallowed. "Apparently, there's been some progress on the case since this morning. I talked to Dave briefly, and he said they found some interesting stuff in a mini-storage unit rented by Darrell Farrell."

My curiosity was divided between wanting to know more about Di's "brief" conversation with Dave and wanting to know more about the "stuff" at the mini storage. The mystery of the storage unit won out.

"What kind of stuff?"

"Oh, it was all their Civil War reenactment gear and whatnot. But get this," she said, stabbing the air with her fork. "According to one of the reserve deputies who's involved in that kind of thing, a bunch of the clothes and weapons and equipment were the genuine articles, not reproductions. And the Farrell boys wouldn't have been able to amass that kind of collection on their salaries."

"So the sheriff thinks they had a cache of stolen goods?"

"Either that or some high-quality counterfeit stuff that only an expert could tell the difference. Dave has contacted some history professor from the University of Memphis to come look at it all tomorrow. Either way, if they were mixed up with theft or a counterfeit ring, it could be what got them killed," Di said.

"I hope Dave nabs a suspect soon. Today I felt like Mrs. Erdman was trying to imply that I had something to do with the murders, or that Larry Joe did.

The Dixieland band I booked for her party may be playing a funeral march if she keeps it up. She makes me so mad," I said before finishing off my margarita.

"Don't let her get to you, Liv. You already know that woman's a nut."

"It's not just her. I haven't wanted to think about it, but while I've had plenty of calls from nosy gossips, my phone hasn't exactly been ringing off the hook with calls from prospective clients since I discovered the bodies."

After dinner, we ordered some coffee to quell the goose bumps stirred up by the gale-force air-conditioning and to offset the stupefying effect of the jumbo margaritas.

Miss Maybelle delivered the coffee to our table.

"Here's something to warm y'all up," she said, setting down the tray and filling two white ceramic cups with steaming coffee. Her white hair was carefully coiffured, and she was wearing a lightweight cardigan, one almost the same color blue as her eyes. "They nearly freeze me to death in here, but most folks seem to like the air conditioner on high. I think spicy food just makes some people sweat, no matter what the temperature."

Seemingly without taking a breath, Miss Maybelle leaned in to the table and continued in a stage whisper. "Olivia, it must have been just awful for you, finding those young men who went and got themselves killed like that."

"Yes, ma'am. I've had better days."

"It's tragic, of course. But I've always found it to be true that those who come to a violent end most often had a hand in bringing it upon themselves. It's no secret their mama's always been on the wild side. While they were alive, her grandparents did the best they could, but I don't think those boys were brought up properly at all. . . . ," she said, breathing a sigh. "Still, it is sad—and so unfair to you, dear. I certainly hope it doesn't put a damper on your little party business."

Someone or something distracted Miss Maybelle, and she breezed away from the table.

"Lord, help me."

"I wouldn't pay too much attention to Miss Maybelle," Di said. "In case you haven't noticed, she's not the most positive or least judgmental woman in the world."

"Maybe not. But she also has a knack for saying out loud what a lot of other people are probably thinking."

Chapter 5

We paid for dinner at the cash register and grabbed a couple of after-dinner mints after dropping a donation in the jar for the Lions Club to help the sight impaired.

"You feel like walking a bit?" Di said.

"I suppose it wouldn't hurt me to burn off a few of these calories," I said, patting my bulging midsection.

"Good. Well, follow me home, and we can take a stroll through the trailer park."

As we made the short drive to Sunrise Mobile Village, I couldn't help thinking what a misnomer *mobile* was. I've watched Di check the tie-downs before tornado season. The anchoring system underneath the trailer includes steel rods several feet long that screw into the ground and steel straps bolted to the rods that fasten around the trailer frame. Nobody could just hitch one of these trailers to a truck and drive away.

We parked in front of Di's place. I got out of the car and automatically started walking toward the duck pond in the center of Sunrise Mobile, or not so mobile, Village.

"No. Let's head in this direction," Di called to me as she ambled off down a side street leading to the outer circle of the trailer park.

"Are we just walking, or are we going somewhere in particular?" I asked, wondering why Di seemed to be choosing the far less scenic route.

"That depends. If you're still in snooping mode, there's a neighbor around back I thought you might like to have a chat with," she said coyly.

I resented the snooping remark, but I still had to ask, "Who's that?"

We walked leisurely, nothing aerobic—it was still too stifling for a jog or even a power walk. But a warm breeze stirred, mitigating, or at least dispersing, the humidity.

Ray Franklin lived in a section of the trailer park set up for visiting RVs, one with temporary hookups. The section was nearly vacant, except for Ray's old Winnebago and another rusty camper. These dwellings actually were mobile, although looking at the condition of Ray's Winnebago, I had my doubts it would start. There are a few retired couples who park their campers here during the winter to be near relatives and to escape the cold and snow of their homes up north. They're sensible enough, however, not to vacation in the South during the long, hot summer.

Ray Franklin, who looked to be in his early forties, had a military-style haircut and the physique of an ex-athlete who had developed a slight paunch. He also exuded a steady stream of smarm.

"Evenin', ladies. What brings you out this way?"

Ray was sitting in a plastic chair just outside the open door to his camper.

"Just walking off dinner," Di said. "You may remember me. I live here, on the front side. I think we met at the Sunrise Village picnic."

"Oh, yes, ma'am," he said. "I do remember you." His eyes scanned her figure without the least bit of discretion.

"This is my friend Liv McKay."

"How d'ya do?" he said, his snake eyes slithering in the direction of my bosom.

I nodded and forced a smile.

"I'm just having an after-dinner drink. Would you care to join me?"

"We'd better not," Di said. "We had drinks with dinner."

"Suit yourself," he said, tossing an empty beer bottle on the ground and reaching into the ice chest beside his chair to fish out another.

"Liv McKay. I suppose you're the one that found the Farrell brothers," he said knowingly.

"Yes. It was just awful. They were so young. Did you know them?"

"Course I did," he said. "Met 'em through Shiloh company. Kinda showed them the ropes. They were good kids. It's a real shame what happened to them."

"That's what their boss said, that they were good kids. Never in any trouble he knew of . . . . They worked for my husband's family trucking business," I added in explanation.

"It just don't add up. It's like I told the deputy. Duane and Darrell kinda confided in me. I think they saw me as some kind of father figure. I served in the Iraq War, which their daddy died in. Maybe I flatter myself, but I like to think if they'd been in some kind of trouble, they would've told me. I'd have done what I could to help them out. But then, I guess we never know people as well as we think we do."

Despite being a crusty character, Ray spoke about the Farrell brothers with what sounded like a genuine fondness.

"Well, good night," Di said. "We should head back."

"Night, ladies," he said, raising his beer to us.

"Some people are so sleazy, just talking to them makes you feel like you need a shower," I said once we were out of earshot.

"He certainly has a gift for undressing women with his eyes," Di said.

"Do you know where he works?" I asked.

"I've seen him trimming hedges and painting fences here in the park," Di said. "I know he was in the army. Maybe he draws a military pension. What I do know is that he didn't really tell us anything new about the Farrells."

"I'm not so sure."

"What do you mean?" Di asked.

"What was it Ray said? Something like he had 'shown the ropes' to the Farrell boys about reenacting. I'd bet you a dollar to a doughnut that if the Farrells were mixed up in stealing or counterfeiting Civil War artifacts, Ray Franklin was right in the middle of it."

I said good night to Di, drove home, and jumped in the shower. After I had bathed the clinging humidity and the impurity of Ray Franklin's gaze off my body, I slipped on a purple nightshirt that had PARTY GIRL emblazoned across the chest. I had just started filing my nails when Larry Joe walked through the bedroom door, took off his tie, and heaved himself wearily onto the bed.

"Rough night?" I asked, leaning over and giving him a kiss on the forehead.

"I've smiled so much tonight, my face hurts," he said. "Some people act like we won't be able to do business, just because we lost a couple of employees. I'm convinced some of them even think Dad and I were somehow involved in killing those boys."

"Oh, honey. People are just tense because there's a murderer still at large. Things will settle down when Dave has a suspect."

I didn't have the heart to tell him that even Mrs. Erdman seemed to suspect us.

I filled Larry Joe in on what the sheriff had told Di about the possible stolen goods in the storage unit. I circumspectly omitted having talked to Ray Franklin.

"Maybe that's the lead Dave needs to get to the bottom of this whole mess," I said.

"I certainly hope so—and soon," Larry Joe said. "It's starting to get to me, but I'm more worried about Dad. He doesn't need this kind of stress. He's getting to be an old geezer, you know."

"Don't worry about your dad. He's one tough cookie. Why don't you try to get some sleep?"

Larry Joe was gently snoring within seconds of his head hitting the pillow, and I drifted off soon after. About 2:00 a.m. our neighbors' car alarm sounded—again. This occurs more often than I'd like to think about. Sometimes it beeps for five minutes; sometimes it goes on for fifteen minutes or more.

At the sound of the blaring *beep-beep-beep*, Larry Joe shot straight up into a sitting position in the bed.

"I'm going to kill the neighbors," he said drowsily.

"Honey, it's two a.m.," I said, glancing over at the alarm clock. "At least wait until after sunrise to kill them. You wouldn't want to accidentally kill the wrong people."

Larry Joe moaned and stuck his head under his pillow. The alarm fell silent after a few minutes, and Larry Joe fell back asleep in an instant. I wasn't so lucky.

Our neighbors with the pesky car alarm, the Newsoms—Larry Joe and I have dubbed them the Gruesomes—live next door to Mrs. Cleats. If the alarm persists for very long, Mrs. Cleats will often call the sheriff to complain.

Mrs. Gruesome insists that Mrs. Cleats's cat is setting off the alarm by jumping on the hood of the car. Mrs. Cleats insists that she always brings Mr. Winky in the house at night, although we all know she doesn't, and there are frequent litters of kittens that resemble him in the neighborhood to attest to it.

Larry Joe tried talking to Mr. Gruesome on a couple of the rare occasions when the neighbor was sober, and even offered to help him disable the car alarm. Gruesome declined because he said he was afraid it would void the warranty on the car. I think he was more afraid his wife would void his right to breathe.

Chapter 6

Thursday morning it was ninety-eight degrees outside, and I was in the eighth circle of hell, arguing with a man over ice.

The ice sculptor I had employed for the Erdmans' party, who had at first been so charming and accommodating, was now trying to tell me he couldn't deliver the sculptures until the day of the party—an hour and a half before the guests were scheduled to arrive. He had previously assured me that if we had freezer space for the sculptures, they would be delivered at least forty-eight hours before the party.

"Ms. McKay, please be reasonable," he said through the phone. He was lucky I couldn't get my hands on him. "You have my word the sculptures will be delivered not a minute later than five thirty."

"You already gave me your word that they would be delivered Wednesday afternoon. How am I supposed to trust your word when you keep changing it?"

There was no way I could risk having the sculptures delivered at the last minute. What if they cracked in transit? What if one of the cherubs had a crack somewhere other than on his little heinie? Mrs. Erdman would have a meltdown.

My borderline insane client considered these sculptures the crowning glory of her elegant supper buffet, and I was not going to let this guy backpedal on his promised delivery time.

"I'm an artist, Ms. McKay, not an assembly line," he said dismissively.

"The work order for the sculptures, which we both signed off on, stipulates that the sculptures will be delivered by Wednesday afternoon," I said, steam slowly escaping from my ears. "If you cannot fulfill the terms of the contract, then consider it voided, and I'll just have to find another artist."

This was a threat I hoped I wouldn't have to carry through with. Ice sculptors weren't exactly plentiful, and I understood that creating large custom ice pieces involved more than pouring vats of water into great big trays.

"This is the first time I've employed your services, and I'd certainly like to be able to do business with you in the future—and recommend your work to my colleagues and clients," I added.

I knew he wouldn't want to risk bad word of mouth from someone who could continue to bring him business in the future. As a party planner, I carried a little more weight than an individual customer, who was likely to be just a one-off sale.

He silently struggled with his pride for a moment before acquiescing. "You drive a hard bargain, Ms. McKay. I'll have to rearrange our project schedule, but your client's order will be delivered on Wednesday."

I hung up the phone and leaned back in my chair. I felt like I'd already put in a full day's work, and it was only 9:30 a.m. I poured a fresh cup of coffee and allowed myself a few moments to decompress before getting back to work. As I gazed vacantly out the window, a parade of four black sedans driving past the office suddenly captured my attention. I jumped up from my desk, hurried down the stairs, opened the front door, and looked out to see the cars circle around the courthouse and come to a halt in front of the sheriff's office.

I turned around and ran smack into Winette and Mr. Sweet, who were peering over my shoulder.

"I wonder who those unmarked cars belong to," I said.

"It's the Feds," Winette said matter-of-factly. "You can tell by those cheap suits and sunglasses."

A gray-haired man in the lead car, along with his driver, had gone into the sheriff's office, while the others waited outside. By this time, we weren't the only ones watching the spectacle. People from inside the barbershop, the diner, and other businesses were gathering in doorways and spilling out onto the sidewalks, gawking at the entourage.

In a couple of minutes, the sheriff emerged from the building with the gray-haired man and Deputy Ted Horton. A guy in a cheap suit and sunglasses opened the back door of one of the sedans and took the arm of an older man who was handcuffed and helped him out of the car.

Heat waves rising off the asphalt distorted the scene I was watching unfold. For a brief moment, I almost convinced myself it was a mirage, just a trick of the light. Voices behind me brought me back to reality.

Winette said, "Whaaa? Huh?" Mr. Sweet muttered something equally unintelligible.

I rushed into the parking area to get a closer look before gasping, "Daddy Wayne!"

In complete shock, I found myself crumpled on the curb. Then Winette and Mr. Sweet each grabbed one of my arms, helped me up, and led me into their office.

"This can't be happening," I said as Winette brought me a glass of water. "I need to call somebody—a lawyer or my mother-in-law."

"You need to call Larry Joe," Winette said calmly.

"You're right." Just as I picked up my cell phone, it rang. It was Larry Joe.

"Honey, they've arrested your dad and—"

"I know. I'm sorry I didn't have a chance to give you a heads-up. I've been on the phone with our attorney."

"Larry Joe, what's this all about? There must be some mistake."

"It's something about some drugs they found on one of our trucks in Oklahoma."

"But that's crazy. How can they think your dad has anything to do with that?"

"I don't know. I'm sure Bill Scott will have Dad out of jail within a few hours. What I really need you to do is to go over and be with Mama. I told her Dad had been taken in for questioning, but you know her phone will start ringing off the hook pretty soon."

"Sure. I'll head over to your mama's right now. Keep me posted."

In the car, on my way over to my mother-in-law's,

I decided I had better call my own mother before she
phoned Miss Betty or me. Since my husband and I
had both grown up in Dixie, I'd known his parents
pretty much all my life. As seemed to be common in
the South, I grew up calling all my mama's friends
"Miss Betty," "Miss Sylvia," and so on, while I addressed most of their husbands as Mr. Smith, Mr.
Brown, and so forth. When Larry Joe and I got married, it seemed a bit formal to keep calling his dad
Mr. McKay, so he ended up being Daddy Wayne,
while his mom remained Miss Betty to me.

"Hi, Mama. . . ."

"Dear Lord, Liv. What in the world's going on?
I just had a call from Sue Maynard, saying she
saw some men take Wayne McKay into the police
station—in handcuffs."

"He's been taken in for questioning about drugs
found on one of the trucks. But Larry Joe has already talked to their attorney, Bill Scott, and I'm sure
he'll have Daddy Wayne out of there soon. I'm on
my way over to be with Larry Joe's mom right now."

"Of course, hon. You tell her we're praying for her
and Wayne."

Mama hung up, and I knew instinctively she'd be
right back on the phone, calling all the ladies in her
prayer circle. *That should keep her busy for a while*,
I thought.

I pulled into the driveway of Wayne and Betty
McKay's house, located just a few blocks on the
opposite side of the town square from where Larry
Joe and I lived. While our neighborhood is a hodge-
podge of houses dating from around 1900 to 1940,
their street is a mix of houses built mostly in the

fifties and sixties. The house Larry Joe grew up in is circa Ozzie and Harriet.

I slipped in through the kitchen door, which is never locked, knocking as I entered. My mother-in-law was sitting at the kitchen table, clipping coupons, still wearing her pink terry-cloth bathrobe.

She stood to give me a hug.

"Olivia, thank goodness. Larry Joe called and told me not to answer the phone until you got here. Has someone died?"

"No, Miss Betty. Nobody's died. The police are just questioning Daddy Wayne about drugs they found on one of McKay's trucks in Oklahoma."

"Well, that's what Larry Joe said. I thought there must be more going on than what he was saying. Telling me not to answer the phone and all."

"He just doesn't want nosy busybodies calling and worrying you, that's all. In fact, why don't we just take the phone off the hook for a while and have a cup of coffee?"

"Oh, no. We can't do that. What if Larry Joe calls back?"

"I have my cell phone," I said, taking it out of my purse and laying it on the table. "If he needs to get in touch, he'll call this number."

"All right, dear. Whatever you think's best. I'm too jumpy to talk to anybody right now, anyway."

After almost thirteen years of marriage, it still astounded me how generally compliant my mother-in-law is. No way would my own mother have stayed off the phone until I arrived, or agreed to take the phone off the hook. Betty McKay is only six years older than my mother, but it seems some generational shift occurred during that interval. Or maybe

it's just that Mama is bullheaded, a trait Larry Joe
would say I inherited.

My mother-in-law poured us two steaming cups
of coffee out of what looked like a freshly brewed
pot. I surmised that she had busied herself with
making coffee and clipping coupons after Larry Joe
called.

I leafed through her stack of coupons and did my
best to make benign conversation. She suddenly
blurted out, "How could that nice Sheriff Davidson
make such an asinine mistake as to think Wayne
could have anything to do with drugs? I don't think
Wayne's ever even been to Oklahoma."

I was a bit taken aback, since "asinine" is probably as close to profanity as my mother-in-law would
ever venture.

"I don't think Sheriff Davidson really had anything to say about it. Since it had to do with crossing
state lines and all that, it was federal agents that
brought in Daddy Wayne for questioning."

"That explains a lot," she said.

My mother-in-law doesn't really trust anyone who
wasn't born and raised right here in Dixie, so it explained a lot for her. This was an attitude she and
Mama happened to share.

"Miss Betty, why don't you go get dressed and put
your face on? Just in case we need to go out later."

Fortunately, she complied. I needed a break. Once
she was upstairs and out of earshot, I called Larry Joe
for an update. His phone went straight to voice mail.
I hoped that meant he was talking to either his dad
or their attorney.

As I was about to put the phone down, it buzzed,

alerting me that I had a text message. I hit the
RETRIEVE button to find a message from Di.

Handcuffs?

I spent most of the morning and half the afternoon with my mother-in-law. As the hours dragged
on, Miss Betty kept busy with her knitting project,
and I spiraled deeper and deeper into enveloping
boredom. I actually spent an inordinate amount of
time studying my mother-in-law's vast collection of
salt and pepper shakers. A whole wall in the kitchen
is devoted to it, with 114 specimens—yes, I counted
them—on wooden shelves Daddy Wayne had built
specifically for the collection.

Some of the shakers made sense, at least as much
as any collection of never used objects makes sense.
She has lots of shakers from her travels over the years,
from Route 66 to Graceland to the Golden Gate
Bridge. She has a set of tiki salt and pepper shakers
she brought back from the thirtieth-anniversary trip
she and my father-in-law took to Hawaii. These
kinds of souvenirs I can understand. But some of the
sets, such as the pair that looks like shotgun shells
or the one of a peasant woman pushing two pigs in
a cart, just don't compute with me.

Just before 3:00 p.m., Larry Joe finally arrived,
with his dad in tow. Daddy Wayne looked as pale as
if he'd just survived a bloodletting. Larry Joe took
me aside and briefly brought me up to speed. His
dad hadn't actually been charged with anything.
Apparently, the handcuffs were only because he got
belligerent when the agents attempted to bring him

in for questioning. Ralph Harvey and the attorney were coming over to his parents' house later in the evening to go over paperwork, look for any irregularities in shipments, and brace for an audit. Larry Joe said I should go on home and not to expect him for supper.

After I arrived at the house, I pulled a page from my own playbook and took the phone off the hook. I figured anyone I really wanted to talk to would call my cell phone, anyway. I left a trail as I dropped my purse and kicked off my shoes on my way to the den. I stretched out on the sofa and promptly dozed off to the droning of some television talk show.

I woke up a little after 4:00 p.m. With Larry Joe out of the picture for supper, I called Di to see if she had dinner plans.

"I was just about to call you," she said. "Dave phoned and asked me if I could drive home the professor that came to look at all the Civil War stuff in the storage unit. His car won't start, and Dave says he can't really spare a deputy to drive him to Memphis. You want to come along for the ride? That way I'll have someone to talk to on the drive back."

"Are you sure you don't want to have the distinguished professor all to yourself?"

"No. I think he's some old coot. Dave says he's harmless but chatty. Maybe we can find out something about the Civil War gear he examined."

"Okay. Count me in. When do we leave?"

"Ted was just about to run the professor over to Town Square Diner. They skipped lunch, and he was getting hungry. Dave said he was sure the professor would enjoy the company if we wanted to join him for supper."

I texted Larry Joe to let him know where I'd be, put on some lipstick, hurried over to the square, and parked in front of my office. Less than a minute later, Di pulled in next to me. We walked past the court-house to the other side of the square. Deputy Ted was just getting the professor settled into a corner booth when we arrived at the diner.

"Professor, may I introduce Ms. Souther and Mrs. McKay? Looks like you're going to be treated to the pleasure of their company for dinner."

The professor rose in a gentlemanly fashion and greeted each of us with a nod and a smile. We slid into the booth, facing him. He waited for us to be seated before sitting down again.

"This is Dr. Maurice Shapiro, ladies. Now, if you'll excuse me, I better get back to work," Ted said, put-ting on his hat and turning toward the door.

"Ladies, I'm charmed. I'm also grateful for a ride home. I understand the nice sheriff has pressed you into service on my behalf. I hope it's not too much of an inconvenience."

"Not at all," Di said. "It's our pleasure."

"Do you recommend anything particular on the menu?" he said.

"The daily special's always a safe bet," I suggested.

"Excellent. I shall have the chicken-fried steak."

Dr. Shapiro was as cute as a baby's bonnet. He sported a tweed jacket and a bow tie, a neatly trimmed white beard and round horn-rimmed glasses.

The professor asked about our town's history, noted the charm of our town square, and commented about how much he was looking forward to some down-home cooking. Most of his chatter might have been simply polite conversation. It was obvious, however, that he was serious about the down-home meal by the way he tucked into his supper.

As the dinner crowd swarmed into the diner, Di and I silently agreed to save any questioning of the professor about the Confederate collectibles for the drive to Memphis. As Dr. Shapiro noisily scraped the last bit of gravy and green beans off his plate, I couldn't help noticing he looked somewhat less dignified with corn-bread crumbs peppering his beard.

He insisted on picking up the tab for dinner, and then we loaded into my SUV, with Di in the back and the professor in the front passenger seat, cradling a black briefcase between his calves.

Just after we turned onto the highway, Dr. Shapiro spoke up. "The sheriff told me that you two would probably have a lot of questions about the Civil War relics I examined today."

I heaved a sigh of frustration, assuming the sheriff had invoked a gag order.

But the professor continued, "Sheriff Davidson also suggested that I could save myself considerable aggravation by simply answering your questions. So, ladies, what would you like to know?"

I glanced over my shoulder at Di.

"You're the expert, Dr. Shapiro," Di said in a saccharine voice. "Why don't you tell us what you found most interesting about the collection?"

The professor waxed academic about some of the items and went off on a tangent about a couple of important Civil War battles. But by the time we made it to East Memphis, we knew everything we needed to know about the items in Darrell's storage unit, and then some. All but a couple of things were authentic. Many were valuable, and some were extremely rare and expensive.

"The only articles I could not authenticate with confidence were some Confederate currency," he said. "That's not my area of expertise." From his long-winded lecture, which included his curriculum vitae, I knew his area of expertise was weapons. "I'm flattered that the sheriff considered me trustworthy enough to take a couple of samples to a colleague of mine for examination and authentication," Dr. Shapiro added, patting the briefcase, which was leaning against his knee.

"I always thought Confederate money was worthless," Di said.

"To the people who possessed it at the time, it was. By the end of the war, it wasn't worth the paper upon which it was printed. Now, however, it is quite valuable. Even a fairly common twenty-dollar note can be worth one hundred to three hundred dollars," he said.

We dropped the professor off at a handsome bungalow on a tree-lined street just a few blocks from the main campus of the University of Memphis. He thanked us profusely. Di climbed into the front seat for the ride home.

About twenty minutes outside Dixie, Di's cell phone buzzed. She told me it was Dave and put the call on speaker.

"How did your fact-finding mission go?"

"I resent that," Di said. "This was a mission of mercy."

"Okay. Whatever it was, I'd appreciate you keeping anything the professor told you to yourselves.

I'm a little nervous about having so much valuable stuff sitting in that storage unit. The fewer people who know, the better."

"You're just going to leave it there?" I asked.

"I don't really have any choice," Dave said, with more than a hint of irritation. "The FBI won't take it, and I don't have room for all that stuff in the tiny property room at the sheriff's office in Dixie. At least people have to enter a code to drive into the mini storage, and it has security cameras. Ted put a new heavy-duty lock on the storage locker. That's the best we can do for now," Dave said before ending the call.

I pulled in front of my office on the square, next to Di's car, and switched off the engine. We both fell silent for a long moment.

"The biggest crime in Dixie is usually some guy driving off from the gas pump without paying. Now we have a double murder, a stash of valuable Civil War items that were likely stolen, and maybe a drug-smuggling ring all in the same week," Di said.

"It's too big a coincidence," I noted. "They have to be connected."

"I hate to point it out," Di said, "but the only obvious connection I can see is McKay Trucking."

"I know," I said quietly.

"It looks bleak right now, but there is an upside to all this," Di said.

"What's that?"

"They're making progress on the murder case. I mean, the drugs on the truck and the stolen collectibles have to somehow be connected to the Farrell brothers getting killed. Now that Dave has something to go on, he should be able to solve the murders."

"I hope so. I'm just afraid that before the cops get around to figuring it all out, the business Larry Joe's grandfather started may be damaged beyond repair. Not to mention Daddy Wayne's health. You should have seen him, Di. He looked like he should be in the hospital."

"I'm sure a good night's sleep and some of Miss Betty's cooking will have him in the pink by tomorrow," Di said.

Chapter 7

It was almost 1:00 a.m. when Larry Joe finally made it home, ready to drop. I tried to talk him into setting the alarm clock for a later wake-up call, but he insisted he had to get to the office early.

"I told Dad to come in late, that I'd go in early to handle anything that comes up," Larry Joe said.

I knew the chance of Daddy Wayne going into the office late was as remote as me convincing Larry Joe to go in late, but I didn't say so. I understood that Larry Joe was worried about his dad—and so was I.

He was out cold by the time his head hit the pillow, and I finally drifted into a fitful sleep around 2:00 a.m.

Larry Joe had already left for work by the time I woke up, but a half pot of coffee was still on the heat when I stumbled, only half awake, into the kitchen. Two cups of coffee and two pieces of toast brought me nearly to a state of lucidity. All I needed now was a shower. The upstairs shower hadn't been operational for months. I told myself to be thankful that at least the toilet worked. Of course, I had threatened to kill Larry Joe if he ripped out the commode and forced me to go traipsing down the stairs in the middle of the night, should nature call.

As I started gathering everything I needed to take with me to the downstairs shower—clothes, make-up, and so on—my face began to flush with anger. I could, at the very least, put on my make-up in the upstairs bath if Larry Joe would just install the light fixture that he had dragged me down to Home Depot to pick out months ago. It was sitting on the floor, still in the box, even though I had asked Larry Joe over and over to put it up. He kept telling me that he would, just as soon as he had cut a hole in the ceiling for it. The single bare bulb hanging over the sink offered barely enough light to brush my teeth by.

I'd had it. *How hard can it be to cut a freaking hole?* I thought. Since I didn't have to rush to the office this morning, I decided to tackle it myself.

I left the clothes and other things on the bed and went into the spare bedroom, where Larry Joe had all his tools strewn about. I grabbed a ladder, a drop cloth, some safety goggles and a small electric saw thingy that looked like it would be perfect for cutting holes. I opened the light fixture box to measure how big the hole would need to be and found a handy template for the hole size tucked next to the instructions.

After tracing the outline for the hole on the ceiling with a pencil, I plugged in the saw and ascended the ladder. I switched on the saw, and its vibration shook me so violently, I nearly fell off the ladder. I realized I wouldn't be able to steady myself on the ladder and operate the saw at the same time.

If only I'd given up at that point.

In a stroke of brilliance, I deduced that it would be much easier to cut the hole from the attic side of the ceiling, instead of teetering on a ladder. So I scrounged a long nail from the toolbox in the spare bedroom and hammered it through the ceiling to mark the center point of the hole that I wanted to cut. I went up to the attic, with saw, goggles and template in hand, and located the protruding nail I had driven through from the underside. Piece of cake.

I placed the template over the nail, traced the outline with a pencil, and put on the safety goggles, and after a couple of minutes of getting acclimated to using the saw, I started to get the hang of it. I cut a nearly perfect circle. I was sweating, I was covered with sawdust, and I was feeling pretty pleased with myself. But after pushing out the wood and plaster, I looked down through the hole at a bird's-eye view of my bed. Apparently, the nail I had driven into the ceiling was not the only nail sticking up through the attic floor.

After muttering curses for a few minutes, I gathered my wounded pride and picked up the cell phone. I started to call Larry Joe but just couldn't bring myself to punch in his number. Why should I give him the satisfaction? I could fix this, or at least I could hire somebody to fix this, I thought. After pouring myself a glass of iced tea from the refrigerator and taking some aspirin out of the medicine cabinet, I called Winette.

"Sweet Deal Realty, Winette speaking. How may I help you today?"

"It's Liv. I'm in desperate need of someone to repair a ceiling. Can you recommend anybody?"

"I thought Larry Joe was your handyman."

"Don't taunt me, Winette. I've had a rough morning. I need someone who can repair a ceiling quickly— and preferably discreetly."

"Mmm-hmm. Well, I do have a friend at church whose nephew does odd construction and repair jobs. He does good work and charges reasonable."

"Anything else I should know about him?" I asked sheepishly.

She paused. "He's a recovering drug addict, but he's been coming to church real regular since he got out of jail."

"He's hired. What's his phone number?"

"I'll have to find out and call you back in a few minutes."

True to her word, Winette called back in less than five minutes.

"His name is Kenny. The only catch is you'll have to pick him up. He doesn't have a car, or a driver's license, for that matter. He lives over at the Howe Apartments on Pine Street."

"Thanks, Winette. You're a lifesaver."

She gave me his phone number, and I arranged to pick up Kenny in an hour.

I showered and got dressed. While I was slapping on some makeup, I remembered reading in the obituary that the Farrell brothers had also lived in the Howe Apartments. Maybe Kenny could be helpful in more ways than one.

The Howe Apartments are comprised of six units, three upstairs and three down, with an outside staircase and front doors and windows facing a small parking lot. I assumed the young man sitting on the stairs with a toolbox was Kenny, so I rolled down my window.

"You Ms. McKay?"

I nodded and motioned him over. We shook hands through the car window, and he introduced himself. Kenny Mitchell, a slender young man with short dreadlocks and wearing a T-shirt that said GOT CHRIST? stowed his gear—a toolbox and a couple of milk crates filled with various boards and other materials—in the back of my SUV before climbing into the front passenger's seat.

"I got material and tools for a basic patch job. If it's complicated, we'll have to go to the hardware store."

"Let's go take a look at the ceiling, and you can figure out what you need."

Kenny was pretty chatty as I drove, making conversation about what a nice lady Winette was and how he had turned things around since he gave his life to Jesus. At the house, Kenny got out of the car and retrieved his gear. He didn't think that fixing the hole would be a problem—news that gave me a great feeling of relief. Kenny went to work from the attic side and told me he'd need a stepladder or a kitchen chair to stand on to finish up from the bedroom side.

I went in the kitchen and checked my voice mail, then retrieved a stepladder from the garage. I helped Kenny push the bed over a few feet. After he had attached some Peg-Board from the attic side, Kenny positioned the stepladder under that spot in the bedroom and used a putty knife to coat the underside with drywall compound.

I told him I wanted to watch him work because,

obviously, my husband and I were in the process of remodeling the old house and still had a lot to learn. He explained step-by-step what he was doing. In between steps, I pumped him for information about the Farrell brothers. After he had applied two coats of compound, Kenny said he'd need to wait about fifteen minutes before applying a third and final coat. I offered him a cold Coke, and we sat down at the kitchen table.

I learned from Kenny that he had lived in his apartment building for only about six months and had pretty much just known the Farrells to speak to. Other than an occasional visit from various shapely females, the only people Kenny remembered seeing at their apartment were Ray and sometimes a friend of Ray's, someone they called Bobo.

"Duane, you know, the slow one, would sit on the steps sometimes, writing in this little notebook. I'd stop and talk to him for a minute. I felt sorry for the guy. I had a feeling Darrell sent him outside when he was entertaining a lady."

"Did you ever go in their apartment?"

"Yeah, just once. They had a Fourth of July party and said they were inviting everybody in the building. It was pretty obvious they just wanted an excuse to invite over the new girls who had moved in downstairs without seeming too bold, you know? I dropped in for a beer, just to be neighborly. But I didn't stay too long. They had all this Civil War crap sitting around the apartment and a big rebel flag on the wall. It kinda creeped me out. And when one of the girls Darrell was trying to impress started looking me over, I knew it was time to leave."

"Was Ray or Bobo at the party?"

"Yeah, Ray was there. Then Darrell got a call on his cell phone. Darrell and Duane excused themselves for a minute, saying they had to take care of some business, and Ray went with them. The three of them went down to the parking lot to talk to Bobo, all urgent like."

"Could you hear any of what they said?"

"Naw. I was standing by the window, but they had music playing. I could see 'em. It looked like Bobo was all worked up about something and they were trying to calm him down. Bobo drove off after a few minutes, and the rest of them came back in. I left right after that."

"What does this guy Bobo look like?"

"He's a scary-looking white dude, heavyset with a shaved head," Kenny said. "He's got these deep-set eyes, and his eyebrows are so faint, it looks like he ain't got any."

Kenny said the final coat of compound on the ceiling would need to dry for twenty-four hours. After a light sanding, it would be ready to paint. I paid him the price we had agreed on and drove him back to his apartment. He said he'd be glad to come finish the job for no additional charge, but I told him I thought I could manage the sanding and painting part myself.

After dropping Kenny off, I headed to the office to go over details for a couple of upcoming events with my assistant, Holly Renfrew. Actually, referring to Holly as my assistant is akin to referring to Batman as Commissioner Gordon's little helper. A recently widowed admiral's wife who is experienced in hosting parties for dignitaries around the globe and who doesn't really need the job for the money, she's been absolutely invaluable to the business. "Doesn't really need the money" is especially crucial, since I could never possibly afford to pay Holly what she's worth. Of course, her cachet has just enough quirk attached to it to keep things interesting.

Her personal style is Jackie Kennedy—the Onassis years, complete with oversize eyeglasses in a changing array of colors, and gypsy-chic head scarves in batik fabrics. She refuses to work on January 8 or August 16—Elvis Presley's birthday and his date of death, respectively. However, all this is a small price to pay for her expertise and enthusiasm.

After going over a few items for the Erdmans' party, I stuffed some papers for a bridesmaids' tea we had booked into my satchel, and the two of us moved across the square to the diner for a late lunch. With the lunch crowd cleared out, we had relative quiet in which to work. Gert Carter, called Meemaw by everyone in town, including me, had enlisted Liv 4 Fun to plan her granddaughter's bridesmaids' tea. Meemaw has six grandchildren, but Andrea is the only girl in the bunch, so she wanted everything to be perfect—and so did I.

While bridal showers can run the gamut from very casual to quite formal, bridesmaids' teas or luncheons are typically a more formal affair. Bachelorette parties, while gaining popularity, are still not a given in the South, but bridesmaids' teas generally are. This occasion provides an opportunity for the bride to spend some quality time with her best girlfriends and to present them with their bridesmaids' gifts. The tea is usually held about a week before the wedding, although it may be held a day or two before the big day if some of the bridesmaids are traveling in from out of town. The bride and her mother may host the bridesmaids' tea, but it's typically hosted by an aunt or cousin or, in this case, a grandmother.

Meemaw's instructions to us were, "Simple Southern elegance."

"I think the menu and the decorations we have planned so far exude the Southern elegance Meemaw is looking for," Holly said, pronouncing *for* as "fo-wah," her accent shaped and polished by a proper Southern finishing school. "But we're still missing that . . . sparkle."

The waitress refilled our iced teas, and Holly's clunky bracelet clanked against the glass as she stirred in some Splenda.

"Tea lights in the afternoon wouldn't add much sparkle to an outdoor event," Holly said absently.

"Mason jars filled with crystals?" I offered. "No," I added. "Too New Agey."

"I know," Holly said with a pleased look. "We should go through Meemaw's costume jewelry and scatter some on the table, among the flowers and china."

"That's absolutely perfect," I said. "It's personal, and I bet Andrea even has memories of playing dress-up at Meemaw's house with some of that jewelry when she was growing up."

Holly said she'd set up a time with Meemaw to rummage through her costume jewelry.

The key to throwing a successful party—and keeping your sanity—is meticulous planning. Even more important than my glue gun and duct tape, which have helped me avert disaster on any number of occasions, are my checklist and timeline for every party. The checklist, which may start out sparse and grow exponentially, includes every single item needed for a particular event, along with every contact name and number. The timeline starts weeks or months before the event and then counts down to the days leading up to the party, with descriptions of what to do, and finally, it becomes a schedule for the day of the actual event, broken down into fifteen-minute increments.

Holly and I fleshed out the remainder of our lists over a well-earned slice of peach pie.

Despite having wasted a good chunk of my morning cutting and repairing an errant hole in the ceiling, it turned out to be a productive workday. I even managed to get caught up with some odds and ends that had been simmering on the back burner for a while.

Chapter 8

I had supper ready when Larry Joe made it home a little after six. He usually scarfs down second helpings of my meat loaf and mashed potatoes. When he didn't clean his plate, I knew worries about the business and his dad were taking a toll on his appetite, despite the fact that he tried to be upbeat during dinner and convince me things were really okay.

"Dad seemed in good spirits today. And our lawyer says all the company paperwork is in order. We shouldn't have any problems with an audit."

"That's great, honey," I said, although neither of us seemed to believe a word we were saying.

I tried to persuade Larry Joe to watch some television with me or go out to a movie. I really felt like he needed a break. But he holed up at the computer in the den after dinner, saying that he'd been so busy putting out fires, he was way behind with regular work stuff. After Larry Joe retreated to the den, I placed the dishes in the dishwasher and went upstairs to give Di a call.

"Di, have you heard Dave mention anything about a guy named Bobo?"

"Seriously?" she asked in a tone that peeved me.

"Yes, seriously. He hangs around with Ray Franklin and apparently made several visits to the Farrell brothers' apartment. And, according to Kenny, one of those times Bobo was real upset about something."

"You lost me. Who's Kenny?"

"He lives in the same apartment building as the Farrells did."

"And you questioned him?"

"In a manner of speaking."

"Are you crazy? How do you know Kenny wasn't involved with drugs or whatever the Farrell boys were into? And how do you know he isn't involved with Bobo or even isn't this guy Bobo, for that matter?"

"Kenny is *not* Bobo," I explained calmly. "Bobo is a heavyset white guy with a shaved head and no eyebrows to speak of. I wonder if he has a thyroid condition. Anyway, Kenny barely knew the Farrell brothers, and he is not a drug smuggler. Besides, he's given his life to Jesus. And Winette knows him."

"Well, if Winette knows him, that does make me feel a little better," Di said.

"Forget about Kenny and Bobo for the moment. I've been wondering, why were the Farrell brothers' bodies left in that garage?"

"It was certainly out of sight," Di said.

"Yeah, but there are thousands of acres of woods all around here where someone could bury a body and it might never be discovered. And we're not too far from the river. If you dumped a body in the river, it could get swept miles away by the current."

"So you're saying the murderer wanted the bodies to be found?"

"I don't know about that. But maybe the murderer had to stash the bodies quickly for some reason. What it does tell us, I think, is that the house was convenient. It must be close to where the brothers were killed."

"I hate to be the one to point it out, but McKay Trucking is not too far from there."

"I know. That had already occurred to me."

"Unfortunately, you don't really want to steer the investigation in that direction."

"No, Di. As much as I hate it, I can't ignore the McKay connection. A lot of people work for the company—especially when you take into account all the part-time workers and casual labor and independent contractors. I plan to spend tomorrow afternoon seeing what I can find out about the Farrell brothers and the murders and the drugs on the truck. Don't try to talk me out of it."

"I wouldn't waste my time trying to talk you out of anything. But, honestly, what can you do that the police haven't done already?" Di said.

"I can avoid wasting time by looking at Larry Joe or Daddy Wayne as having any kind of involvement. I may not be objective, but I am certain of their complete innocence in all of this. Plus, I should be able to snoop a bit and wrangle any information that might be helpful from the trucking company without arousing too much suspicion. That's as good a place to start as any."

"Oh, snooping around reminds me of something Dave said."

"Really?" I said with prurient interest.

"Yeah, the cops are doing some kind of stakeout or special surveillance tonight. He wouldn't tell me what it's all about. But he acted like it was a big deal, so it's probably related somehow to the murders. It's not like we have that much big crime here in Dixie."

I let Di go hurriedly when I heard Larry Joe coming up the steps.

"I just had a call from Ralph," he said. "Seems one of our contractors has bailed on us. I'm going to have to drive to Huntsville tomorrow to pick up a load. I better try to get some sleep."

"Honey, I'm worried about you. You're pushing yourself too hard. Can't you hire someone else to drive to Huntsville?"

"I'm afraid we're already calling in favors just to cover orders, since the FBI has detained a couple of our regular drivers in Oklahoma."

Larry Joe stripped down to his boxers and climbed into bed. I snuggled up next to him, nuzzling my face against his scratchy nine o'clock shadow. Staring straight up, he said, "There's Spackle on the ceiling."

"I thought it might be nice to paint the ceiling in here a different color," I said innocently.

"Did you have that thought before or after you knocked a hole in the ceiling?"

"I'll plead the Fifth on that one."

"Look, Liv, I know I haven't been spending much time with you lately," he said, pulling me closer. "When all this is over, we'll get away for the weekend—just the two of us. Promise."

"Mmm, that sounds good. But you're still getting behind on your chores around here," I teased. "You did promise me an upstairs shower—and a light fixture in the bathroom. Remember?"

"I promise you shall have a working shower and a light by Thanksgiving. If I can't finish it, I'll hire somebody."

Larry Joe dozed off, and I knew he must be delirious, offering to pay someone to work on the house. I brushed my teeth, slipped on a nightshirt, and got back into bed beside my snoring husband. I was glad at least one of us could sleep.

The next morning I offered to cook Larry Joe some breakfast, but he said he'd rather just have cold leftover meat loaf on toast. Not a first for him, and at least he ate something, instead of just dashing out the door with a mug of coffee.

Since it happened to be a rare Saturday that I didn't have an event to work, I had called Winette to see if Residential Rehab was working on a project this weekend. They were. I had signed up for the morning work crew, and Di had volunteered to join me. Residential Rehab, chaired by Winette, collects donations of money and supplies and brings together volunteers to do home repairs for the elderly and disabled in our community—a cause I wholeheartedly support.

Today's work site was the home of Miss Lacey Canon, who, at eighty-five, was still as spry as a spring lamb. She had made enough homemade biscuits to feed a platoon and served them up with a choice of sausage or peach preserves. She kept coaxing the dozen or so volunteers working on the house to eat more.

Miss Lacey brought a plate of hot biscuits out to the front porch, where Di and I were scraping wood, prepping for a fresh coat of primer and a buttery shade of yellow paint.

"Now, precious, you better eat something," Miss Lacey said. "I know you young folk rush out the door in the mornings with nothing 'cept a cup of coffee. That ain't no good for a body. You need some real food."

"Miss Lacey, if I eat any more of your scrumptious biscuits, I'm going to pop," I said.

She turned her attention to Di, who was up on a ladder, scraping paint from above a double-hung window.

"No, thank you, ma'am. I've had my fill for now, too."

"I'm keeping some warm in the oven if you change your mind, precious," she said, giving Di's calf a little love pat before she shuffled back into the house.

"It's sweet the way you're spending your day off working on somebody else's house, considering the shape yours is in," Di said.

"It's honestly a relief to work on somebody else's house for a change," I said. "It's especially nice to be able to see progress actually being made."

Earlier in the summer, the RR team had put a new roof on Miss Lacey's house. Kenny Mitchell, the godsend who had speedily fixed the punctured ceiling at my house, was inside, working with another guy to repair a water-damaged ceiling in Miss Lacey's living room and hallway. The rest of us were getting the exterior ready to paint.

Kenny passed through the porch on his way out to a truck in the driveway to get some supplies. When he came back up the front steps, I introduced him to Di.

"Nice to meet you, Ms. Souther. Good to see you again, Ms. McKay," he said. "Be sure to call me if you have anything that needs fixing."

"Will do," I said.

"Why don't you take him up on his offer?" Di said after Kenny had disappeared into the house. "Next time Larry Joe's out of town for a couple of days, why don't you hire a plumber—or maybe a crew of plumbers—to get your upstairs bathroom working, and let Kenny patch up after them? Larry Joe might be miffed, but he'd get over it."

"I've certainly entertained the idea," I said. "In fact, the thought of a working shower upstairs is a frequent subject of my fantasies."

"If you fantasize about plumbing, you have bigger problems than renovating your house. You should see a shrink."

"The thing is, Larry Joe really believes he can fix up the house himself, despite all the evidence to the contrary. And he does try. He puts in untold hours working on the place—albeit without much to show for it. If I gave up on him, I think it would break his heart."

"You're more patient than most wives," Di said. "Though, Lord knows, Larry Joe has his own cross to bear being married to you."

I dipped my paintbrush into a bucket of primer and flicked the brush in Di's direction, spattering the back of her shirt.

"Oh, you don't want to go there," Di said. She reached over and tried to wrest the paintbrush from my hand, and we both burst out laughing.

Winette walked out, clapping her hands. "More painting and less playing, ladies."

With insincere looks of contrition, we straightened up and got back to work.

"Winette's a real taskmaster," I said.

"Yeah. I bet if she was supervising Larry Joe, he'd have that bathroom finished by now."

I plopped down on the porch and started scraping a badly peeling board near the porch floor.

"You've gone all quiet. What's wrong?" Di said after a short interlude of silence.

"Nothing really. I just started thinking about the renovations on my house."

"That could be depressing if you think too much about it."

"It's not the work that depresses me," I said. "You know my business has definitely dropped off since the murders. And I don't think Larry Joe's having to turn away new customers at the moment, either. If this trend continues, we may have to tighten up the belt financially speaking. And since we like to eat, we'd probably have to put renovations on hold."

"Snap out of it," Di said. She climbed down the ladder, knelt on the porch beside me, and began plucking off the paint chips stuck to her arms. "You know every business has its ups and downs. Liv 4 Fun and the trucking company will be fine. In fact, I predict such glowing recommendations from Mrs. Erdman after their anniversary party that you'll have crackpots lined up around the block, waiting to book your services."

She turned to ascend the ladder, and I dipped my brush in the primer and smacked her on the butt with it.

Di and I wrapped up our four-hour shift at about noon. I grabbed a couple of sausages and biscuits to go for my lunch and drove home to get cleaned up.

Larry Joe had said he would be on the road to Huntsville by noon at the latest. So a little before 1:00 p.m. I drove out to McKay's to do some snooping. I hoped Ralph would be out to lunch. He wasn't. I made some lame pretext of coming by to pick up some papers for Larry Joe. Ralph nodded and gave me a faint smile as he kept on walking. I was in luck. Ralph, and everyone else, for that matter, was too busy to pay any attention to me. Now, if I only knew what I was looking for.

I knew better than to wander into the locker room. Some of the truckers might be changing clothes. Besides, I was certain the Farrells' lockers had already been cleaned out by now. So, after I made sure Ralph wasn't looking, I skulked just around the corner from the locker room to eavesdrop on the guys, hoping to pick up any useful tidbits of information. All I heard were a couple of off-color jokes, one of which I didn't even understand.

I decided to look around upstairs. I headed in the direction of the garage office where bills of lading and various other kinds of paperwork are dropped off temporarily before being delivered to the front office. It would be the most likely place for me to go if I actually was picking up something for Larry Joe. Directly across the hall from that office was the door to the security office, which, to my chagrin, was locked. I ambled up the hall and noted that Ralph was still out of his office. His top desk drawer was ajar, revealing an unattended key ring. I stood in the doorway to his office, stretching my arms and massaging my neck. With no one looking my way, I backed into the office, reached one hand behind my back, and scooped up the keys.

Fortunately, there were only three keys on this ring, and even more fortuitously, the second one I tried fit the security office door. After a quick glance around, I slipped inside the office, closed the door behind me, and found myself standing in a dark, windowless room. After a moment of fumbling, I happened upon the light switch.

The office was small, about nine by nine feet. I've measured enough rooms for party arrangements that I can usually size up a space pretty accurately by sight. There was a desk cluttered with papers, two cabinets along one wall, and a closed-circuit monitor facing the desk, with a live feed from the truck bays below. I watched the action for a moment, before taking a look in the cabinets. In the second cabinet, on the middle shelf, were two sets of videotapes, each numbered one through thirty-one. One set seemed to be for the garage; the other, for the warehouse. Apparently, security tapes were kept for a month before being taped over. I couldn't believe the company hadn't shifted to storing security footage digitally. But then my father-in-law is too much of a cheapskate to buy a new anything if the old one was still working, however inefficiently.

I also couldn't believe the FBI hadn't already confiscated the tapes. I figured maybe they had reviewed the tapes and had found nothing of interest. At any rate, I wasn't going to question my good luck. Unfortunately, four tapes were all I could possibly cram into my purse. Poor planning on my part—which was kind of embarrassing for a professional planner. I grabbed two tapes of garage footage and two tapes of warehouse footage covering the two days preceding the discovery of the bodies.

I checked the monitor but couldn't spot Ralph on the feed. I walked to the door, shut off the light, and eased the door open a crack. Not hearing anything, I stepped out and gently pulled the door shut, then checked the handle to make sure the door had locked behind me. I walked toward the stairs, anxious to make my escape, and ran smack into Ralph as he stepped out of his office.

"'Scuse me, Mrs. McKay. Are you okay?"

"Fine, fine. It was totally my fault. Should watch where I'm going."

"Did you find what you were looking for?"

I paused, frozen for a moment, thinking I had been caught. Then I remembered I had said I was picking up something for Larry Joe.

"Oh, yes, I did. Thanks," I said, patting my purse.

Although Ralph must have thought I'd been drinking by my goofy behavior, he was too polite to say so. As soon as the top of his head had disappeared from sight down the stairs, I stepped into his office, dropped the keys in the drawer, and left the building before anyone else had a chance to speak to me.

Luckily, we still have an old VCR hooked up in the den for VHS tapes that Larry Joe can't bear to part with—mostly of his high school football games. I poured a glass of iced tea, opened a bag of pretzels, and settled in for some serious reviewing of the days leading up to the murders.

I started with the first garage tape so I could see what Darrell had been up to. Since I didn't find him in the early part of the tape, I realized he must have worked the three-to-eleven shift that day. I fast-forwarded to the shift change and spotted him coming in. After watching Darrell perform the same boring maintenance routine a couple of times, I fast-forwarded, scanning for any new people coming into view. There were periods of time when I couldn't see Darrell, such as when he was working under the truck in the pit area.

He talked for a few minutes with a guy named Joe—the patches on their coveralls gave me their names. Darrell and Joe left for a few minutes, for a cigarette break or whatever. A few minutes after he came back from his break, Darrell got into a scuffle with a guy named Rudy. There was no sound on the tape, but it seemed like Rudy had taken some of Darrell's tools and Darrell was ticked off about it. There was some shoulder shoving and chest-thumping, but the two men didn't actually come to blows.

At the end of Darrell's shift, I decided I was ready for a break, too. I made a pot of coffee and grabbed a half-full pint of mint chocolate chip ice cream from the freezer. I was going to need significant quantities of caffeine and sugar to stay alert, or even awake, through the rest of the tapes.

I saw Duane pass through the garage a few times. Unlike his brother, who spent the majority of his time working in the same garage bay, Duane wandered around, performing various maintenance and janitorial duties. At least while he was on-screen, he didn't talk to anyone and no one talked to him.

I switched over to the first warehouse tape and had just about despaired of watching trucks getting loaded when one of the truck drivers caught my eye. I backed up and replayed that section of the tape to get a better look at a shaved head with deep-set eyes and no discernible eyebrows. Unfortunately, the guy didn't have a name patch on his shirt. Wondering if this could be Bobo, I let the tape continue playing at regular speed, and suddenly I had my answer. I saw a man in the background climbing out of the passenger side of the truck cab. I freeze-framed the image. It was definitely Ray Franklin.

Chapter 9

I knocked on the door of Di's trailer, busting to share my newfound information. She came to the door, apparently just out of the shower, her hair still damp and infused with the aroma of lavender. She was wearing jeans and a ZZ Top T-shirt.

"Hey," she said, stepping back so I could pass through. "Isn't it about feeding time for Larry Joe?"

"He had to drive down to Huntsville to pick up a load."

"Did you eat yet?"

"Nothing but pretzels and ice cream."

"I can't top that, but I do have a couple of low-fat TV dinners in the freezer."

"Thanks. It probably wouldn't hurt me to eat something a little more nutritious than ice cream."

Di peeled the corners back on the frozen entrées and stuck them in the microwave. I sat down at the kitchen table and waited impatiently.

"Di, I've got so much to tell you. I don't know where to start."

"I've got some news for you, too," Di said. "You first, since you look like you're about to burst," she added, grabbing a pitcher of iced tea from the fridge and pouring a glass for each of us.

"Okay. I now know that Bobo and Ray Franklin were at McKay's two days before the Farrell boys' bodies were discovered. Bobo was driving a truck and may or may not have had a legitimate reason to be there, but Ray was just along for the ride."

"Somebody saw them?"

"*I* saw them. On the surveillance tapes from the company security office, which I kind of . . . borrowed this afternoon."

"Borrowed?"

"Well, I intend to put them back. Eventually. The point is, whatever Duane and Darrell were mixed up in—probably the drugs they found on that truck in Oklahoma—Ray and Bobo are involved, too." I paused for a moment. "What's your news?" I asked.

"Dave told me Professor Shapiro is in the hospital."

"What happened?"

"Somebody broke into his house and stole that Confederate money he had in the briefcase. In the process, they fractured his skull."

"Oh, no. That poor, sweet little man," I said. "Is he going to be okay?"

"I hope so. Dave didn't have any details," Di said. "Can you think of anything we can do to catch this SOB before anybody else gets hurt?"

As I pondered Di's question, my cell phone rang. "It's Larry Joe. I better take it."

"Hey, honey. Have you made it to Huntsville already? I didn't expect to hear from you until—"

Larry Joe interrupted. "I haven't made it to Huntsville. Ralph just called and said the FBI came late this afternoon with a warrant for our security tapes. But when he took them into the office to get them, some of the tapes were missing. Ones from around the time of the murders."

I held my breath, waiting for the other shoe to drop. But, apparently, Ralph hadn't mentioned my visit to the garage today.

"As if things didn't already look bad enough for us, now this. Liv, would you mind checking on Dad first thing in the morning? I'll get back as quick as I can. It'll probably be at least mid-afternoon before I can make it in."

"Okay, honey. I'll look in on your dad. But don't you try to drive all the way back without getting at least some sleep."

"I can't pick up the container until four thirty in the morning, so I'll catch a few z's before then. Love ya. Tell Di I said hello."

My complexion must have matched the sick feeling in the pit of my stomach, because Di immediately asked what was wrong.

"Larry Joe said the FBI came to get the surveillance tapes and found some of them missing."

"Oh, crap."

The microwave beeped, coinciding with my complete loss of appetite.

"Liv, you've got to put those tapes back somehow."

"I can't do that. Even if I could get away with it, it would just make things look worse for Larry Joe and his dad—like the tapes had been altered or switched out or something. But I have to do something. Maybe I should tell Sheriff Dave about Bobo."

"Tell him what? That Ray Franklin has a truck driver friend named Bobo who looks like Uncle Fester?"

"I guess you're right," I said. "By the way, did Dave mention anything more about their big stake-out last night?"

"Unfortunately, no. And I did try to get him to talk. But when he gets into his tight-lipped official lawman mode, you couldn't force information out of him with a cattle prod."

"Yeah, I know. But . . . ," I said with a pregnant pause as the cogs in my brain started churning. "I'm sure you'd have better luck getting information from Deputy Ted, if you just tried."

"Oh, no," she said. "There's only so far I'm willing to go for a friend, and going out with Ted Horton is above and beyond the call of duty."

"I'm not suggesting you sleep with him or even go on a real date. But you could talk to him after your yoga class, let him walk you to your car, maybe get a cup of coffee. You know, just a little harmless flirtation."

"Absolutely not," she said. "Why don't *you* indulge in a little harmless flirtation with Ted to get the information?"

"Because I'm married. And flirtation doesn't look harmless when you're a married woman, especially in a small town."

Di's lips were clamped shut, like those of a child refusing a spoonful of medicine, and I could tell it was useless to pursue the matter any further. But I also knew I had to figure out some way to make up for the predicament I'd put Larry Joe and Daddy Wayne in by taking the security tapes.

"Di, did Dave mention which hospital Dr. Shapiro is in?"

"Baptist, I think. Why?"

"I'd like to go visit him. I can't stand the thought of him laid up with a cracked skull. You want to go with me?"

"Yeah, I do. I'd like to see how he's doing."

"Good. Let's go. And after we get back, I'm going to finish watching those security tapes if it takes all night."

After grabbing a couple of bottled waters for the trip, we took my SUV. I drove the back roads to the interstate, then finally exited onto Walnut Grove Road. Baptist Hospital, known as Baptist East until the downtown hospital was torn down, is located on the eastern edge of Memphis, which borders the upscale suburb of Germantown.

We stopped at the information desk in the lobby to ask for the professor's room number. I was relieved to hear he was in a regular room rather than in intensive care, partly because being in the ICU would have meant we couldn't get in to see him after driving all the way out there, but mostly because it suggested that he wasn't in critical condition.

We took the elevator to the third floor and tapped on his door, which was slightly ajar. We said hello, and I was worried for a moment when Dr. Shapiro's eyes didn't register a glimmer of recognition for the two women he'd shared dinner and a long car ride with just a couple of days before. But then he reached over to the bedside table to retrieve his glasses.

With his specs on, he immediately said, "Ah, Mrs. McKay, Miss Souther, this is a pleasant surprise." His head was bandaged on the back and along one side. He seemed a little drowsy but was lucid.

Di pulled over the side chair, and I sat down on the end of his bed. We inquired about his condition, and he explained that it was just a hairline fracture and that, luckily, there was no swelling in his brain.

"I was quite fortunate, from what I'm told," he said. "The intruder struck me on the back of the head, and I fell to the floor, remaining in an unconscious and semiconscious state until my housekeeper discovered me the following morning."

He described to us how someone had broken into his home during the night on Thursday, the same night we had driven him home. He was in bed when he heard a thud, and got up to investigate.

"I thought it was my cat, Henry. His eyesight is very poor, and sometimes he bumps into and knocks things over. I caught a glimpse of a shadow on the wall out of the corner of my eye, and the next thing I knew, I was lying prone on the floor."

"Did you get any impression of the intruder, like how tall or heavy he was?" I said.

"No," he said. "It was dark, and I got only a brief glance at a distorted shadow. The burglar absconded with the two Confederate banknotes the sheriff had given me for authentication. Oddly, nothing else was stolen. I feel badly that the artifacts Sheriff Davidson entrusted to my care are now missing."

"You have no cause to feel bad," Di said. "I can assure you that the sheriff, and everyone else, is concerned only about you getting better."

We chatted with the professor for a few minutes more, until he seemed to be getting tired. We asked if we could bring him anything or if he'd like us to check on his cat.

"No. That's very kind," he said. "But Mrs. Bonds, my housekeeper, took Henry home with her to look after him. And the nurses here are taking very good care of me."

He was so cute, I just wanted to tweak his cheeks, but I gave his hand a squeeze instead.

On the way to the elevators, we walked behind a male patient who was slowly pushing his IV bag on a pole down the hall, mooning us off and on as his hospital gown flapped open and shut.

"That man had more hair on his ass than on the top of his head," Di said matter-of-factly as soon as the elevator doors had fully closed.

We stopped by the ladies' room and bought a couple of Diet Cokes from the vending machine in the lobby before getting into the car for the trek home. I felt I needed a shot of caffeine to stay alert on the road.

"Well, it looks like the professor is going to be okay," Di said. "He looked pitiful, though, with his head wrapped up in bandages."

"Yeah. Bless his heart. But it could have been a lot worse," I said. "There's a good chance that whoever conked Dr. Shapiro over the head and stole that Confederate money is the same one who killed Darrell and Duane."

"We don't know that," Di said.

"The professor said the banknotes Dave had given him were the only things that were stolen. Your run-of-the-mill burglar would have taken electronics or cash. And Dr. Shapiro is an expert in Confederate weapons, so he's likely to have some antique firearms in his house, too. But nothing like that was taken. It doesn't make sense, unless the Confederate bills were specifically what the thief was looking for."

"You could be right, but I don't see how the thief, or anybody else, could have known that he had the Confederate money. Besides Dave and Ted and us, who even knew?"

I took a gulp of Diet Coke and mulled that over for a minute. "I can think of only a couple of possible answers to that question—and both give me a creepy feeling."

"What are you thinking?" Di said.

"Neither of us told anybody, so only someone who was in that storage unit when Dr. Shapiro was looking over the artifacts, or someone who was watching it while he was there, could have known he had the Confederate money."

"You know as well as I do, Dave or Ted wouldn't hurt Dr. Shapiro. Dave didn't have to let him take the money with him to begin with."

"I know it wasn't Dave or Ted. But remember what Dave said when they first discovered the stuff in the storage unit? One of the reserve deputies who's involved in Civil War reenactments was the one who told Dave the stuff looked genuine, too expensive for the Farrells to have bought themselves."

"That's right. I'd forgotten about that," Di said. "I wonder who that was and how long he's been a reserve deputy. It's scary to think Dave could have a thief or maybe even a murderer on his staff."

"The alternative might be even scarier. If there was somebody watching the action from a safe distance, say through binoculars, they wouldn't have known Dr. Shapiro's name or address."

"Which means they probably followed us when we drove him home that night," Di said, a note of uneasiness in her voice.

"Exactly."

"What should we do?" Di said.

"I'm going home to watch the rest of day two on the tapes to see what else I can find out. And tomorrow I'm putting Ray Franklin under surveillance. He was close to the Farrells, and he was at McKay's with Bobo. I think it's time to see what he's up to."

Chapter 10

A pot of coffee kept me awake through most of the remaining footage. I woke up on the sofa in the den just after 6:00 a.m., stumbled to the bathroom, and splashed cold water on my face. My right cheek boasted a clear impression of the brocade pillow I'd fallen asleep on.

After stashing the videotapes in the one place Larry Joe would never venture—the laundry room— I performed mental yoga, trying to decide if I should start my surveillance of Ray Franklin early or go to church first. Guessing that he wouldn't get an early start on the day, and knowing my mom would call if she didn't see me at church, I swung by to check on Daddy Wayne, then headed to the eight o'clock service.

My usually stoic father-in-law honestly looked as if he'd been crying. He insisted he was having sinus issues, and Miss Betty and I talked him into going back to bed.

I slid into the pew and sat next to my mom just as the organ pealed the chords for the entrance hymn, signaling the congregation to stand. I rarely make it to Dixie Community Church's early service, which is my mother's service of choice. I prefer to go to the 10:00 a.m. service and usually only see Mama in passing as she's coming out of Sunday School and I'm going into the late service. I tell Mama we attend the ten o'clock service because Larry Joe doesn't get up in time for the 8 a.m. service, and he won't go to church at all without me, which is only partly true. The fact is, I don't like getting up so early on Sundays and Larry Joe's church attendance is sporadic, at best. When I do attend the early service, my mother expects me to sit with her, as if I'd misbehave if I sat with my friends.

The nondenominational church is housed in a rather nondescript building devoid of any ornamentation on the exterior, save a sign with the church's name on it. Inside isn't any fancier, with a tiled vestibule and a carpeted sanctuary. The matching padding on the pews and the carpet are a color that can best be described as mauve—an unfortunate decorating decision made in the eighties. But at least the pews are padded, something for which I am very thankful.

At nearly six feet tall, Mama towers over my five-foot-three frame. I got my height, or lack thereof, from my daddy's side of the family. Too vain to wear her reading glasses, she held our shared hymnal at a height that worked for her, and I peered over the page at the lyrics as best I could. The preacher read a scripture passage from one of those prophets tucked near the end of the Old Testament, but I had no idea what the sermon was about. My mind was fixated on finding out what Ray Franklin might be up to.

After the final amen, my mom pressed me to go to brunch with her and her friend Sylvia. The only person I know who can talk more than Mama is her friend Sylvia. She finally let me off the hook for brunch after I promised to go to lunch with her and to go shopping at the mall in Hartville on Monday afternoon.

I headed for the door as quickly as I could, pausing along the way for the obligatory handshakes and shoulder hugs. After shaking hands with the preacher and telling him how much I appreciated the sermon, I finally made a clean break and hurried to the car.

I stopped by the house, changed out of my church clothes, and took off on assignment with a notebook, a pair of binoculars, and a can of postman-grade pepper spray, which Di had given me just in case things got dicey.

About 9:25 a.m., I drove just far enough down the road where Ray lived to catch sight of his blue pickup truck. *Good*. He was still at home. I parked beside the convenience store/gas station across the street from Sunrise Mobile Village, which gave me a clear view of the only driveway in or out of the trailer park. After purchasing provisions—coffee and doughnuts—I settled in and waited. It was nearly 10:30 a.m. when Ray finally pulled out and headed toward the highway.

I followed and tried to keep at least one car between us. With sunglasses on and my hair pulled back in a ponytail, I hoped I wouldn't be easily recognizable to Ray, since I'd met him face-to-face on only one occasion. Ray's first stop was for gas at a little two-pump station. Afraid to get that close, I pulled into the parking lot of a small shopping center across the highway that housed a beauty salon, dry cleaners, and a cell phone store. There were enough cars pulling in and out to give me good cover.

Just as I started mulling over the idea of calling my own hairstylist to schedule a cut, Ray's pickup pulled back onto the highway. Despite a good bit of traffic, I was able to keep close to him without much trouble. Ray drove into a mini-storage site, another place where I couldn't really follow him without risking being seen. I turned into the next driveway, which belonged to a concrete company. The business was apparently closed on Sundays, so I circled around behind the building and stopped next to a chain-link fence that overlooked the mini-storage place.

With binoculars, I spotted Ray and made a note of the building and the unit he was accessing. Since I knew Ray lived in a small camper, I suspected that he used the storage unit to store his Civil War reenactment gear, like Darrell and Duane had. I also wondered if any of the stuff in his unit might be stolen. He opened a padlock, slid up the garage-type door, and went inside, then pulled the door about halfway closed. It was too dark and too far away for me to see anything inside the unit. He was inside for only a couple of minutes, and he wasn't carrying anything when he emerged.

I couldn't help but notice through the binoculars that Ray was dressed up pretty spiffily for him and even had his hair slicked down on top. The thought that a lady might be on his mind was further implicated when he stopped at a vegetable stand and bought a bouquet of flowers. Ray headed back in the direction of Dixie before turning off onto a county road that led eventually to McKay Trucking. As soon as there were no cars between us, I backed off to avoid being spotted and occasionally lost sight of him as we went over hills and around curves.

I panicked when I lost sight of the truck and didn't spot it once I'd made it around a curve. I sped up just in time to catch a glimpse of his truck disappearing down the gravel road that led to Tonya Farrell's farmhouse.

Chapter 11

"Can you believe the nerve of that guy?" I asked Di via cell phone as I drove back to town. "There he goes, flowers in hand, to see the Farrell brothers' grieving mother. He'll probably even try to seduce her."

"That may be just what she wants," Di said. "As hard as it may be for us to believe, some women might consider Ray Franklin a catch."

"I can't believe he could get a date without roofies and a Taser," I said, still shuddering at the thought of any sort of fleshly contact with the man.

I told Di I was on my way to the trailer park. "I should have at least twenty minutes to search Ray's trailer."

"You're insane," Di said, before adding, "Swing by my place and pick me up on your way."

All the way to Ray's, I was worried about whether I'd be able to jimmy open the lock on his camper door. Before I could even fish the nail file out of my purse, Di had reached inside the concrete block serving as a step to the camper door and had pulled out a key.

Once inside, Di and I warbled a collective "Eeew" at the general state of uncleanliness. Di suggested that she start searching at the front, I start at the back, and we meet in the middle. In the back of the camper was a built-in bed. I tugged at the mattress to check for anything that might be hidden under it. The sheets were stiff and visibly stained; I wished I had brought gloves with me. I was looking in the fridge, again wishing I had gloves, when Di said she had found something in a box stacked in the corner.

"Here's a picture of Darrell and Duane when they were little kids. At least it's got their names on the back."

I glanced at the photo and immediately recognized their mother's house. "That's definitely them," I said.

Even weirder, Di said she had found a postcard addressed to Bobby Farrell at an APO address in Iraq with Duane's and Darrell's childish signatures, along with Xs and Os, scrawled on it.

Finishing my search of the freezer, I noted that a TV dinner felt much heavier than it should. I carefully opened the end tab and slid out a small book from inside. It looked like a diary. Di and I found a book of a similar size and weight to put back into the carton, hoping Ray wouldn't notice the diary was missing, at least for a while. After trying to make sure everything looked as we had found it, we left. Although the place was such a mess, it could have been ransacked before we arrived.

I drove away from Ray's and started to pull up in front of Di's place. But I didn't want Ray to see my car when he returned, since I had been tailing him all morning, so I drove to my office on the square instead.

"By the way, Liv, I mentioned our doubts about that reserve deputy to Dave. The thought had already crossed his mind after he heard about the attack on the professor."

"Good. At least he knows to watch his back until he knows for sure about that guy."

We went upstairs to my office, and I laid the diary on my desk. Di pulled a chair from opposite the desk up beside me, sat, and peered over my shoulder as I paged through the diary we had found at Ray's. The first entry was from just over a year ago.

> *D. laid out the plan for us today. If we're careful, we should be able to raise enough money for the move in about two years.*

"I wonder who D. is?" Di mused.

"If the diary belonged to one of the Farrell boys, it could be referring to his brother—either Darrell or Duane."

"Flip through a few pages and see if any names stand out."

> *First package was delivered, no problem. I feel like I can breathe easy again for the first time in a week. Bro says to relax, but there are so many ways things can go wrong.*

"Bro could certainly be one of the Farrells referring to his brother," I said.

"Check the date of the final entry. See if it is close to the time of the murders," Di said.

The last entry was made three days before the bodies were discovered.

Another lie. Bro says it's one lie too many.

"Oh, my gosh, Liv. It sounds like the brothers discovered the truth about whatever they were mixed up in, and it got them killed. We have to give this diary to Dave."

"No."

"What do you mean, no?"

"I mean Dave won't be able to use this diary as evidence, because it was obtained illegally. I'm going to take the diary home and read the rest of it. Hopefully, I'll glean some information that Dave can use as grounds to get a search warrant for Ray's trailer. Then we'll have to put the diary back where we found it so the sheriff can discover it legally."

"Okay," Di said. "Just keep in mind there could be information in that diary that already got two people killed."

At home, I once again cracked open the diary, sunlight streaming through the window to illuminate the pages. The light began to fade into early evening shadows. I reached up to switch on the lamp when it suddenly occurred to me that I should have heard something from Larry Joe by now. I dialed his cell phone, but the call went directly to voice mail. For an awful moment, I imagined my husband lying unconscious and perhaps seriously injured in a hospital somewhere between Huntsville and Dixie. Maybe he had fallen asleep at the wheel. I called the warehouse number at McKay's and was panic stricken when there was no answer.

Pull yourself together, I told myself. *Of course there's no answer. It's Sunday.*

After a few deep breaths, I had the presence of mind to call Ralph Harvey at home. He would have heard if the shipment Larry Joe was delivering had not arrived.

He finally picked up the phone after the sixth ring.

"Ralph, this is Liv McKay," I said, trying not to sound hysterical. "Have you heard from Larry Joe today? I know it's silly, but he hasn't called, and I was beginning to worry that he might have had engine trouble or maybe even an accident on the way back from Huntsville."

There was a long pause before Ralph mumbled, "He made it home safe and all, but, er . . . well, I'm sure he'll call you as soon as he gets a chance. He, uh . . ."

"Ralph, please just tell me what's going on."

"Well, I'm sure it's just routine, but . . . the FBI seized the truck before we could unload it and took Larry Joe in for questioning."

I think I said thanks or good-bye before hanging up the phone, but I can't be sure. My mind seized up as emotions took over. Larry Joe had been hauled off by the FBI, and it was all my fault. I never should have taken those tapes. And what if the FBI were to suddenly burst through the front door with a search warrant? They'd find not only the tapes but the diary, too. It would look like Larry Joe was systematically removing evidence.

I'd have to call and turn myself in, tell them I stole the tapes. No, that was no good. They'd just think Larry Joe and I were in on it together. What could I do? Finally, my sanity began to return. If Larry Joe had been allowed one phone call, he would have called our attorney, Bill Scott.

I called Bill and left what I hoped was a slightly coherent message, telling him to call me if he'd heard from Larry Joe, and to call me even if he hadn't heard from Larry Joe, because he would be needing his help. In a few minutes, Bill returned my call. I began to babble again, frantically, before he could get a word in.

"Liv, calm down and listen," he said in a steady voice. "I'm at the FBI field office in Memphis right now, in the process of getting Larry Joe released from custody. He hasn't been charged with anything, and I should have him home in a couple of hours."

"Oh, thank you, Bill. Is he okay? Is there anything I can do?"

"He's fine. Just sit tight. I've got to go now."

I heaved a huge sigh of relief. But my relief quickly turned to anger as I thought about how the FBI was wasting precious time harassing my husband and my father-in-law while drug smugglers and murderers were on the loose.

With a renewed sense of determination, I went back to reading the diary, carefully studying each page. I didn't want to miss a single detail that might point to the murderer.

A couple of hours later, I heard the front door

open and quickly stashed the diary under the sofa. I ran to the front door, threw my arms around Larry Joe's neck, and soaked his shoulder with my tears.

"It's okay, babe," he said softly. "I'm fine. I've had proctology exams that were less thorough, but I think the FBI has lost interest in me as a serious suspect. Or maybe that's just wishful thinking on my part. Anyway, they let me go and just told me not to leave town again without checking in with them first."

I stepped back and took a long look at my husband. He looked dead on his feet.

"I'm sorry, honey," I said, wiping the tears from my face and trying to compose myself. "Here, you've been through hell, and you're having to comfort me. Tell me what you need."

"I want to drink a beer and then go to bed and sleep for at least twelve hours."

"You've got it. Take off your shoes, put up your feet, and I'll bring you a cold beer."

As he downed the last of the beer, Larry Joe could barely keep his eyes open. I put him to bed and snuggled up beside him. I figured he would be out cold as soon as his head hit the pillow. And I was right.

With Larry Joe down for the count, I slipped downstairs to the den to read the rest of the diary. As much as I wanted to skip to the last pages, I knew some of that information might not make sense without reading the earlier entries. Most of the entries were dated, some weren't, but they were definitely in chronological order. The first entry was from the end of June last year, and the last entry was from just a few days before the Farrells' bodies were discovered.

Sept. 2 – Bro had a close call with the boss today, while working on one of the trucks. Luckily, I was nearby, and he was able to pass off the stuff to me.

Since Darrell worked on the trucks, he must be Bro, I thought. That would mean this was Duane's diary. That made sense, because Tonya had said that Duane started keeping a diary as a kid, and Kenny had mentioned that Duane would sit on the apartment steps, writing in some kind of notebook.

Sept. 9 – BB nearly went ballistic when we told him about the delay. He chilled when Bro told him things got back on track today.

Hmm. BB must be Bobo, I thought.

Oct. 14 – D. had to hide in the closet when Mama dropped by. I still think she has a right to know, but D. and Bro say no way we can let her get mixed up in this. I guess they're right.

Okay, clearly Bro and D are two different people, I mused. *And D. must be somebody their mother knows, since he hid in the closet to keep her from seeing him. Maybe Bobo's first name or last name begins with a* D. *Could be he's a cousin or a schoolmate of theirs that their mom knows is bad news.*

Nov. 3 – Just got back from reenactment camp in Missouri. First one with D. since everything came out. Our unit did so great. Everybody was right on cue. D. said he's so proud of his boys.

Dec. 17 – We just bought D. a Christmas gift. We got him a Leech & Rigdon field officer's sword. I'm excited about our first Christmas with D. Actually, Bro says it's not the first, but of course I don't remember anything about those early ones.

Hmm, I thought. *"Our first Christmas with D. . ."* Clearly, D. is someone very special to Duane, a father figure. Maybe Ray Franklin? But what's the D. stand for?

Oh my God. Dad! D. is Duane and Darrell's dad!

Chapter 12

After drowsily reading through entry after entry, I was suddenly wide awake, jolted by this new revelation: Ray Franklin was Duane and Darrell's father. I kept trying to wrap my mind around the revelation. D. had to be Ray Franklin. He had spent so much time with the boys. And he had that picture of them and that postcard they'd sent when they were little. Not to mention the diary.

But their dad was supposed to have been killed in Iraq. If he'd been alive all that time, why had he waited so long to contact his kids?

As huge as this discovery was, I knew I needed to read the rest of the diary before morning—and I hoped something turned up that pointed to the murderer.

July 2 – BB says we have to ramp up operations again. We can't do that without getting caught. Bro says there's been too many close calls already.

*July 4 – BB really blew up. He says if we
don't get more stuff going soon, it's going
to get complicated for us with his boss.
D. says to let him worry about BB. He's got
experience in hand-to-hand combat if it gets
rough.*

Sounded like the Farrells were really in over their
heads.

*July 19 – Bro says knowledge is power and
it's time we knew more details about the
operation. He's planning to dig up info on
BB, follow him and stuff. I tell Bro maybe we
should let D. handle it, but he says that's too
risky. D. needs to stay under the radar. Tells
me not to mention anything to D. I don't know
what to do.*

This was less than a month before the murders. It
sounded like Darrell was wading into dangerous
waters. My heart was racing as I read the final pages.
I found myself hoping Duane and Darrell would
escape unharmed somehow, even though I already
knew this story had a very unhappy ending.

*July 28 – Bro says a lot of things are starting
to add up, but he won't tell me what's going
on. He says he has to be sure first, because if
he's right, the shit's really going to fly.*

*Aug. 1 – Reenactment went well. Bro says to
get ready, because we may have a real battle
to fight soon. Says he should have some*

answers in a day or so. I promised I wouldn't
say anything to D., but maybe I should. I'm
real worried. Bro's barely eaten or slept in
two or three days.

Then I reread the ominous final entry.

Aug. 5 – Another lie. Bro says it's one lie
too many.

I slipped quietly into the garage and stashed the
diary under the driver's seat in my SUV before heading back upstairs to bed. Larry Joe didn't so much
as twitch as I slid beneath the covers. I couldn't sleep
with words from the diary running over and over in
my head.

At just after 5:30 a.m., I slipped on some jeans, a
T-shirt, and a ball cap and tiptoed downstairs, leaving Larry Joe snoring away. I was dying to tell Di
what I had learned, and wanted to catch her before
she left for work. As I turned onto Maple Street, I
was startled to get a glimpse of myself in the rear-
view mirror. I had left the house without putting on
make-up or so much as dragging a brush across my
bed head.

The light was on in Di's kitchen when I arrived. I
tapped lightly on the front door.

"Come on in," Di called out.

When I walked into the kitchen, she was at the
counter, with her back to me.

"I can't believe you'd just holler, 'Come on in,'
without bothering to see who's at the door."

"I knew it was you," she said, digging a spoon into
a bowl of Cheerios. "Who else would be knocking

on my door at this hour of the morning?" Di sat down at the table and invited me to pour myself some coffee. "You look like you could use a cup. I'm guessing you found something interesting in the diary."

"Interesting? Try absolutely shocking."

Di looked irritated as I punctuated my statement with a long pause.

"Wait for it," I said. "Ray Franklin isn't just a father figure to Darrell and Duane. He is their long-lost father—who apparently didn't die in the Iraq War, after all."

Di, who's rarely at a loss for words, sat in a stunned silence. I filled her in on the other stuff I had learned from the diary, like Darrell and Rudy getting into a shoving match and Darrell getting suspicious about something and secretly following Bobo to find out what was going on.

"He's their dad," Di mumbled, obviously still mulling over the big news. "I guess it adds up. I mean, we did find the postcard from the boys and the old photo of them in his camper. But why would he show up after all these years? Do you think he actually killed his own sons?"

I admitted I didn't know what to think.

"Maybe he came back here to hide out," Di said. "And whatever danger he was running from ended up being dangerous for his kids."

We batted around countless scenarios to explain the "death" and delayed reappearance of Papa Farrell, aka Ray Franklin. We hypothesized that he could be a deserter on the run from the military. He could have been part of a secret military operation that went horribly wrong and left him for dead behind enemy lines. He could have gone undercover to infiltrate a terrorist group.

"Liv, does anything about Ray Franklin strike you as noble or heroic?"

"No. He mostly strikes me as sleazy and useless."

"Exactly. I don't think he was ever part of some secret military action or undercover operation. I think he's a deserter. Maybe his unit thought he was dead, and he let them keep on thinking that—and he's been on the run ever since."

"It's true that if he's trying to evade U.S. authorities, he wouldn't be able to get a real job. It would be easy to become involved with illegal activities, like drugs," I said.

"Well, I better get moving and get to *my* real job," Di said.

Di went to the back of the trailer and returned a few minutes later in her uniform. She grabbed her purse, paused at the door, and looked back me.

"You know, the sun's up now," she said. "You're welcome to help yourself to any of the makeup and hair products on my bathroom counter."

"I really look that bad, huh?"

"Unless you think advertising what the morning after a wild party looks like will help drum up business, you should probably pull yourself together."

Chapter 13

After Di left, I thought about going home to make myself more presentable for public view. But Larry Joe was probably still at the house. I had left him a note saying I had some early morning errands to run, and I didn't want to go home and have to explain what I'd been up to at this early hour. I poured another cup of coffee and decided to do the best I could with whatever paints and potions I could find in Di's bathroom.

I pulled up in front of the office at a little after seven and was surprised to see through the window that Winette was already at her desk.

"Mornin', sunshine," Winette said as I walked through her front door.

"You're up and at 'em kinda early, aren't you?"

"I have a lot I want to get done today, so I decided to get an early start. Besides, I'm just a morning person," she said with too much perkiness for my taste. "But what are you doing in so early? We both know you are not a morning person. You're not meeting clients looking like that, are you?"

I felt momentarily insulted, then realized that despite my lame attempts at primping, I was still wearing a T-shirt and old jeans.

"No. No clients. Is Mr. Sweet in yet?"

"Lord, no. He's still drinking coffee at the diner with the other old men."

I helped myself to a cup of the coffee Winette had brewed and sat down at the desk next to hers. She was putting together information packets, collating photocopies printed on different colored papers into neat color-coded stacks and humming as she stapled the packets together. She looked over at me, waiting for me to say what was on my mind.

"Winette, could I ask your advice about something, confidentially?"

"You know I don't tell tales out of school. But don't ask me what I think, unless you want to hear the truth."

"That's exactly what I want to hear."

I explained, without giving too many details, how Di and I had found Duane Farrell's diary and how it had information that could have a bearing on the murder investigation.

"Problem is, we 'found' it in somebody's home while they were out, and we didn't exactly have permission to be there. If I give it to the sheriff, I'm afraid he won't be able to use it, because of how it was obtained. And if I put it back, I don't know if the sheriff will be able to get a search warrant based on what I tell him."

Winette, who had continued stapling while I talked, put down the stapler and swiveled in her desk chair to face me. "At the very first opportunity, you and Di need to put that diary back where you 'found' it," she said, punctuating the word *found* with air quotes. "Then phone in an anonymous tip to the sheriff that you've seen Duane's diary at this person's house. And go ahead and add that you think this person may be selling drugs, just for good measure. The sheriff's a smart man. He'll figure out how to get a warrant."

"Thanks, Winette. You're absolutely right," I said, breathing a shallow sigh of relief.

"Now, can I ask *you* a question?"

"Shoot."

"I know you're a crazy woman, willing to live in a construction zone when there's perfectly good houses to be had in town. But Diane Souther strikes me as a sensible person. Why does she still live over in that trailer park? Not that there's anything wrong with living in a trailer, but . . ." She paused for a moment. "She's bound to make decent money working for the post office. Now, I'm not hounding you for a new client. I'm just genuinely curious."

"Well, you know how ugly a divorce can be, having been through one yourself."

"Lord, don't I," she said, shaking her head.

Winette had taken her ten-year-old son and had walked out on an abusive husband with just the clothes on their backs. He had tried to block the divorce, had fought for custody and, as far as I knew, had never paid a cent of child support. Yet she had managed to raise a well-adjusted, bright young man, who was now a sophomore in college, and she had worked two jobs while she studied for her real estate exams.

Di had divorced Jimmy Souther when he went to prison. And she had got saddled with his IRS problems and his sky-high credit card debt. I don't know all the details, but I do know the IRS garnished her paycheck at one point.

"I've tried to talk her into buying a house whenever you and Mr. Sweet have mentioned some really good deals on the market, like that foreclosure last year that she could have had for a song. But she says the trailer is paid for, and she's saving up for a comfortable retirement."

"A home that's paid for is a beautiful thing," Winette said. "No doubt about that."

Winette took a phone call, so before getting down to work, I decided to stretch my legs. I stepped outside and ambled down the block. I thought I'd buy a snack to tide me over until lunch.

Suzanne Bagley owns Farmers' Market, on the northeast corner of First Avenue and Main Street, just a few doors down. She runs the store, while her husband, Stan, works on their farm. Suzanne says she and Stan plan to keep the store after he retires from farming. The market features local produce, including tomatoes and peppers from the Bagleys' farm; fruit and preserves from a local orchard; locally milled sorghum; and a few organic products, such as peanut butter, shipped in from elsewhere.

I'm a regular customer because I like to support local business—and because the locally grown produce is much tastier than the stuff shipped in to the supermarket.

"Mornin', Liv," the proprietress said, looking up from the counter as I walked through the front door.

A good bit older than me but younger than my mom, Suzanne is a tall woman with a mop of salt-and-pepper curls and amazingly good posture.

"Hey, Suzanne. What looks especially pretty today?"

"Well, I've got some beautiful tomatoes—we're at the peak of tomato season."

"I'll take a few of those tomatoes and a pint of blackberries for later, and add this apple to the bill," I said, laying a Red Delicious on the counter.

Suzanne bagged and totaled my purchase.

"How's your mama?" Suzanne inquired politely.

"Sassy as ever."

"Good for her," Suzanne said, smiling. "I guess this whole business with the Farrell boys has been pretty hard on Larry Joe's dad."

"He does look tired," I said.

"And I'm sure you're tired of folks asking you about finding the bodies. My nephew actually worked with the Farrells."

"Oh. I didn't know you had any family working at McKay's."

"I think he's been working there for a year, or close to it. He's twenty-five years old and still living in his mom's basement, but my sister's just thankful he's finally straightened up and gotten a job."

"Is he a driver?"

"No, he's a mechanic. You'd probably remember him if you've seen him. He's got hair dyed jet black, except for a couple of splotches that are bleached blond. It's too bad, because he wouldn't be a bad-looking kid otherwise. Of course, this is his aunt talking," she said, flashing a broad smile. "His name is Rudy."

She handed me change from a twenty-dollar bill.

"Thanks, Suzanne."

"Thank you. And you be careful out there. It's pretty scary knowing there's still a killer on the loose."

Stepping from the air-conditioned store into the stifling heat nearly took my breath away. I polished the just purchased apple on my sleeve before taking a bite. So now I knew it was Suzanne's nephew Rudy Johnson who'd nearly come to blows with Darrell Farrell shortly before he died. I made a mental note to try to find out more about him. I strolled back down the block, feeling a bit lazy. I had slacked off with work a bit too much recently, so I dutifully went back to the office. I knew I really needed to wrap up a few things before I left to meet Mama for lunch and shopping.

I sat down at my desk and noticed the light on the answering machine was flashing. I hoped it was a call from a potential client, since business had been a bit scarce. No such luck. It was a message from Mrs. Erdman. She said she couldn't remember if we had discussed details about the tablecloths for her anniversary party. She said emphatically that it was "absolutely essential" that the tablecloths for the buffet table were crisply starched and ironed, like those at fancy restaurants. She would be "absolutely mortified" if the tablecloths were limp. I sighed and added these minutiae to the checklist for the Erdmans' party.

Mama was waiting for me, sitting in a rocking

chair on her front porch, when I pulled into the driveway and parked next to her Cadillac. I stepped out of my car and she came down the front steps toward me.

"Let's take my car, hon. Would you mind driving?" she asked, opening the front passenger-side door without waiting for an answer.

Virginia Walford is a big woman, with a personality and an attitude to match. Her plus-size clothes are always freshly pressed, if a bit on the flamboyant side. And her chemically enhanced black hair is always perfectly styled—thanks to twice-weekly trips to the beauty shop. Maybe it's her striking green eyes, but something about my mama makes people take notice. Men of a certain age can't seem to take their eyes off her—not that she'd ever let anyone get away with ignoring her.

I knew without asking where we'd eat lunch in Hartville, but Mama, nonetheless, felt it was necessary to state the obvious.

"I thought we could have lunch at the Victorian Tea Room. How does that sound, darlin'?" she said as I backed out of the driveway.

I thought, *Predictable*. I said, "Wonderful."

The waitress at the tea room seated us next to a window. I ordered a soup and half-sandwich combo. Mama ordered a large salad and a plate of tea sandwiches I'm pretty sure were meant to be shared. I asked if she planned to shop for anything in particular at the mall, and she told me one of the stores was giving away a free compact mirror with the purchase of her favorite perfume, which always envelops her like a miasma.

After Mama filled me in on all the gossip she had gathered from Sylvia after church, I decided she might be a good source from which to find out more about Suzanne's nephew, Rudy. If he'd ever been in any kind of trouble, she'd most likely have heard about it.

"Mama, do you know Suzanne Bagley's nephew, Rudy Johnson? He's her sister's boy. I think he's in his midtwenties."

"Evelyn Taylor's son? I think so. Why do you ask?"

"Suzanne mentioned he works as a mechanic at McKay's. I didn't know that. Wouldn't have thought he was old enough. I don't know if I've even seen him since he was just a little kid."

"He was a cute little boy. Sucked his thumb till he started kindergarten. Last time I saw him, he'd done something crazy with his hair. His mother, of course, thinks he's wonderful. I think he does help out some, fixing things around the house and keeping her car running. But then, Lord knows, he should, since he's a grown man living rent free in his mother's basement, for heaven's sake. I think he went away to college for a year or so but got involved with drugs and ended up flunking out. After he came home, he spent a couple of months in a hospital. His mother told everyone he had pneumonia, but Sylvia said he was really holed up at some kind of rehab center.

"I'm glad he has a good job now. I hope he stays out of trouble. His mother has enough to bear, what with Rudy's father running off with that floozy and now having to put up with Rudy's stepfather," Mama said, pursing her lips.

"What about her current husband? Does he run around with other women, too?"

"I hardly think so, given his, shall we say, 'shortcomings.' But he does drink and gamble away money at the casinos."

"That's too bad. By shortcomings, do you mean he's not able to perform as a husband?"

"Well," Mama said, "probably not very well. His ex-wife says he's hung like a Vienna sausage."

I couldn't believe I was having this conversation with my mother.

Mama cleared her throat and moved on to less prurient interests. My mind was stuck on Rudy's past drug problems. I wondered if he had any current drug issues and if that could have prompted his fight with Darrell on the videotape.

And as hard as I tried not to, I kept getting this visual image of Rudy's stepfather's "shortcomings" as compared to canned meat.

After lunch we went to the mall. Mama dragged me from store to store, trying on nearly every pair of dangly earrings in stock and looking for a skirt in just the right shade of blue. She didn't have any luck with the skirt chase, but I bought a cream-colored blouse that would work perfectly with a navy blue or black suit. My mom bought her signature perfume to get the compact mirror they were offering as a free gift with a purchase. I had to admit it was kind of cute. And, of course, even on the other side of the county, we kept running into people Mama knew, and had to stop and chat with each and every one of them for what seemed like hours.

I finally got a chance to sit down when Mama suggested we stop at the food court for some ice cream. She has remarkable stamina for a woman of her age and girth.

"So how are Wayne and Betty doing? I didn't see them at church yesterday," Mama said.

"I think the whole business of finding drugs on one of the trucks and two employees getting murdered is weighing heavy on Daddy Wayne. Even though he obviously has nothing to do with any of it."

"Well, of course not," Mama said. "The whole thing is completely ridiculous. Dragging him into the police station in handcuffs, for heaven's sake. Maybe I'll bake a chocolate pie and take it by."

About that time I heard someone squeal, "Virginia," and I looked up to see a squat redheaded woman making a beeline toward us, waving jazz hands.

Mama smiled and called out, "Maureen," then whispered to me out of the side of her mouth, "Brace yourself, hon. This woman never knows when to shut up."

That was rich coming from my mother—and frightening. Mama stood up to hug Maureen, who nodded to me and then began prattling on and on, with an auctioneer's speed. Even Mama could barely get a word in. I drifted into a semiconscious state and was contemplating ordering more ice cream— since they don't sell liquor at the food court.

Finally, Mama stood up, which silenced Maureen just long enough for Mama to say, "I wish we could stay and chew the fat, but Liv and I have a little errand of mercy we have to take care of." Mama patted Maureen on the shoulder, gathered up her purse, and started walking away. I scrambled to catch up.

When we hit the door, I turned to her and said, "So, what's our little errand of mercy?"

"I don't know what yours is, but I just rescued you from brain-numbing boredom, didn't I?"

I wrapped my arm around her waist. "Thank you, Mama. I owe you one."

"You're welcome, darlin.' But you already owe me more than you could ever possibly repay—starting with sixteen hours of labor and a giant head." She paused. "Which reminds me. If you don't mind, could we stop by the grocery store on the way home? I need to pick up some ground beef. Earl's coming over for supper, and I'm making meat loaf."

I didn't want to know why my oversize baby head reminded Mama of ground beef. She said, "Earl's coming over for supper" like it was a special event, which it wasn't. Either Earl Daniels comes over for dinner or they go out to eat pretty much every night of the week, although his car is never parked at her house overnight.

My daddy passed away four years ago, God rest his soul, and Mama and Earl had been seeing each other steadily for about two years now. She cooks for him, and he makes little repairs around her house and escorts her to any events that she prefers to attend with a man on her arm. I wouldn't call Earl good-looking, but he is taller than Mama, has a full head of hair, and still has his own teeth.

Mama insists they are nothing more than friends, and I suppose I believe her. But I can't help thinking Earl smiles an awful lot.

Chapter 14

After I dropped Mama off at her house, I drove around for I didn't know how long. Bits and pieces of all that had happened over the past few days darted around in my head like a Pac-Man game, running through an endless maze of dead ends.

Larry Joe pulled in the driveway just ahead of me. I threw together a quick supper of canned chili and a tossed salad. After dinner, we retired to the den and pulled up a movie to watch on Netflix. It was some goofy comedy, but it was good to see my husband laughing like his old self, enjoying some downtime after an intense few days.

Unfortunately, it didn't last long. About thirty minutes into the movie, Larry Joe answered a phone call from a driver who had been in an accident on I-40. Thank God no one was hurt. But Larry Joe spent the next couple of hours making calls to get the wrecked truck taken care of and the freight trans-ferred and delivered on time. Mentally exhausted, we called it an early night. I drifted off to sleep, thinking about the next day's main event—the Farrell brothers' funeral.

Tuesday afternoon I changed into a short-sleeved navy-blue dress and helped Larry Joe pick out an appropriately somber tie.

"We better get moving," I said. "I always hate walking in late for a funeral."

To me, it seems even tackier to come into the church after the casket than to trail in after the bride at a wedding.

"Will your mama be at the funeral?" Larry Joe asked as he was backing out of the driveway.

"She didn't say, but do you really think she'd miss the spectacle of a double funeral?"

"Silly question."

We pulled into the parking lot of the First Methodist Church with plenty of time to spare before the one o'clock funeral for Duane and Darrell Farrell. We squeezed into a pew near the back, next to Larry Joe's parents. The church, which probably seated more than two hundred people, was packed.

The organ played a mournful tune, striking more than a few sour notes, as two gray coffins were rolled on gurneys up the main aisle. Six pallbearers, all wearing Confederate uniforms, flanked each casket. The officers wore long frock coats and brimmed hats, while the enlisted men sported short jackets and visor-fronted caps. It was a surreal sight. After escorting the coffins to the front of the church, the reenactors took off their hats and placed them over their hearts before taking their seats on the front pews to either side of the center aisle.

Ray Franklin was among the men in gray. Tonya Farrell was seated on the second row. I spotted Ralph Harvey and some other people I recognized from McKay Trucking sitting a couple of rows ahead of us on the opposite side of the church. I caught a glimpse of Mama sitting near the front. I recognized her favorite funeral hat.

Reverend Goodwin, the pastor at First Methodist, is relatively new to Dixie, having been assigned to the church here less than a year ago. After the organist had struck the final painful, off-key chords of "In the Garden," the congregation exhaled a collective sigh of relief. The slender, thirty-something-year-old minister nervously approached the pulpit, a visible perspiration mustache above his lips. My guess was this was the reverend's first double funeral—and likely his first standing-room-only service.

Following the funeral, Larry Joe and his dad offered their condolences to Tonya Farrell and chatted briefly with Ralph Harvey and the other guys from work. We decided to skip the graveside service, since it looked like a respectable number of folks had pulled their cars into the lineup for the procession to the cemetery. Larry Joe kept tugging at his collar, as if to let steam escape. And honestly, Daddy Wayne looked like he needed to lie down.

We talked my father-in-law into going home, and Larry Joe headed back to the office for a few hours. I briefly considered crashing the funeral luncheon to see if I could pick up any helpful bits of information, but decided it would be tacky. Besides, I needed to go to the office and make some phone calls before my appointment at the country club.

I had a date with the head bartender at the Dixie

Country Club to sample some different versions of the mint julep. It was a tough job, but somebody had to do it. Mrs. Erdman had originally been scheduled to go with me to the tasting. I always like to involve my clients in some fun aspect of the planning process, and with Mrs. Erdman, I figured drinking liquor while we were at it would make it more enjoyable, at least for me. She wanted to be sure we served the ultimate mint julep at her Moonshine and Magnolias Anniversary Party. But at the last minute she called to cancel, saying she had a sick headache. My best guess: her headache's name was Walter Erdman.

Her cancellation caused me a moment of panic. I didn't know if we'd be able to schedule another time for the sampling before the party, and we really needed to place the bar order right away. She said she didn't want to leave something "so important" to chance—meaning leaving the decision up to the bartender, which made perfect sense to me. She reluctantly said she'd trust my judgment, but trying to figure out what would please Mrs. Erdman was not a responsibility I wanted on my shoulders.

Then I thought of Holly. Mrs. Erdman had shown an obvious admiration for Holly's pedigree—from one of Dixie's most prominent families, world traveler, elegant manners. I suggested taking Holly along for the tasting, an idea that elicited enthusiastic approval from Mrs. Erdman. Fortunately, Holly was available on such short notice. I'd rightly reckoned that the prospect of sipping mint juleps wouldn't be disagreeable to her.

I drove up the winding drive to Holly's stately Tudor-style home, vintage 1920s. She had inherited the house from her mother, who had died just a couple of months after Holly's husband had passed away. It had obviously been a difficult time for her emotionally. But Holly said that when she returned to Dixie to sort out her mother's estate, it felt like being wrapped in a warm, welcoming blanket. She knew instantly that moving back into her childhood home was just what she needed.

Holly came out the front door, dressed in a sleeveless turquoise turtleneck, matching eyeglasses, and wide-legged pants, her hair pulled back in a Karl Lagerfeld ponytail. Not a look everyone could pull off, but it worked for her.

On the ride to the country club, Holly filled me in on her morning meeting with Meemaw Carter. Rummaging through our client's costume jewelry had turned up some pieces Holly thought would add a nice bit of sparkle and whimsy to the table for the bridesmaids' tea, and it had also been a pleasing trip down memory lane for Meemaw. I've learned never to underestimate the value of personalizing parties with items belonging to the clients, as well as of making the process of planning the party an enjoyable one for them.

Hunky head bartender Mark DeAngelo treated us to a tasty variety of mint julep recipes. Like any bartender worth the salt on his glass rims, he flirted with us as he mixed drinks. Holly was laughing loudly and was flirting back, which I found a little surprising for my usually decorous assistant. It started to make sense when I learned she had already had a two-martini lunch with an old friend. By the third mint julep sample, I was catching up to her. Mark's biceps flexed when he muddled, and I was feeling turned on as I watched him bruise mint sprigs.

The amount of bourbon in the mint juleps ranged from one and a half to three ounces per serving. They all tasted good to me, but in the end Holly and I settled on the recipe with the most liquor and a slightly expensive brand of bourbon, believing that after having a few of these, even Mrs. Erdman would be too mellow to complain.

Mark reached over and rubbed Holly's bare upper arm and remarked that she had goose bumps. If she didn't before, she did after he touched her. He told us they always kept the air-conditioning on a little too cool for the ladies, and said he'd be right back with a fresh pot of coffee to warm us up. It was a smooth way of saying we needed to sober up a little before operating an automobile on public roads, but we weren't drunk enough to take offense. The two of us sat at the bar, enjoying the steam rising from our cups and off of Mark's body as he cleaned up the glassware and took the bar order for the Erdmans' party.

After I dropped Holly off at her house, I picked up two chef's salads from the diner for supper. When I arrived home, a fly came in through the back door with me. I chased it around the kitchen for ten minutes like a woman possessed before I finally silenced its buzz with the splat of a flyswatter against the windowpane. Larry Joe came in from the garage just as I collapsed into a chair at the kitchen table.

"You look tuckered out," he said, bending down to plant a kiss on the top of my head. "You been doing one of those dancercise videos?"

"No. I've been managing pest control."

Larry Joe grabbed a beer for himself and the pitcher of iced tea for me from the fridge while I plated up our salads and mixed a simple vinaigrette dressing.

"I'm worried about your dad. He was looking kind of green around the gills today."

"Yeah. When he gave in to going home after the funeral, I knew he must be feeling poorly," Larry Joe said. "If he won't go to the doctor, I think I'll see if Dr. Chase can drop by the house and have a look at him."

"I think you should, honey. Your mom's going to make herself sick worrying over him."

After we finished eating, Larry Joe insisted he needed to mow the lawn before the neighbors started to complain.

"Honey, are you sure you're up to it? You've been working yourself to death. I can call that kid down the street tomorrow and get him to come over and cut the grass."

"Aw, you know I don't like the way he cuts it. Anyway, I'll probably just run over the front yard and save the back for another day."

"Take a bottled water out with you," I hollered as he headed upstairs.

After Larry Joe had changed clothes and had gone outside to tend to yard work, I curled up on the sofa in the den. I stared at a game show on TV but didn't manage to fill in any of the letters before Vanna made them appear. I thought to myself that I should do some laundry or paint some more in the living room. Instead, I lay on the sofa with the TV remote in my hand, clicking from channel to channel with the energy of a three-toed sloth.

Unfortunately, my mind wouldn't give in to the laziness my body so readily embraced. I couldn't help wondering who had put Darrell and Duane in that garage. Couldn't help wishing the killer had stashed the bodies somewhere else. Couldn't help thinking Winette was right and I needed to get that diary back into Ray's trailer.

Problem was, even if I could work up the energy to drive over to Ray's trailer, I couldn't do it tonight. Di plays bunco one night a month with a group of other mail carriers, all women except for one retired guy. And this month was Di's turn to host. It sounds pretty cutthroat: they play for money, although Di insists it's just chump change. And the parties are BYOB, with the host or hostess providing light snacks. Di says it helps her keep up with post office politics and gossip. And the gossip gets even more cutthroat than the bunco. There was no way I'd risk one of those tongue waggers spotting my car driving past Di's on the way to Ray Franklin's place.

After channel surfing for a long while, I hit the OFF button, wondering why we paid for cable. At some point, my mind finally stopped racing, and I dozed off to the drone of the lawn mower.

I was awakened with a jolt by the sound of Larry Joe's panicked voice.

"Liv, put your shoes on. We've got to go."

Chapter 15

I sprang up to a seated position and could see my husband through the doorway kicking off his shoes and hurriedly peeling off his sweat-soaked T-shirt. He was obviously shaken up.

"Honey, what's wrong?"

He suddenly stood very still and looked at me with misty eyes. "Mama just called me on the cell. Daddy's had a heart attack."

We both looked at each other helplessly for a moment, before Larry Joe resumed his frenzied activity.

"Grab your purse," he said. "We're heading out just as soon as I wash my face and put on a clean shirt."

I pulled on my shoes and, even though it was the middle of August in Tennessee, instinctively grabbed a sweater from the entry closet. I thought it might be chilly at the hospital. After a moment, I heard Larry Joe's feet thundering down the stairs. I offered to drive, but he said he was fine.

Neither of us was fine.

I was actually relieved when he said he'd drive, though. I felt a little unsteady and slightly nauseated.

We pulled onto his parents' street just in time to see an ambulance racing away, lights flashing, sirens blaring. One of the firefighters, who apparently had been among the first responders, walked to the curb when Larry Joe stopped in front of the house and rolled down his window. I recognized him as Jeff Kovacs, who had played high school football with Larry Joe.

"Where's my mama, Jeff?"

"She's in the ambulance with your dad. You go on and follow 'em to the hospital. They're taking him to County General."

"How's Daddy?"

"He's a feisty old cuss—hanging on with both hands," Jeff said before slapping the car door twice, signaling for Larry Joe to drive on.

We rode in silence to the hospital, holding tightly to the nugget of hope Jeff had given us.

We parked the car outside the emergency room, and I struggled to keep up with Larry Joe, who was walking faster than I could run. We entered through the automatic doors and spotted Larry Joe's mom at the check-in desk, talking to a nurse. She seemed to be steadying herself against the counter just to remain upright.

Larry Joe walked up beside his mother, wrapped his arm around her waist, and guided her over to a chair in the waiting area. I sat down with Miss Betty, while Larry Joe went back to the desk to take care of paperwork. I gave my mother-in-law a hug. Her arms were ice cold, so I draped the sweater I'd brought with me around her shoulders.

"They wouldn't let me go back with him."

"Well, we'd just be in the way right now."

"He was breathing, though. I could see he was breathing."

I felt tears welling up in my eyes and a lump in my throat getting so big, I could barely swallow. Unable to speak, I just reached over and grabbed her hand.

Larry Joe came over, took the seat on the other side of his mom, and put his arm around her. She placed her head on his shoulder and started to sob.

"That old goat better not die on me," she said.

"Now, we both know Daddy's too stubborn to die. He's just had a lot on him lately. He's gonna have to slow down some, that's all."

After what seemed like hours but registered only as thirty-two minutes by the clock on the wall, a nurse came through the swinging doors and called out, "McKay family?"

We jumped to our feet in unison and rushed toward her.

"Come on back," she said.

We followed her until she stopped in the hallway, in front of some chairs like the ones in the waiting room, and told us to have a seat.

"The doctor will be out to talk to you in a minute."

We were all relieved to see that the man in the white coat was Evan Chase, doctor and longtime golf partner to Larry Joe's dad. He came and knelt in front of my mother-in-law.

Before he could speak, she said, "Don't sugarcoat anything for me, Evan. Give it to us straight."

"He's had a major heart attack. We've started a clot-buster medicine in his IV, and we're moving him up to the ICU. Our biggest concern at the moment is an arrhythmia, which could cause him to have another heart attack in the next twenty-four hours. We'll keep him hooked up to an EKG to monitor for that."

"Can we see him?" Larry Joe said, rising out of his chair as the doctor stood up.

"After we get him settled upstairs. The last visiting period in the ICU is ten p.m. After that, I suggest y'all go home and try to get some sleep. The next visiting period won't be until eight o'clock in the morning."

Larry Joe shook hands with Dr. Chase, and we walked to the elevators to make our way up to the intensive care waiting room. We sat in the ICU waiting room, listening to Larry Joe's mom fret over whether to call Daddy Wayne's brother and sister. We all agreed there was no point in calling and worrying Aunt Nora, who was the oldest sibling and was in frail health. As the clock ticked toward ten, we finally decided it was too late to call Uncle Ed, especially since none of us could remember if he was in the central or eastern time zone.

At straight up 10:00 p.m., the desk nurse announced visiting time. We were among eight or nine people who lined up for a brief visit with loved ones.

Daddy Wayne looked pale but seemed to be steadily breathing oxygen through a tube affixed to his nose. The nurse told us not to worry if he didn't wake up, since he had just been given a sedative.

I slipped out of the crowded, curtained-off corner that housed Daddy Wayne's hospital bed and monitoring equipment, where Miss Betty was holding my father-in-law's hand and Larry Joe was holding his mom's hand. The clock in the waiting room showed it was almost 10:15 p.m., so I texted Di on my cell phone.

Is bunco over? I'm @ hospital.

In less than a minute Di texted back, Call me.

The sign on the wall said cell phone use was prohibited in the waiting room or the ICU, so I stepped into the hall and stood next to the elevators.

I dialed, and Di picked up without bothering to say hello. "What happened? Who's in the hospital?"

I brought her up to speed on what had transpired thus far and what little we knew about Daddy Wayne's condition. She insisted on coming to the hospital, even though I told her she didn't need to. I reminded her she could enter the hospital only through the emergency room entrance after 10:00 p.m.

Larry Joe and his mom walked back into the waiting room at the same time that I did. The large room began to clear out a bit as family members of some of the patients said their good-byes for the night. Others started staking out the sofas and recliners scattered around the room for a place to sleep. Miss Betty had stopped to chat with an acquaintance, and I told Larry Joe he'd better grab a recliner for his mom before they were all taken.

"I'm going to try to get her to go home."

"Good luck with that," I said.

With a look of resignation, he put his mom's purse on a recliner, and we sat on the sofa next to it.

"Di's on her way over," I said.

"Why don't you get her to run you home? You can

drive my truck tomorrow, and I'll have the car here if we need it."

"I'll stay. I hate leaving you here alone with your mom. What if something happens?"

Larry Joe and my mother-in-law both insisted I go home. So after Di and I had hugged them both and admonished them to get some rest, we headed to the parking lot.

"I don't know why I'm leaving," I said. "I know I won't be able to sleep a wink tonight."

"Where's Duane's diary?"

"In my car."

"Good. Ray Franklin pulled out of the trailer park just ahead of me. So, if you're feeling up to it, let's grab the freaking diary and stick it back in the freezer for Dave to find."

"Why not? No time like the present," I said.

I retrieved the diary, which I'd stashed under the seat of our SUV, in the emergency room parking lot.

Chapter 16

Di retrieved the spare house key from inside the cement block, and we entered Ray's camper the same way as before. Without the forethought to bring a flashlight, we made do with the little penlight on my key chain. Since we'd been there before, I figured that would provide enough light to find the freezer and replace the diary.

I froze for a moment when I thought I heard the scurrying of tiny paws. "I'm sure that's just a cat under the camper," I said out loud, refusing to entertain the possibility that I was stumbling around a dark room with a mouse.

I found that the book we had slipped into the empty frozen dinner carton was still in its place, and I felt relieved that Ray apparently hadn't noticed the diary was missing. I pulled out the book, placed the diary in the carton, closed the freezer door, and turned around just as the camper door was flung open and a huge flashlight beam smacked me in the face. Di and I both stood silent and stunned, like deer in headlights, fearing what Ray's next move might be.

Then a familiar voice spoke from behind the blinding light. "Just what in the hell do you two think you're up to?"

"Oh, Dave. Thank God it's you," Di said as we both heaved a sigh of relief.

The sense of relief was premature. Dave let us know he was in no mood to be lenient.

"Step outside, ladies," he said, motioning with the flashlight. We followed his instructions.

"I saw your car parked out here, and I was worried something might have happened to you," Dave said, a slight tremor in his usually rock-solid voice. "Only to find out you and Liv McKay are just doing a little breaking and entering."

"We didn't break in. We used a key," I said hopefully. Di held up the key as proof.

"So, you have the key to Ray's trailer. Well, I'll just call him and get this whole mess straightened out."

Dave took his cell phone out of his pocket, and Di and I said, "No" in unison.

"Wait, Dave. We can explain everything if you just give us a chance," Di said in a sweet-as-molasses voice. "Let's all go back to my place and talk about this over a cup of coffee."

Dave took a deep breath, and I could see his nostrils were flaring. In my experience, it's never a good sign when a man's nostrils flare.

"We're going to talk, all right. Down at the station."

"Dave, you can't be seri—" Di began, but Dave interrupted.

"Damn skippy, I'm serious. Diane Souther, you

get in your car and drive straight to the station." He shifted his icy gaze in my direction. "And, you, get in the police car with me. I don't want y'all cooking up a story on the drive over."

We both stood there for a moment with a hangdog look on our faces, but Dave wasn't about to give us a break.

"Move it," he said.

And we did.

Terry, the dispatcher, watched quietly as Dave marched us through the station and into what I presumed was called the interrogation room.

"Terry, I don't want to be disturbed for anything short of a homicide."

Terry said, "Yes, sir." And that was the last voice, other than mine and Di's and Dave's, I heard for the next three hours.

There was obviously more going on between Dave and Di than the situation at hand. My best guess, based on their current behavior and my own assumptions about their clandestine relationship, was Dave felt betrayed that Di hadn't confided in him about our snooping. And Di, rankled that Dave was giving her such a hard time, was dropping the temperature in the room with her cold shoulder and frosty stares in Dave's direction.

Unfortunately, this prompted Dave to shift his attention toward me. I managed to remain guarded in my answers for a while, telling Dave about the diary, since he had caught us red-handed. I tried to avoid telling him about other activities, like stalking Ray and stealing the security tapes from the trucking company. But as I felt the long arm of the law reaching across the table and putting me into a psychological choke hold, I finally caved. I ended up confessing everything I'd ever done that was wrong, all the way back to stealing a T-shirt from Carol Gompers while we were at church camp in the sixth grade.

I sat limp and spineless in my chair. Dave, apparently moved to compassion, asked Terry to bring us some coffee and doughnuts. Di turned up her nose at the stale doughnuts, but I was devoid of pride at that point.

Satisfied I had told him everything we'd been up to, Dave finally relaxed, at least momentarily, and assumed a friendly demeanor.

"Since I saw for myself that you didn't remove anything from Ray's camper, and you did have a key, I suppose we can forget about that, for now. And seeing how you ladies have provided information that may prove to be helpful—although you should have come to me with it sooner—I'll keep you in the loop on the investigation to the extent that I can, which hopefully will encourage you not to do any more snooping around on your own.

"Rudy, the one you saw having a scuffle with Darrell on the tape, is a person of interest. The Feds have him under surveillance. Their people took apart that truck in Oklahoma and discovered a hidden compartment for drug smuggling. It was smartly done. Basically, the power drive had been fixed to transfer all the drive power to the front-drive axle. The rear axle continued to turn like normal, but the junction box and rear axle liner were used to hide drugs—in this case, about half a million dollars' worth of heroin. Took a skilled mechanic to fix it up, so I'm thinking it was Darrell, and maybe Rudy, too."

Dave adjured us not to tell anyone, including Larry Joe, about the hidden compartment just yet. "In addition to keeping their eyes on Rudy, the Feds are following other trucks and checking for hidden compartments as they can. Hopefully, this trail will lead to the drug trafficking ring that's been operating through Dixie."

Dave was intrigued by the diary's implication that Ray Franklin could be Duane and Darrell's father. "Based on what you've told me, I'm going to bring Ray in for questioning tomorrow about some possibly stolen Confederate artifacts. But what I really want is to get him to drink a Coke or some coffee so we can retrieve a DNA sample for the lab. If he is a deserter, I'll gladly lock him up and hold him for the military police," Dave said.

"Now, I've got a couple of things to wrap up here, but I will arrive at my house in exactly thirty minutes," he said, his face suddenly stony and his nostrils flaring. It's creepy the way he can turn his bad cop look off and on as if with the flip of a switch. "When I do, I'd better find a box of videotapes that have a bearing on a certain murder investigation left on my front porch anonymously, which I'm obligated to share with the FBI. If I don't find said package when I get home, I know two people who will be arrested and charged with obstruction of justice before sunrise. Are we clear?"

I nodded vigorously.

Di just looked at me and said, "Let's go."

I felt as pale as the moonlight, but I savored

breathing unrestricted air again as Di and I walked out of the station and got in her car.

"I can't believe Dave was being such a jerk," Di said, slamming the car door. "He knew good and well we weren't stealing anything from Ray's."

"Yeah, but he also knew we were poking around in a murder investigation."

Di appeared to have nothing else to say on the matter, so I dropped it.

"I guess it's just as well I wasn't planning to sleep tonight, since it's almost a quarter to three," I said. "Di, maybe you should call one of your bunco buddies and get them to sub for you today."

"I'm not that old and decrepit yet. I'll just get to bed early tonight . . . or tomorrow night. I don't even know what night it is anymore."

Di pulled into my driveway.

"You go on home," I said. "I'll drive Larry Joe's truck to take care of that little errand for the sheriff."

Chapter 17

After I got back from dropping off the tapes at Dave's house, I checked the answering machine and double-checked my cell phone for texts or missed calls but found none. I figured no news from the hospital was good news.

Despite my concerns about insomnia, sleep came easily. Feeling as wrung out as a dishrag, I collapsed into bed and didn't awaken until the alarm clock went off at 6:15 a.m.

I arrived in the ICU waiting room a few minutes before seven to find my husband and my mother-in-law looking haggard and swilling coffee out of Styrofoam cups. While they both looked tired, Miss Betty's eyes were red, as if she'd been crying. When she excused herself to go to the ladies' room, I asked Larry Joe about her.

"Did your mama not get any sleep?"

"Off and on. Actually, she did pretty well until about five o'clock. Mr. Coburn, one of the ICU patients, passed away. And that's when they told his family. Mama got all emotional then."

"I'm so sorry, honey. Maybe we can get your mom to go home and rest awhile after the eight o'clock visit."

But rest would have to wait.

Dr. Chase came to talk to us just after we had gone in to see Daddy Wayne.

"Betty," he said, "I don't like the looks of this morning's readings. I'm scheduling Wayne for angioplasty at ten this morning, and we'll put in two stents while we're in there."

Despite Dr. Chase's assurances that angioplasty was a very safe and widely used procedure, when we went in to see my father-in-law before they took him up for surgery Larry Joe and I squeezed his dad's hands, as if we were seeing him for the last time. Then we slipped out to let my mother-in-law have a few minutes alone with him before his surgery.

My husband and I wrapped our arms around each other and stood silently in the hall until his mom came out of the room.

"I guess we should make some phone calls," she said. "I'll call the preacher and your uncle Ed."

We spread out, leaving a few feet between each other, and Miss Betty made her calls, Larry Joe phoned the trucking company, and I called my mother. Mama was miffed that I hadn't called her last night, but she softened when I told her Daddy Wayne was scheduled for stents at ten o'clock.

"I'm on my way," she said.

My mom muscled her way in to see Daddy Wayne, even though it wasn't visiting hours. Then she came out and sat with us in the waiting room. The three of us McKays were too tired to talk, so Mama carried the conversation—something she has a gift for. In a bit, Mama jumped up and said she was going to phone to see what was keeping the preacher.

Larry Joe took his mom's hand and asked if she wanted us to call any of her friends.

"No. I've got my family here," she said, holding tight to Larry Joe's hand and reaching over to pat me on the knee. "Brother Caleb will put Wayne's name on the prayer list for the Wednesday night service. By the end of the week, church folks will be swarming."

"Maybe Daddy Wayne will be home by then," I said, trying hard to sound hopeful.

A hush fell over the room, and all eyes turned as Mama walked through the door, accompanied by Brother Caleb Duncan in a three-piece suit, with slicked-back hair, and with a Bible tucked under one arm.

The three of us stood in unison. Brother Duncan clasped Miss Betty's hands between his and assured her of the church's prayers and support. He invited us to go with him to pray over Daddy Wayne. Larry Joe and his mom followed along behind Brother Duncan, and Mama and I decided to remain in the waiting room.

"Did y'all go out to the graveside service yesterday?" Mama asked.

"No. We talked Daddy Wayne into going home to lie down, which should have been a sign. I wish we had made him go on to the hospital right then. Maybe he could have avoided having this heart attack."

"Now, you know dang well you couldn't have dragged that bullheaded man to the hospital. I'm surprised you were able to talk him into going home to lie down. Hopefully, after this wake-up call he'll take better care of himself. Betty's just going to have to put her foot down if he won't behave. And speaking of misbehaving, I had to put my foot down with a certain make-believe colonel yesterday," Mama said, barely taking a breath.

She went on. "Junior Price grabbed my bottom during the funeral lunch, as I was pouring iced tea in his glass. Sitting there, all decked out in his Confederate uniform . . . He may be an officer, but he's certainly no gentleman. I gave him my best squinty-eyed look. If Junior had put his hand on my fanny a second time, he was getting cooled off with a pitcher of iced tea to his crotch."

In the South, a man can still be called "Junior" decades after the "Senior" is dead and buried. I guessed Junior Price to be in his midseventies. However, I know from experience that Mama's mean, squinty-eyed look was pretty scary at any age.

"What were you doing at the funeral lunch? I thought the Methodist women were taking care of it."

"Liv, you know me. I'm not the kind who waits around to be asked to do something. Sylvia and I just naturally pitched in. Besides, that little Methodist group obviously needed some help. Pitiful lack of planning there. Three different people brought potato salad, for heaven's sake."

I wouldn't say Mama didn't have good intentions, but in this case I tended to believe her motivation might have been more about gossip than gospel. I didn't scold her, though. One, because it wouldn't do any good, and two, because I wanted to hear whatever gossip she might have picked up.

"I'm glad Wayne went home to rest. Ralph Harvey was there, so McKay Trucking was represented, and

Ralph seemed to know some of those Civil War actors. Wasn't that the strangest thing you've ever seen, all the pallbearers in Confederate uniforms? But at least they were dressed nice. I've been to some funerals where the pallbearers didn't even wear a tie. . . ."

Mama went on for a good while but didn't tell me anything useful to the investigation. If Tonya Farrell had any family still living, they didn't come to the funeral, which was sad.

"I happened to see Junior Price handing a thick envelope to Tonya Farrell," Mama said. "I assumed the Civil War actors passed the hat and gave the money they collected to Tonya to help with funeral expenses, which I thought was real nice. Only time I saw that poor woman smile all day, bless her heart. It was almost sweet enough to make me forgive Junior Price for pinching my bottom—but not quite."

It seemed like hours before they took my father-in-law to the operating room, and the hour and twenty minutes for the procedure seemed even longer. Afterward, Dr. Chase came into the waiting room, still dressed in scrubs. He said the procedure went well, but Daddy Wayne's blood pressure was still too high. They'd have to monitor him closely, and he likely would be in the intensive care unit for a couple more days.

We all breathed a sigh of relief that Daddy Wayne had made it through surgery. Mama left after hearing the doctor's report, and Larry Joe finally talked his mom into going home and they left to get a bite to eat and to get some rest. I volunteered to stay in the ICU waiting room until they returned. I knew my mother-in-law wouldn't leave unless somebody was keeping vigil.

Di arrived to keep me company just after 7:00 p.m. with take-out plates from the diner.

"How was yoga class this evening?" I asked as I speared a green bean with a plastic fork.

"It was fine. And you'll be pleased to know, against my better judgment, I did your bidding and invited Deputy Ted to join me for some ice cream after class. I guess your father-in-law being in the hospital made me feel charitable. Plus, I'm still not speaking to Dave."

"Did you find out anything?"

"Yeah. I found out Ted's a sloppy eater. But he also told me they scored with their surveillance operation the other night."

I listened with rapt attention as Di laid out the details. The manager at the mini-storage place had called the sheriff after spotting some guy walking around outside of Darrell Farrell's storage unit—the one with all the expensive Civil War gear in it—and taking a real close look at the lock. So Ted had set up surveillance that night to see if the guy would come back and try to break in, which he did. The sheriff had instructed Ted not to arrest the guy until he came out of the storage unit. Dave wanted to know what he was after. Thought it might be important to the case.

"Ted said it was pretty obvious the thief wasn't a professional, since it took him, like, fifteen minutes to get the lock open," Di said before downing the last of her bottled water and reaching across me to take a drink of my Diet Coke. "I guess that ice cream made me thirsty."

"So what was the man after in the storage room? Were there drugs hidden inside some of the stuff?"

"No. He just nabbed one sword. Apparently, it's a pretty rare piece, according to Professor Shapiro. But he also had a camera with him and took digital photos of nearly everything in the storage unit."

"Hold that thought," I said.

I got up and walked over to the vending machine area adjoining the waiting room to buy Di a Diet Coke of her own. I'd say my mind was racing, but I was operating on too much of a sleep deficit for that. It was more like my mind was stuck in second gear, trying to forge up a steep hill. I wondered why anyone would go to the trouble to break into a room full of expensive collectibles, only to steal just one item and take some photographs.

Di resumed telling me the story, pausing occasionally when prying ears moved past us.

It turned out the not so professional thief was a legitimate dealer of Civil War goods and was named something Adams. He had owned a store near Nashville for the past ten years. He said he had bought some stuff from Darrell Farrell a while back that turned out to be stolen. He found out when a dealer friend of his was in town, visiting, and spotted something in the store that had been burgled from one of his longtime customers, some real big-time collector. And the collector had insurance photos to back up his claims.

Adams said he returned the stolen goods. The only problem was, he'd already sold a couple of items he had bought from Darrell. He paid the ripped-off collector market value for the sold items, and the victim agreed not to report it to the police or tell fellow collectors. Adams said he was ticked off to be out of the money, but he was really more worried about his reputation as a dealer. It could ruin his business if word got around to serious collectors that he had bought or sold stolen goods.

Adams said he took pictures of all the stuff Darrell had in storage to find out if any more of it was stolen. He figured if he had proof, he could get Darrell arrested—and probably collect a reward from the owners for the return of their collectibles.

"But why did he take the sword?"

"Supposedly, it's an expensive, really rare sword. Adams said he was pretty sure it hadn't been stolen, because he figured he would have heard about it if a piece like that had gone missing. He said he wouldn't risk trying to sell it, but he wanted it for his personal collection. Considered it payment for the stolen stuff Darrell had pawned off on him," Di said. "That's his story, anyway."

"Do the police think this guy, Adams, is the one who assaulted Dr. Shapiro? Could he be mixed up in the murders?"

"He swears that he had nothing to do with the Farrells' deaths, that he heard about the murders only after he had tracked down Darrell's address in Dixie. But it seems to me he had a pretty good motive, especially if he had confronted the Farrells about the stolen merchandise. He apparently has a solid alibi for the time of the robbery and assault at the professor's house, but he doesn't seem to have an alibi for the time of the murders."

"What is Dave going to do with him? Has he been charged?"

"He was charged with breaking and entering, but he made bail this morning. Dave told him he could go home to Nashville, but he has to check in with the cops there. And Dave let Adams keep the pictures he took after downloading copies to the computer at the police station. Dave told the guy he could discreetly show the photos to some collectors that have been robbed. If he can document that any of the stuff in Darrell's storage unit is stolen and who it was stolen from, it could give Dave a new lead in the murder investigation."

"And you were able to prod all this information out of Ted over an ice cream sundae? You're *good*," I said.

Di replied to my comment with stony silence.

Chapter 18

Larry Joe and his mom made it back to the hospital in time for the last visiting period of the day, and Di said her good-byes. Daddy Wayne seemed to be resting comfortably when we looked in on him. Larry Joe and I went back to the waiting room, while Miss Betty stayed beside the bed, holding tightly to her husband's hand.

Later we tried to talk my mother-in-law into going home for the night. But she refused to leave while Daddy Wayne was still in the ICU, and Larry Joe couldn't let her stay all night in the waiting room by herself. Although I offered to stay the night with his mom so Larry Joe could sleep in a real bed for a change, he wouldn't hear of it. I fervently hoped the doctor would be able to move Daddy Wayne into a regular room soon.

I pulled out of the hospital driveway, thinking of all the things I needed to do in the morning. I needed to go to the grocery store. I needed to call Mama. I really wanted to find out more about the stolen

Confederate artifacts and how they might tie in with the drug smuggling. And I desperately needed to catch up on some work.

Despite all the questions running through my mind about what I had learned from Di, I was asleep by the time my head hit the pillow, and I didn't stir until well after 7:00 a.m. I started the coffeemaker and took a long, steamy shower. Savoring a hot cup of coffee, I sat at the kitchen table, looking out my window at blue skies streaked with white and gold. I felt almost like a normal human being again after days of losing sleep and being worried sick about the murders, my father-in-law's health, and the family business, not to mention getting caught breaking into Ray's trailer and being grilled by the sheriff for hours. Oh, and I almost forgot about the whole "finding two dead bodies in a garage" incident.

My cell phone, which was still in vibrate mode, the mode I had switched it to at the hospital, suddenly began to buzz and dance across the tabletop. I was surprised to see it was a text message from Di, since she rarely calls while she's working.

When I opened the message, a photo popped up of Ralph Harvey and Bobo standing on a porch, talking. Di had texted, If this is Bobo, call Dave. House in 400 block of W. Spruce couple minutes ago.

I had never seen Bobo in person, but it was definitely the same guy I'd seen on the tape with Ray Franklin, so that was confirmation enough for me. Why would Ralph be talking to Bobo? I followed Di's advice and called the sheriff. I filled him in and then forwarded the photo to his phone. Dave said he'd have an unmarked car check it out. I then texted Di to let her know what was happening.

I felt queasy at the thought that Ralph, a longtime trusted employee at McKay's, could possibly be involved in smuggling drugs or maybe even murder.

So much for things feeling normal again.

I tried to busy myself by unloading the dishwasher and sorting laundry. More than an hour passed without my hearing from Dave. I called his cell, but my call went straight to voice mail. As anxious as I was to find out something, I knew only too well that Dave was much more into receiving information than doling it out.

I dressed and drove to the office. I figured that staying busy was the best thing I could do. I touched base with a couple of clients. The phone rang, and it was a potential client. If I'd had the energy, I would have done a little happy dance. I made an appointment to meet with the parents of the bride about a formal engagement party.

As a rule, I don't do weddings anymore, although on occasion I still get roped into planning a wedding for family or close friends. Weddings just bring too much drama. I mean, it's usually not a huge deal if a guest shows up at a party and he's already been hitting the bottle. But if it's a wedding and the drunk in question is the father of the bride, it can spell disaster. Been there, done that. As a party planner, I just find bridal showers and engagement parties—and pretty much any event other than a wedding—to be much less stressful.

I was humming a lively tune after I got off the phone with the new clients. We had scheduled an appointment for them to come to my office. They had called because a good friend of theirs had given me a glowing recommendation—which was always nice to hear. And it sounded like they had a large and lavish celebration in mind, which could add up to a very nice payday for me.

Next, I gathered up my notes and headed downstairs to Sweet Deal Realty's office for an 11:30 a.m. conference. I had a meeting with Winette, Dixie Chamber of Commerce director Bryn Davenport, a local pastor, the mayor's secretary and a couple of other people to go over plans for a Halloween party fund-raiser to benefit Residential Rehab. This wasn't a moneymaker for me or for anyone else involved. It was strictly volunteer, but for a very worthwhile cause. The meeting broke up around 12:20 p.m. Just as the others were leaving, I stepped away to answer my cell phone. More good news. Larry Joe had called to say they were moving his dad to a regular room.

"That's the biggest grin I've seen on your face in a while," Winette said as she walked from the conference table back to her desk.

"It's the best news I've had in a while. They're finally moving my father-in-law to a regular hospital room."

"That *is* good news."

"You're pretty dressed up, Winette. Do you have some house showings today?"

"Naw. I've got a funeral to go to."

"I'm sorry. Was it someone close?"

"It's a lady at my church. She was ninety-eight, I think. Anyway, she hadn't been doing too well for a long while. She's got lots of children and grandchildren and great-grandchildren. I'm going to help out with serving lunch to the family after the funeral."

I couldn't help wondering how much potato salad they'd have.

As Winette left for the funeral, I wandered over to the diner. All the booths and most of the stools at the counter were already filled with the lunch crowd. I nabbed a small table for two against the wall, one wedged between the hall to the restrooms and the swinging doors to the kitchen. Since I'd had nothing but coffee for breakfast, I ordered a vegetable plate with turnip greens, fried squash, and glazed carrots.

I had just placed my order and was handing my menu back to the waitress when I caught sight of Deputy Ted Horton over her shoulder, walking in my direction.

"Diner's about full up. Mind if I join you?"

"Pull up a chair. I'd appreciate the company."

Our waitress had disappeared momentarily and reappeared with a glass of iced tea for Ted. "You want the special, hon?" she inquired, touching Ted on the shoulder. He nodded, and she padded away in orthopedic shoes.

"What is today's special?"

"I don't remember what it is on Thursdays," Ted said. "I just always order the special."

I was dying to ask Ted if they'd learned anything new about the guy who had broken into Darrell's storage unit or if any of the Civil War collectibles at the mini storage really were stolen. But that would be admitting that Di had told me everything he'd said to her over an ice cream sundae. I decided that would be bad form.

Ted interrupted my thoughts to ask how my father-in-law was doing.

"He's improving. In fact, they're moving him out of the ICU and into a private room today."

"That's really good news. I'm sure the investigation into the murders and the drugs has been pretty stressful for him," Ted said, sounding apologetic.

This gave me the perfect opportunity to ask about Ralph Harvey and Bobo. After all, I was the one who had sent Dave the photo.

"I'm afraid it's going to be really upsetting to Daddy Wayne if it turns out Ralph Harvey is somehow involved in all this. Do you know what his connection is to Bobo?"

"No, but thanks for the information about him and Ralph."

I was afraid my inquiry had come to a dead end, but after Ted took a big gulp of iced tea, he continued.

"The Feds are tailing Bobo. They had lost track of him but are back on his trail, thanks to your call. They hope he'll lead them to the top guys in the drug-smuggling operation."

One waitress set our orders on the table, while another breezed over and refilled our iced teas. Turned out the special of the day was chicken and dumplings.

"What about Ralph?" I asked in a hushed tone after the waitresses had walked away.

"We're keeping an eye on him. The Feds aren't really interested in him right now. If he's involved in the drug ring, it's only as a two-bit player. They may question him later, once something turns up with Bobo. But now that it looks like he might be linked to Bobo and the drug smuggling, the sheriff thinks there's a chance he could also know something about the murders."

"Whose front porch were Ralph and Bobo standing on? I know Ralph doesn't live on that street."

"It's Ralph's mama's house," Ted said. "She's in bad health. Doesn't get out much."

"Ralph's worked for the company for years," I said. "It's just so hard to believe he could be mixed up in any of this."

"Unfortunately, we don't have enough information to bring him in at this point. I'd appreciate it if you kept this information under wraps for the time being. We definitely don't want to tip off Ralph that he's a suspect."

I made the gesture of turning a key in my lips and throwing away the imaginary key as a vow of silence.

"Just out of curiosity, Ted, is Bobo a first name, last name, nickname?"

"Last name. His first name is Milton," Ted said with a smirk.

Chapter 19

I was relieved to hear the Feds had Bobo under surveillance. But it blew my mind that Ralph might somehow be involved. He's a key player at McKay's, with knowledge of and access to just about everything that goes on in the company. Larry Joe and Daddy Wayne trusted him implicitly. I didn't want to believe it was possible he had betrayed their trust and had put them and the company in danger.

Dave had too many pots boiling at the moment to keep an eye on all of them, so I decided it was up to me to stir this one. I needed to get the lowdown on Ralph But, who would know?

I couldn't very well talk to his mama. She probably wouldn't know anything about his dirty dealings, anyway. Then it hit me. I'd have to go to the gossip merchants. I didn't want to, but desperate times called for desperate measures. So I phoned the beauty salon to see if I could get an appointment for this afternoon. If there was any dirt to dish, Nell Tucker and her crew would have it by the spades full.

I needed a haircut, but a quick cut wouldn't give

me much time to gather information. I decided to go all in and get a perm, as well. The receptionist told me they'd had a cancellation, so if I came straight over, Nell would be able to work me in for a perm and cut.

I walked through the front door of Dixie Dolls Hair Salon and was greeted by the pungent odor of perming and dye solutions and a fog of hair spray.

The raspy-voiced receptionist, Pat, greeted me without enthusiasm and advised me to take a seat. By my best guesstimate, Pat weighs over 350 pounds. I think she's short, although I've never actually seen her rise to a standing position from her padded bar stool, its edges overlapped by her hips and thighs.

Nell waved to me from her station, where she was putting the finishing touches on a ninety-year-old woman's coiffure, sealing it in a double layer of either varnish or hair spray. I wasn't sure which it was. I flipped through a dog-eared magazine of hairstyles. The date on the cover was 1985. This should have been a warning, but I was absentmindedly flipping through the magazine while I tried to figure out how to bring up Ralph's name in a casual way.

Nell's elderly client shuffled up to the desk to pay, and Nell hollered for me to come on back and take a seat. She flung a black plastic cape over me and fastened the Velcro strip noose tight around my neck. She inquired about my mama and Larry Joe's dad, and I asked about her husband and son. After we had covered all the pleasantries, including the weather, I took an opening.

"This is the first serious health issue we've had to deal with since my daddy died. Of course, he went quickly, collapsing on the golf course with a major heart attack. I'm hoping Larry Joe's dad takes care of himself and sticks around for a long while yet. Speaking of which, I didn't know until recently that Ralph Harvey's mother was pretty much home-bound. Do you know what her condition is?"

As I had suspected, Nell knew all about Ralph's mother's first and second strokes, as well as how she would probably have to start dialysis soon.

Our conversation continued from the sink to the chair and back to the sink and back to the chair over the next hour and a half or so, as my hair got washed, rolled, permed, neutralized, trimmed, and styled. I should have been paying more attention to what Nell was doing when she started rolling up my hair on rollers as skinny as toothpicks.

The conversation got off track a few times as we chatted briefly with other customers as they came and went. But in a nutshell, I learned that Ralph had got cleaned out in his divorce. His ex-wife, Kay, had claimed he cheated on her and got abusive when he drank. But according to Nell, Kay had had some extramarital action of her own going on. Despite getting fleeced in the divorce, Ralph still helped take care of his ailing mother and had a daughter attending a private college.

"And yet he just bought a new fishing boat," Nell said. "Paid cash for it, too, or at least that's what the guy at the boat dealership told my Billy while they were playing golf."

Nell's opinion, and the general consensus in the beauty shop, was that Ralph was making money on the side by gambling, and most likely cheating at it. But I was more worried he was taking in extra cash by running drugs through my family's trucking company.

I tried to hide my alarm when Nell spun the chair around toward the mirror to give me a look at the finished product. My perm was fried. I looked as if I'd been electrocuted.

"Of course, it'll loosen up quite a bit after you wash it," Nell said unconvincingly.

After I paid her for abusing my hair, I went straight home and washed my hair three times. It didn't loosen up one bit.

Tired and depressed, I took two aspirin and had a nap. When I woke up, I hoped the whole perm thing would turn out to be just a bad dream. That worked until I looked in the mirror.

Still suffering from a cumulative sleep deficit, I heated a cup of leftover coffee in the microwave and stepped out onto the patio for a breath of fresh air and a hit of sunshine to warm me up.

The way Southerners cope with our sweltering summers is a bit of an enigma. When it's miserably hot outside, we keep it cold enough indoors to hang meat. If the temperature were to drop that low in the winter, we'd be cranking up the heat and pulling on sweaters.

An overnight rain and plentiful sunlight made it seem like the grass had grown an inch or two just since yesterday. And it was already a bit shabby before Larry Joe's dad went in the hospital. So I phoned Kenny Mitchell to see if his handyman skills extended to lawn care. He seemed happy to pick up a quick thirty bucks.

I tried for a few minutes to rearrange my hair into something approaching normal looking, to no avail.

I accepted the ugly truth that I'd have to leave the house sometime before my perm grew out. I grabbed a straw hat out of the hall closet and pulled it down on my head as far as it would go. My voluminous hair made it spring back up, and it sat like a tiny clown hat on the top of my head. I tossed the hat onto the kitchen table and headed out to pick up Kenny.

I dropped Kenny off at the house and told him I'd be back to pick him up in an hour or so, but to call me if he finished up sooner or had any questions. After opening the garage so he could access the lawn equipment, I drove to the hospital to check on my father-in-law.

I tapped on the door as I entered his hospital room. My mother-in-law was sitting in the chair next to the bed. The head of the bed was raised, putting Daddy Wayne nearly in a sitting position. His coloring had definitely improved; his cheeks were starting to pink up. He even looked over and said hello as I walked in. I couldn't help but smile. What a difference a day can make!

I gave my father-in-law a peck on the cheek and walked around the bed to give Miss Betty a hug. My mother-in-law's eyes scanned my hair, but she was too polite to comment. Daddy Wayne, being a man, probably didn't even notice.

"Larry Joe has gone to the office for a while," she said. "But he said he'd check in later and stay the night if Wayne needs him to."

"I don't need anybody to stay the night," he said, his hackles up. "I've got a bevy of nurses that come running if I push this button," he added, pointing to the call button dangling by a cord from the bed rail.

"Besides, the doc will probably let me go home tomorrow."

"We'll see," Miss Betty said doubtfully.

I shared her skepticism that the doctor would let him go home so soon. But it was really good to see Daddy Wayne full of spit and vinegar, like his old self.

My father-in-law was on the mend. I had an appointment with a new client. The Feds were on Bobo's trail. It was shaping up to be a pretty good day, except for the perm debacle, which I tried to put out of my mind.

I returned home and stepped into my formerly shabby backyard to find a finely manicured lawn. Kenny had not only cut the grass in a neat crisscross pattern, but had even edged along the walkway and patio.

Kenny finished sweeping up the walk and stowed the lawn equipment in the garage. As we walked to the car, I noticed his perspiration-streaked face. I cranked up the air-conditioning. On the way back to his apartment, I drove through one of the fast-food joints to order a couple of flavored slushy drinks.

"Kenny, do you prefer cherry or cola flavor?"

"Cherry, definitely."

"Me too."

While we slurped our frosty drinks in air-conditioned comfort, I gave Kenny a physical description of Ralph Harvey and asked if he remembered ever seeing him around the apartments with the Farrells or Ray or Bobo.

"Can't say as I do. But that don't mean much. I'd

go days sometimes without catching sight of Duane or Darrell coming and going."

As I drove along, both of us silent, I nearly sprained my brain trying to think of any pertinent questions about the Farrells I should ask Kenny while I had the opportunity. Finally, one popped into my head.

"Kenny, you mentioned before that you thought Darrell invited everyone in the apartments to that Fourth of July party as an excuse to get to know the girls who had moved in downstairs. Did he ever get together with one of them, or was there any particular girl you know of that he went with for a while?"

"I don't think things ever heated up between him and Amy. She's the new neighbor he had his eyes on. But he was crazy about the girl that was living in that apartment before Amy and her roommate moved in."

"What was her name?"

"Candy," he said. "She was on again, off again with some guy named Brad. Whenever Brad was out, Darrell was in, you know."

"Do you know why she moved out of her apartment?"

"Can't say for sure, but my guess is that Brad didn't want her so handy to Darrell. He was the jealous type big-time. I heard him yelling and banging on her door late one night, saying he knew she had some guy in there, and she'd better open up, or he'd break the door down. She told him to go away and sober up, but he kept at it. It finally got quiet, and I looked through the blinds to see if he was leaving. I didn't see him, so I figured she had let him in.

Thing is, just a few seconds later I see Darrell coming from around the side of the building and sneaking up the stairs, real quiet like. He was carrying his shoes and didn't have a shirt on. I ciphered he had slipped out the back window at Candy's place before she let Brad in. Not too long after that, she moved out."

"Do you have any idea where she works or where she lives now?"

"No, ma'am, but I know she really liked going to karaoke night at that little bar out on Bass Road, halfway between here and Hartville."

"What does Candy look like?"

"Dark hair. Small waist. Big everything else," he said.

"What about her boyfriend?"

"He looks like trouble."

I thanked Kenny, then handed him his pay, including a fat tip, before he got out of the car.

"Anytime, Ms. Mac."

I stopped at the grocery store to pick up a few necessities, like toilet paper, and decided to get the fixings for a nice supper. Larry Joe had been surviving on fast food and hospital cafeteria fare since his dad had been in the ICU. It would be nice to have a sit-down meal at home, just the two of us. It would be even nicer to have him back in our bed, since I felt certain his dad would flatly refuse to let anybody stay with him overnight at the hospital.

I quickly mixed together some mayonnaise, celery seed, cider vinegar, salt, pepper, and sugar in a mason jar, then shook it well and put it in the fridge to chill. Next, I dusted some fresh catfish fillets with seasoned cornmeal and a bit of flour, carefully laid each piece in a pan sizzling with melted shortening, and cooked them for three or four minutes on each side. With the fried catfish fillets draining on paper towels, I mixed a bag of shredded cabbage and carrots with the coleslaw dressing I'd prepared in the mason jar.

The aroma of fresh fried fish brought a broad smile to my husband's face as he walked into the kitchen, and this was followed by a big kiss on the lips for the cook. He stepped back, did a double take, and said, "Your hair looks kinda *big*. Did you do something different to it?"

"No," I said in a tone that let him know I didn't want to talk about it. We'd been married long enough that he knew to let it go.

Larry Joe filled glasses with ice and tea, while I plated up our supper and retrieved a jar of sweet pickles and a squeeze bottle of tartar sauce from the refrigerator. We held hands as Larry Joe said a heartfelt thanks for our meal and his dad's improving health, before he stabbed a fork into his catfish.

After we'd topped off our meal with some fresh blackberries and whipped cream, we ambled into the den, turned on *Wheel of Fortune*, and flopped down on the sofa. I leaned back against Larry Joe's chest as he wrapped his arms around me and rested his chin on the top of my head, or more accurately, on top of four inches of spring-loaded hair.

"Thanks for the nice supper, hon. I don't think I could face another plate of that hospital slop."

Larry Joe then told me that things seemed to be settling down at work, that everyone had been pulling together since his dad's heart attack. I wanted so much to warn him that Ralph Harvey might not be as trustworthy as we had thought. But I had promised Ted I wouldn't say anything. Besides, we really didn't know anything for certain, just gossip. There was no need to lay another burden on Larry Joe's broad shoulders, unless it became absolutely necessary, I reasoned.

"As nice as this is," he said, giving me a peck on the cheek, "I better get down to the hospital. I don't plan to stay the night, unless it's the only way I can get Mama to go home. With the geezer laid up, we sure don't want Mama making herself sick."

"I think your dad will help you on that front. He seemed to be feeling pretty feisty earlier today. I bet he tells you both to go home."

After Larry Joe headed for the hospital, I phoned Di to fill her in on what Ted had said over lunch, as well as on what I'd picked up at the beauty shop. She suggested I come by her place and tell her about it over a glass of wine.

Di opened the front door and said, "Hey, you've got kind of a retro thing going on with your hair. I didn't know you were thinking about changing hairstyles."

"It wasn't exactly intentional. I'd rather not talk about it."

"Uh, okay."

After settling into Di's recliner, I kicked off my shoes and took a couple of sips of wine. "Mmm. This is pretty tasty. What is it?"

"I don't know," Di said, stretched out on the sofa. "It comes in a box."

I told her what I'd learned from Ted.

"Milton, huh? No wonder he goes by Bobo."

"It's a good thing you sent that photo," I said. "At least now the FBI is back on Bobo's trail."

"I've seen Ralph a bunch of times coming in or out of his mama's house in the mornings," she said. "In fact, I doubt I would've thought anything about seeing him talking to that guy, if it hadn't been for your vivid description of Bobo."

"Well," I sighed, "maybe there is some reasonable explanation as to why Bobo was there. I can't believe Ralph would bring a thug to his mother's house."

"I wouldn't let him off the hook so quick," she said. "Wait a minute."

Di went to the fridge and placed our glasses under the wine box tap for refills; then she said that she'd talked to Dave this afternoon. Apparently, he was still trying to smooth things over with her after the nasty inquisition he put us through at the sheriff's office.

"They checked a little into Ralph's finances and found out he's been having some money troubles. Seems his wife cleaned him out in the divorce, his daughter's at an expensive college, and he also helps out his mom financially." She drew a long sip of wine. "And yet he recently bought a new bass boat. The dealer in Hartville says he paid cash for it." Di punctuated the sentence with raised eyebrows.

Her eyebrows went up, and my shoulders sagged, along with my heart and pretty much every part of my being, except my hair. I had sacrificed my hair

and half my afternoon for absolutely no reason.
Dave had told Di every single thing I had "learned"
from Nell.

I went straight home and washed my hair with
laundry detergent.

Still nothing.

Chapter 20

I woke up the next morning nuzzled against the prickly, unshaven face of my gently snoring husband and started to nibble on his earlobe. He roused in more ways than one. We had a little time before the alarm was set to go off. Lazy cuddling led to more aerobic activity, which reached a heart-racing conclusion in sync with the alarm clock buzzer.

Larry Joe headed out the kitchen door with a travel mug of coffee and a smile on his face. He planned to run by the hospital to look in on his dad before going to the office.

I hummed during my shower, towel-dried my hair, since blow-drying it was out of the question, and took extra care putting on my makeup before donning a white skirt and a striped, nautical-inspired blouse. I'm not generally a hair bow person, but I stuck a navy-blue bow on top of my head in an attempt to minimize my hair's height. I was meeting with the new clients about planning an engagement party and wanted to look my best, such as it was.

I stopped by the bakery and picked up some

fresh-baked apple-walnut mini muffins and brewed a pot of freshly ground Kona coffee to offer Mr. and Mrs. Dodd. They wanted to discuss a formal party to officially announce the engagement of their Ole Miss–schooled daughter to a Mississippi State graduate. If the bride-to-be's family and her fiancé's family started talking football at the party, a brawl could break out. But the meeting went great, and they hired me to plan the party.

After starting a file for the Dodds' event, I freshened my lipstick and headed to the hospital, stopping by the convenience store on the way to pick up a couple of magazines I thought my father-in-law might enjoy paging through. On the way into the hospital, I ran into Ralph Harvey, who was on his way out.

"Oh, hey, Ralph. I suppose we're here to see the same patient."

"Yes, ma'am. I just dropped off a get-well card that a bunch of the guys had signed for Mr. McKay."

"That's nice. How's he doing?"

"He seems okay. He was complaining about how there's nothing on the television worth watching. I see you've brought a couple of magazines. He might enjoy looking at those, or maybe you could bring up some videotapes—if you happen to have any just lying around the house," Ralph said with a knowing look. I had more than an inkling that he was trying to let me know that *he* knew I had filched the security tapes from the office. Maybe he even knew somehow that I had tipped off the cops about Bobo.

"Are you trying to tell me something, Ralph?"

"No, ma'am. I wouldn't presume to tell you anything. I'm the kind of guy who tries to mind his own business. Seems like a good policy to me." Ralph tugged at the bill of his ball cap while giving a nod and said, "G'day, Ms. McKay," before sauntering away.

I seethed at the thought that Ralph was trying to menace me with some kind of subtle blackmail. What I knew that he didn't was that the sheriff already had in his possession the security tapes I had taken. Of course, Larry Joe and his dad didn't know about the tapes, and I'd just as soon keep it that way. Still, under no circumstances would I let Ralph Harvey get away with running drugs through McKay Trucking Company—or maybe even committing murder.

My face flushed hot with anger. I knew I needed to calm down a bit before I made an attempt to cheer up Daddy Wayne. After wandering into the gift shop, I left my magazines with the cashier while I browsed. I hoped that gazing at angel statues, teddy bears, and key chains inscribed with Bible verses would bring me serenity. After about fifteen minutes, I figured I had summoned all the inner peace I could muster and headed to the elevator.

When I walked in the room, Miss Betty was sitting on the loveseat, listening to their neighbor, Mrs. Finch, chatter nonstop, while Daddy Wayne looked as if his head might explode. He was genuinely pleased to see me.

"Liv, darlin', come on in," he said.

I gave him a peck on the cheek, along with his magazines, which he started perusing immediately. Mrs. Finch stood and said she'd better be going since Wayne had more company. Even my ever polite mother-in-law didn't try to dissuade her from leaving.

After hugs all around, she departed, with promises to keep Daddy Wayne in her prayers.

When she was a safe distance down the hall, my father-in-law said, "I'll say a prayer. Thank you, Jesus." He raised his hands to heaven. "I thought she'd never leave."

"I have to admit, I was ready for her to go home," Miss Betty said.

"Did she catch you up on any good gossip?" I asked my mother-in-law.

"Now, Olivia, you know I don't listen to gossip," she said loudly. Then, as she hugged me, she whispered, "I'll fill you in later."

Flipping through the fishing magazine I'd handed him launched Daddy Wayne into a familiar story about the one that got away. He lit up as he described the event in animated detail. We both listened attentively, in a deliberate attempt to boost his morale. After he finished his fish tale, he started to get out of bed.

"Wayne, what are you doing?"

"I'm going to the bathroom, woman. They finally took out that damn catheter, remember?"

"You know you're not supposed to get up without help," she said, leaning across the bed and pushing his call button to the nurses' station.

"I think I can go to the bathroom by myself. Been doing it for years," he said gruffly.

I walked around the end of the bed to try to steady my father-in-law. After about two steps, he stumbled forward, and we both nearly took a tumble onto the cold tile floor. Fortunately, Larry Joe walked through the door just in time to grab hold of his dad.

"Guess I'm still not too steady on my feet," Daddy Wayne said, obviously embarrassed, as Larry Joe helped him into the bathroom.

After they had closed the door, Miss Betty said, "His leg, where they ran the heart catheter, is giving him trouble. But he wants to go home so badly, he won't admit it."

After visiting a bit, Larry Joe tried to get his mom to go with me to get a bite to eat. She said she'd eaten a late lunch, and insisted the two of us go out for dinner instead.

She walked us to the elevators. "Son, I'm not sure your dad should be on his own tonight."

"Don't worry, Mama. I'm going to come back and stay the night. I think I should," he said, looking over at me.

"I agree, honey. The last thing we want is for your dad to end up falling and maybe breaking something."

Chapter 21

Larry Joe drove to Town Square Diner, where we both ordered a plate of pinto beans and crawfish corn bread. During dinner three different people stopped by the table with well wishes for Larry Joe's dad—one of the nice things about living in a small town. Of course, everybody knowing your business can have its downside, as well.

"I'm sorry about having to spend the night at the hospital again, hon."

"Don't be silly. I certainly enjoy having you at home," I said, brushing my leg against his under the table. "But I don't trust your dad to buzz the nurses' station for help any more than you do."

I told Larry Joe about my new clients from rival schools.

"I think people from different religions have a better chance of making a marriage work than couples with opposing football loyalties. But I wish them all the luck in the world," Larry Joe said.

"I've learned to put up with you," I said, "so anything's possible."

"Ditto," Larry Joe replied between bites of corn bread.

"Seriously, I can't complain. We have a home. We have each other. And it looks like your dad is going to be okay."

"I'd order a beer and drink to that," Larry Joe said, "but it's going to be hard enough sleeping with one eye open tonight without adding alcohol into the mix."

"Maybe you should tie a string around your dad's foot so you'll feel a tug if he tries to get up during the night."

"If he tries to get up again on his own, I might just hog-tie him with that string."

After supper, Larry Joe drove toward our house before heading back to the hospital.

"I'll take the car to the hospital, and Mama can drive home in my truck," he said.

"Honey, I can drive your mom home. That way, you'll have the truck and I'll have my car."

"Trust me, Liv, Mama won't leave the hospital tonight until the nurse throws her out. There's no reason you should have to hang around waiting for her. I'll leave in the morning, as soon as Dad's awake, and I'll head home for breakfast and a shower. Then you can drop me at Mama's, and I'll take her to the hospital on my way to the office. Unless, of course, you need the car for some late-night carousing."

"Don't worry. I can always get a ride," I said with a wicked grin.

Larry Joe pulled up in the driveway. I leaned over

and gave him a quick kiss. He pulled me closer to him and gave me a nice long kiss.

"Good night, babe."

"'Night, honey. Be patient with your dad. You know his pride is hurting as much as his leg."

"Yes, ma'am."

Larry Joe idled in the driveway until I was safely inside. I found his protective streak endearing, if unnecessary.

As I started through the house, Larry Joe's remark about late-night carousing got me thinking. It wasn't late, actually. The clock on the microwave read 7:52 p.m. I rummaged through a stack of local newspapers lying on the coffee table in the den, looking for the weekend entertainment section. I flipped through until I found what I was looking for: a notice for "karaoke every Friday at Buddy's Joint." The address was on Bass Road, so I surmised that this must be the place Kenny had mentioned. Here was my chance to find Candy and have a chat. Maybe Darrell was one of those guys who talked a little too freely when it came to pillow talk.

I called Di and told her I was going to Buddy's with or without her, which was a hollow threat since I had no car. Fortunately, it took only a couple of minutes to convince her to come along. I changed into some clothes I thought would be a little more appropriate for a karaoke bar and waited for Di to pick me up.

It took about fifteen minutes to make the drive. On the way, I reminded Di about what Kenny had said about the angry boyfriend and gave her his description of Candy. As Di pulled up to a four-way stop, the only four-way intersection between Dixie and Hartville, we spotted Buddy's Joint just ahead, on the left. The gravel parking lot was surprisingly full. As we stepped out of the car, someone opened the front door of the concrete-block building, unleashing a cloud of smoke and a roar of music.

"I'm guessing there isn't a no-smoking section in this place," Di said.

There was no cover charge, but a large sign at the entry announced a two-drink minimum. It was one of those places that features free peanuts in the shell as bar snacks. I shuffled through discarded peanut shells, regretting my decision to wear sandals.

Scanning tables as we walked to the bar, I spotted only beer bottles and shot glasses. Resigned to the fact that margaritas and daiquiris were clearly not on the drinks menu, I ordered two light beers, and Di ordered a beer and a tequila chaser. The bartender's low-cut top revealed an ample bosom with a dragon tattoo on one breast, its tail disappearing into an abyss of cleavage. She took our money without offering change and handed us our drinks without comment.

Some guy was onstage, singing "Three Times a Lady," pronouncing the word *twice* as if it had a *t* on the end. We zigzagged our way through the crowd. I looked around the room as if I were looking for a suitable table, not that there were many to choose from, as the place was packed. What I was really looking for was Candy. Di and I finally sat down at a table by the wall on the far side of the room from the bar. I was beginning to worry that Candy wasn't there when I spotted someone fitting her description emerging from a hallway beside the bar, which presumably housed the ladies' room.

My eyes followed her across the room to a table near the stage. She sat down beside a guy with tattooed arms the size of tree trunks. The woman I hoped was Candy turned in our general direction and waved excitedly to a young woman who had just entered the bar. My Candy candidate certainly lived up to Kenny's description. She had a small waist and big everything else: big hair, big teeth, big boobs, and a round fanny. And the guy she was with looked like bad news to me.

The noisy room quieted to a dull roar of chatter and laughter as one singer left the stage and another stepped up to the mike. I communicated to Di where the woman I thought was Candy was seated, and we both tried to think up ways to approach her. Unfortunately, since she had just come from the direction of the ladies' room, I doubted we'd have another opportunity to catch her alone in the restroom anytime soon, unless she had a tiny bladder.

I cracked open a couple of boiled peanuts to munch on and was surprised to realize that I had already finished the first of my two beers.

Candy and her newly arrived friend made their way over to a table by the stage on our side of the room. They began flipping through a notebook that, I surmised, had the list of songs available for karaoke. I nodded to Di, and we headed for this table. There were actually two identical notebooks there, so we stood on the other side of the table, flipping through one notebook, while they faced us, perusing the other. Both notebooks were bolted to the table like a bank pen to a counter.

Candy glanced up, so I smiled and said, "Hi."

She flashed her huge toothy smile and said, "You two look like maybe the Supremes. Am I right?"

"That's certainly an idea," I said as Di and I shared a doubtful expression. "What about you two? The Bangles or the Spice Girls?"

"Aren't you cute," Candy said. "I guess those old girl bands were a big deal when you were younger, huh?"

"Yeah. Them and Sinatra," Di shot back.

"Oh, well, I guess we're not really up on the current music scene," I said with what I hoped looked like a sincere smile. "What song are you girls thinking about performing?"

"Probably "Call Me Maybe" or something by Adele," Candy said.

Even an old-timer like me knew Candy and her Barbie-double friend didn't have the chops to sing an Adele song with any credibility, but I kept my mouth shut. And, surprisingly, so did Di.

"You pick something. I'm going to run and put on some lipstick," Barbie said to Candy, apparently worried that people with glaucoma might not be able to see the neon shade of coral she already had smeared on her lips.

I seized the opportunity to talk to my new pal Candy alone.

"You look so familiar," I said. "Don't you live in the Howe Apartments?"

She looked nervous.

"It's just that Kenny Mitchell, who lives there, does a lot of repair work and odd jobs for me, and I always pick him up at the apartments, since he doesn't have a car. I was thinking I'd seen you there, is all," I said, trying to sound casual.

"Actually, I used to live there. I moved in with my boyfriend, Brad, not too long ago. That's him over there," she said, pointing him out with the same gesture a model on a game show would use to draw attention to a brand-new big-screen TV.

"Oh, he's handsome," I said. "Were you still living at the apartments when those two brothers were killed? That was just such a tragedy. It must have been unbearable for their poor mama."

"I only knew Darrell and Duane slightly, as neighbors," she said unconvincingly. "Their mother didn't strike me as the motherly type. I always felt sorry for Duane, though. He was a sweet boy, just shy and kind of slow, you know?"

"Yes, that's what I heard. Can you think of any reason someone would want to do them harm? It's hard to imagine, especially since the one boy was, well, mentally challenged."

"Like I said, I didn't really know them well."

Brad came lumbering over. I guessed Candy had been out from under his thumb for too long. She gave him a quick kiss and said, "Hi, baby. Barbie and I are just about to go onstage."

So, plastic girl's name actually was Barbie. Di and I shared a knowing look and bit our lips to suppress laughter.

Candy waved to her friend and hurried over to the deejay to let him know their song selection. Brad crossed his beefy arms and leaned against the wall by the table as the deejay cued up their song and they stood stage left, waiting to make their entrance.

Di seized the bull by the horns.

"Excuse me," she said in a syrupy tone. "Don't you live over in the Howe Apartments?"

Brad glared for a moment. "No, I don't."

"It's just I was sure I'd seen you there. I thought maybe you were friends with those poor boys that got murdered."

Brad turned our way, giving us a frontal view of his brawn. "Lady, I don't live there, never have. And I certainly was not friends with 'those boys.' Too bad they went and got themselves killed like that."

Brad gave us one more dirty look, for good measure, and walked quickly back to his table as Candy and Barbie started singing their song in a shrieking soprano punctuated by giggles. I couldn't help noticing that the same throng of people we had barely elbowed our way through parted like the Red Sea for Brad.

We eased back to our table and decided to make a hasty retreat while Brad was focused on the stage. We scrambled to the car, and Di punched it out of the parking lot, slinging gravel as she turned onto the roadway.

"Candy and Barbie, for real? What kind of names are those, anyway?" Di said.

"The kinds of names that often indicate bigger boobs than brains. Did you notice how Candy said she only knew Darrell and Duane *slightly*? And yet she knew them well enough that she had met their mama and had concluded she wasn't the motherly type?"

"I noticed that her boyfriend is a baboon."

"Kenny was right about Brad being bad news," I said, still a bit shaky after our brief encounter with him. "He certainly wasn't grieved by Darrell's and Duane's demise."

"And Candy actually looked scared when you mentioned the Farrell brothers," Di said.

"She's probably afraid of Brad. I know I am. I think we need to suggest to Dave that he ought to check up on Brad. If he's not a suspect in the murders, I think he should be."

Chapter 22

Di dropped me off at home. By a little after 10:00 p.m., I had showered, put on my jammies, and curled up on the sofa to watch the TV news. I must have nodded off, because I woke up to a late-night talk show host interviewing some starlet I didn't recognize. I turned off the television, and as I stood up, I felt the beers I'd had earlier in the evening weighing heavily on my bladder. I switched off the light in the den and switched on the light in the downstairs bathroom.

Just as I pulled up my pants, I thought I heard some movement in the garage. I initially dismissed it as a neighborhood cat, until I heard the very distinctive squeaking of the door leading from the garage into the kitchen. I started to call out, "Larry Joe, is that you?" But a growing sense of unease trapped the words in my throat. Instead of saying anything or going to investigate, I quietly stepped into the tub and hid behind the shower curtain, wishing my cell phone was in my pocket instead of in my purse, which was sitting on the floor next to the kitchen table.

I steadied myself against the tile wall and listened to the thud of heavy footsteps, followed by the sounds of cabinet doors and drawers slamming. I heard a muffled voice say, "I'll look upstairs." The realization that two men had actually broken into my house caused my Adam's apple to swell to the size of a melon. I tried to breathe quiet, shallow breaths, which is hard to do when your Adam's apple is crushing your windpipe.

Suddenly, I heard the sound of stuff being tossed around in the den, followed by a loud crashing noise. At the sound of the crash, I gasped and my muscles involuntarily jerked, one arm flailing against the shower curtain. I grabbed the errant arm, praying that the intruders had not heard the slap of my arm against the plastic curtain.

A moment later I heard footsteps again, closer now, in the hallway just outside the open bathroom door. I held my breath. At that very moment, the Newsoms' car alarm started blaring. Since it was such a regular occurrence, it barely registered with me, but fortunately, it spooked the intruders.

Cabinet doors slammed in the laundry room. I heard the thunder of footsteps down the stairs and through the kitchen.

"Find anything?" said a muffled voice from the kitchen.

From the hallway, a familiar voice bellowed, "No, but they could have burned the damn tapes by now, for all we know. Let's get the hell out of here before the sheriff shows up to check out that alarm. I'm taking this."

I didn't know what "this" was, but I honestly didn't care what they stole as long as they went away.

Clacking sounds, hurried footsteps, and the squeak of the door into the garage.

I waited a couple of minutes, listening intently. When I felt confident the intruders were gone, I gingerly stepped out of the tub, tiptoed into the hall, and peered carefully into the kitchen. Seeing and hearing nothing, I hurried to my purse, fished my cell phone out, and retreated behind the shower curtain again—just in case they decided to return.

I called Di, figuring she was my fastest, surest connection to Sheriff Dave.

"Don't talk. Just listen. Get Dave to come to my house right this minute. Two men broke in. I think they've gone, but I'm afraid they might come back."

Exactly six minutes later, according to the clock on my phone, I received a text from Dave.

Open front door in sixty secs, or will break it down.

I drew a deep breath, sprinted to the front door, and stepped back as Dave and Ted rushed in, weapons drawn.

"I'm pretty sure they're gone," I whispered.

"Wait right here," Dave said. He looked at Ted and pointed to the stairs. The deputy went upstairs, while Dave searched the downstairs. Di slipped in quietly through the front door, and I collapsed on her shoulder, sobbing.

Di gently guided me over to the sofa, which, along with all the other furniture in the living room, was draped with a drop cloth and covered with dried paint spatter. When the lawmen returned from their search, I was holding on to Di's arm like a drowning man to a life preserver. I wouldn't say I had regained my composure, but I was beginning to inhale and exhale with regularity.

"It's all clear," Dave said, taking off his hat and taking a seat in one of the chairs opposite the sofa. "Stuff's been tossed around, and a couple of things are broken. You'll need to look and tell me if anything's missing. But first, did you get a look, even a brief one, at the perpetrators? Do you think you could identify them?"

"I didn't see them. Just heard them. I have no idea who one of the men was. I only heard his voice from the kitchen, kind of muffled. But the one doing most of the talking was Ralph Harvey."

"Are you absolutely sure?"

"I know Ralph's voice. I talked to him just this afternoon at the hospital. There's no doubt it was him. I'd be willing to swear to that under oath. And I'm also pretty sure I know what they were looking for—and that they didn't find it. Ralph said something like 'They could have burned the tapes already, for all we know.'"

I told Dave—and Ted and Di, who were also listening intently—about Ralph's cryptic comments at the hospital about the videotapes, and how I had wondered at the time if this was some kind of veiled threat.

We looked in the den, and I immediately noticed that the desktop computer was missing. The monitor screen was broken, and the TV was smashed and lying facedown on the floor. It had probably made the loud crashing sound I'd heard. The kitchen was also in disarray, with cutlery and canned goods strewn about. But none of the appliances were missing, and

I didn't think it likely they'd stolen any pots and pans. I went upstairs and did a quick inventory of my jewelry and Larry Joe's guns. Nothing seemed to be missing.

"I have more questions," Dave said. "But if you're sure it was Ralph, I don't want to waste any time before tracking him down. You feel up to riding along with me?"

"Sure. There's no way I'm staying in this house tonight, anyway."

"I'm coming with you," Di said.

We climbed into Dave's truck, and Ted got into the patrol car. They drove first to Ralph's house, but Ralph's truck wasn't there, and no lights were on. Ted peered through the windows, then turned to Dave and shook his head. After a brief discussion, Ted drove out to McKay's to look for Ralph, and Dave drove around the block and parked on the street, with a clear view through the neighbor's yard into Ralph's driveway.

Dave shut off the engine and twisted to face us, while keeping watch out the passenger window for any sign of Ralph. "You're sure there was someone else with Ralph, that he wasn't just talking to himself or maybe talking on his cell phone?"

"No. I definitely heard a different voice say, 'I'll look upstairs' and 'Find anything?' He was in the kitchen, so his voice was muffled. But Ralph, at one point, was standing right outside the bathroom where I was hiding. You know the Newsoms? Their car alarm went off, thank God, and startled Ralph and the other guy. They left in a hurry."

"Maybe the other guy was Bobo," Di offered.

"No. The one person I know it isn't is Bobo,"

Dave said. "The Feds have had him in custody since about six this evening."

"Do you think they intended to hurt Liv? With Ralph making those sly threats at the hospital . . . ," Di said.

"I don't think so. I don't think they thought anyone was at home, since there were no cars in the garage. By the way, Liv, where is your car? And where's Larry Joe?"

"We left his truck at the hospital and went to dinner together in my car. He dropped me off at the house and drove my car back to the hospital. His mom was going to drive herself home in his truck."

"Did his dad take a turn for the worse?" Di asked.

"No. He's better, but he's ornery. He won't call the nurses' station for help getting to the bathroom, and he almost fell this afternoon. We didn't trust him enough to leave him on his own."

Headlights suddenly bathed Dave's truck cab in light as a vehicle swung into Ralph's driveway. We instinctively shrank into the shadows, remaining motionless until the light was extinguished. Dave reached for his cell phone instead of the radio, I supposed to avoid alerting anyone who might be monitoring a police scanner.

"Ted, looks like our man just arrived home." After a pause, he added, "Roger that."

Looking at Di and me, Dave said, "Ted's just pulling into the neighborhood. No matter what happens, you two stay here with the doors locked. If anybody approaches the truck, you lay on the horn to let me know."

Dave got out of the truck, walked through the

neighbor's yard, and leapt over the low picket fence separating the yard from Ralph's.

Di and I each reached out and simultaneously slapped the door locks on the passenger- and driver-side doors. Normally, being told to stay put would have raised my hackles, but I was still very much in "hide behind the shower curtain" mode after the ordeal at the house. Going out to look for trouble, like breaking into Ray Franklin's camper or stalking strangers in a karaoke bar, is much more within my comfort zone than having someone violate the sanctuary of my own home.

We hunkered down on the seat, huddled together, and silently watched the action unfold.

Ted, who must have parked down the block, walked up to the side of the house from the next-door neighbor's yard. Dave signaled to him from the backyard. Then Ted walked around the house to the front door, while Dave positioned himself beside the back door.

In a matter of seconds, Ralph came running out the back door. Dave grabbed him by the collar and shoved him down onto the grass. Ted rushed from the front yard and fastened handcuffs on Ralph's wrists as Dave held him down. The two lawmen grabbed Ralph by his upper arms and helped him up to a standing position. Ted pulled the cruiser into the driveway, and Dave placed Ralph in the back of it.

Dave walked back to the truck, and Di unlocked the door. Neither of us had spoken a word through Ralph's entire capture and arrest.

"Di, if you don't mind, go ahead and drive my truck to the police station. I'm going to take a look inside Ralph's truck and house. Ted will come back here to get me after he puts Ralph in a cell. Liv, I'm going to get you to sign an official complaint against Ralph, identifying him as the man who broke into your house."

We both nodded, and Di slid over behind the steering wheel.

I breathed a sigh of relief, knowing that Ralph was in custody. But I still had an uneasy feeling in the pit of my stomach, knowing that whoever it was that had been with him in my house was still on the loose.

On the drive to the station, Di told me she thought I'd better spend the night at her place. I was grateful, especially since there was no way I was going to spend the night in my own house alone.

"Thanks, Di. I'll take you up on the offer. But why don't you just drop me at the police station and head on home? I'm sure Ted or Dave can run me over to your place after I've finished up. There's no reason you shouldn't try to get some sleep. I can let myself in and crash on the sofa."

"Naw. I'll just hang out at the station with you. I'm too wound up to sleep, anyway."

"Thanks," I said, giving Di a weary smile and feeling thankful to have such a good friend.

"You know you're going to have to tell Larry Joe all about the security tapes and the break-in now."

"Yeah, I know. But I'm not going to the hospital tonight. No need to wake him up, and I certainly don't want to upset Daddy Wayne. Can you drop me off at the hospital first thing in the morning?"

"Of course. Since I don't have to work tomorrow,

I'll even sit with Mr. McKay until Miss Betty gets to the hospital, if you need me to."

Apparently, Dave had told Terry, the dispatcher, we were coming. She offered us coffee and told us we were welcome to wait in the sheriff's office. More telling, she didn't ask us what we were doing there.

Cops must like their coffee extra strong. Three packets of creamer made mine barely tolerable.

"Now that we know it couldn't have been Bobo in the house with Ralph, who do you think it was, if you had to guess?" Di asked as she sat in the sheriff's chair, with her feet propped on his desk.

"I don't know. Maybe Rudy, the mechanic. I don't think he's much of a talker. And if they're both mixed up in this drug-smuggling deal, I could see him tagging along as Ralph's little helper for a break-in."

"By the way, I talked to Dave on the phone after I got home from the karaoke," Di said. "He knows who Brad is and said he'd do a bit of digging into what he's been up to."

"Good," I said. "Even if Brad didn't kill the Farrells, which he certainly seems capable of doing, he's a walking menace."

We were too tired to make idle conversation, so there was a silent hiatus. Di retrieved a file from her purse and worked on her nails and I sipped on muddy coffee and wondered how I was going to tell Larry Joe about everything.

Our respective soul-searching and grooming activities were interrupted when Dave walked in and plopped down in the chair next to me. Di didn't offer to move, and he didn't ask her to. *Hmm*.

"Well," Dave said, "the computer was sitting on the floorboard of Ralph's truck, in plain sight."

"Liv thinks it might have been Rudy who broke into her place with Ralph."

"I'm afraid that's another dead end. I told you we've been keeping an eye on Rudy. He was supposed to be going to Nashville with a group of friends for a concert tonight. Andy, a friend of mine on the Nashville force, does a little moonlighting as a security guard for events at Bridgestone Arena. I called and gave him the seat number on Rudy's ticket, which one of our informants had sneaked a peek at, and asked Andy to e-mail me a photo of who was sitting there. I just wanted to make sure Rudy was where he was supposed to be—and he was."

"I can't believe our two best suspects have alibis—from cops no less," I said, feeling defeated.

"Liv, think carefully. What time did you first hear the intruders in the house?" Dave asked.

"When I clicked off the TV, the clock read a couple of minutes before eleven. It was less than five minutes later when I heard the kitchen door opening."

"Okay, then. I think it's about time I had a talk with Mr. Ralph Harvey, who's been fingerprinted and left sitting in a cell to stew since we brought him in. It's not exactly standard procedure, but since you two are already up to your necks in this business, I'm going to put you in the room next to the interview room and let you listen and watch through the two-way mirror. Don't say a word, don't interrupt the interview, and I'll talk to you after I'm done with Ralph."

A few moments later Di and I were in a dark room, seated on blue vinyl chairs with metal frames, just like the ones in Dave's office. Through a large picture window, we had a full view of the interrogation room, the same one where Dave had grilled Di and me after catching us in Ray's camper.

Ralph waddled awkwardly into the interview room, wearing shackles and handcuffs, with Dave right behind him.

"You really think these damn chains are necessary?" Ralph said, looking like a monkey peeved enough to fling poo. "And, by the way, am I being charged with anything, or is this just harassment?"

Dave took his time, sitting down, shuffling some papers, and clearing his throat, before answering Ralph.

"The shackles are because you tried to evade the police when we came to your house earlier. And, yes, I have enough evidence to charge you with a crime. Now, I have a few questions to ask you. Why don't you start by telling me what you were doing in Larry Joe and Liv McKay's house tonight and why you took their computer?"

"I wasn't in the McKays' house, and I didn't steal their computer. Somebody put that computer in my truck, and I didn't know who it belonged to until you told me just now."

I shot up out of my chair and charged to the two-way mirror. "He's a lying son of a—"

"Liv, be quiet," Di whispered loudly. "Remember what Dave said." She grabbed me by the arm and pulled me back to my chair.

"But he's just a—"

"I know, I know. Just let Dave do his job."

"Well, that's a new one," Dave continued. "Are

people in the habit of putting stolen computers in your truck without your permission?"

"No, sir. This is the first time."

"Who do you think put this computer in your truck?"

"I have no idea who put it there or why."

"Why didn't you report 'finding' this computer to the police? Is it your birthday?"

"I planned to take it to the police station and turn it in first thing in the morning."

"Is that why your fingerprints were all over it?"

Ralph paused for a moment, looking up at the ceiling. "You're right, Sheriff. I shouldn't have touched it. I wasn't thinking. It's just that it surprised me to find it there, and I was taking a closer look at it. I really did plan to turn it over to the police. That's why I left it in my truck. If I'd stolen it, don't you think I would've taken it in the house with me?" Ralph leaned back in his chair with a smug look on his face.

"Where were you tonight while you weren't in the McKays' house, stealing their computer?"

"I ate supper with my mama at her house. We watched a bit of TV, and then I helped her into bed."

"What time did you leave your mother's house?"

"A little after ten. Then I drove over to Rascal's and had a few beers. I guess I got there about ten fifteen."

"What time did you leave the bar?"

"About eleven thirty. That's when I came out and found the computer in my truck."

"Are you sure about the time?"

"Yes, sir. The late-night talk show on the TV in the bar had just gone off before I left."

"Did you see or talk to anybody you knew at Rascal's? Can anybody vouch for you being there?"

"Well, Wally, the bartender, of course. I s'pose he'd remember my being there tonight. And I talked a little with Ray Franklin. I'm sure he'd remember me."

"How do you know Ray Franklin? When did you two meet?"

Ralph suddenly looked a little nervous. His eyes darted around the room. "I don't rightly remember when we first met. It might have been at the bar or at one of those Civil War reenactment shows. Anyhow, you know how it is in a small town. Everybody pretty much knows everybody else."

"Yeah, I know how it is. Did you talk to anybody else at Rascal's besides Ray and the bartender?"

"I don't think so. I don't remember seeing anybody else I know."

"That's kind of odd, don't you think? Seeing how this is a small town and all, where everybody knows everybody else."

Dave stood, left the interview room, and came into the room where Di and I were sitting. I was so mad, my face was on fire.

I jumped up and opened my mouth to speak, but before any sound came out, Dave threw his hands up and said, "Calm down. I know he's lying, but that doesn't help us much."

Dave explained that Ted had gone back to my house to dust for fingerprints.

"But I don't expect to find any," he added. "He'd be a moron if he didn't wear gloves, and he seems pretty confident there's nothing in the house that could incriminate him."

"Aren't you going to check his alibi?" I asked.

"Of course. But don't expect much help there," Dave said. "The bartender will probably remember Ralph being there, but he won't remember the exact time."

"What about Ray Franklin?" Di asked.

"Oh, I'm sure he'll remember the exact time," Dave said. "At least now we have a pretty good idea who Ralph's accomplice was."

"You mean Ray? Not that it surprises me," I said.

"Chances are, Ralph just gave Ray an alibi, and I'm sure Ray will return the favor."

"Speaking of Ray Franklin, were you ever able to get fingerprints or DNA to prove if he really is the Farrells' father or if he's a deserter?" I asked.

"Yes, I did retrieve a DNA sample from his coffee mug, and I received results from the lab late this afternoon. He's not the Farrells' daddy. And he's not a deserter, either. Although he did serve in the military during the Iraq War, same as the Farrells' father."

"I don't understand. It seemed crystal clear in Duane's diary that Ray was their father," I said.

Chapter 23

Di and I both stood there, gobsmacked, for a long moment.

Surmising our confusion, Dave explained, "What was clear was Duane thought Ray was his daddy—or maybe just fantasized that he was. Trust me, it's not at all unusual for people to write fiction in their diaries. Apparently, Duane Farrell was a little challenged mentally, kind of childlike. I guess he and Darrell got to know Ray through the reenactment unit, and he looked up to Ray as some kind of father figure. So he pretended he was his dad."

"But what about that picture of the boys and the postcard we found in Ray's trailer? How come he had those?" Di asked.

"Most likely, Duane gave them to him as some kind of gift."

"I guess that makes sense," I said. "The photo and postcard didn't exactly have pride of place in Ray's camper—not that Ray's camper shows any evidence of pride of place."

I told Dave he should talk to my neighbor, Mrs.

Cleats, in the morning. She doesn't miss much that goes on, and it would be nice to have Miss Snoopy Britches actually helping my cause for a change. Dave said he'd talk to her, but he noted that anything an old lady saw out her window after dark from across the street probably wouldn't hold much sway in court.

"What about Liv's testimony? She clearly heard Ralph's voice," Di said.

"If Mrs. Cleats makes a positive ID, along with Liv's testimony, maybe. But I doubt the district attorney would pursue it. Hearing just isn't as convincing as seeing."

"So you're just going to let Ralph go?" I asked.

"No. I can still charge him with receiving stolen goods. Nobody's going to buy that business about him finding a stolen computer in his truck, especially since he went running out the back door the minute the police knocked on his front door. But chances are his lawyer will have him plead to a misdemeanor and he won't do any jail time. I checked. He doesn't have a record. For now all I can do is put him back in the cell. Then I'll go over to Ray's place and try to rattle his cage."

I collapsed in my uncomfortable chair, feeling like I'd just lost a wrestling match. Dave turned a chair around and sat down, facing me.

"There's one other thing, Liv. I want you to go ahead and sign a complaint against Ralph for theft, listing the computer as stolen and the television as vandalized."

"Okay," Dave said after reading over the complaint form I'd filled out. "I think you two should try to get some sleep. But I will have to talk to Larry

Joe sometime tomorrow, Liv. I'll be talking to him about Ralph and asking him what kind of information was on the computer that Ralph might have been interested in. But I think you better go ahead and bring Larry Joe up to speed on everything. If the Feds end up getting involved in this, there's still a chance of certain tapes left anonymously on my doorstep coming back to bite us in the butt."

"Don't worry, Dave. I'll tell Larry Joe about everything first thing in the morning. I had planned to tell him after his dad got out of the hospital, anyway."

"Good night, ladies," Dave said. "By the way, fistfights and all kinds of drama break out on a regular basis over at Buddy's Joint. I'd recommend you two do your drinking and karaoke somewhere else. I'll check up on Brad."

As we were driving away from the police station, I asked Di to swing by my in-laws' house so I could retrieve the truck from their driveway.

"That way you won't have to drive me to the hospital in the morning. I definitely want to head Larry Joe off at the pass before he walks in and sees that our house has been ransacked."

When we got to my truck, I quietly pulled the door open, climbed in, and waited until I had backed out of the drive before switching on the headlights. Then I followed Di to her place.

I was so tired that just walking up Di's front steps was a chore. It felt like I was wearing cement shoes. Once inside, I plopped down on the sofa. Di latched the dead bolt and started toward her bedroom.

"Di, thanks for everything. I know I've been kind of high maintenance lately."

"Lately?" she said with her usual charm. "By the way, there's a baseball bat under the edge of the sofa. Good night."

"Good night."

Maybe the baseball bat warded off evil spirits and bad dreams, but whatever the reason, I slept soundly in spite of everything that had happened. I awoke to see Di making coffee under the glow of the tiny lightbulb over the stove.

"Hope I didn't wake you. I'm used to getting up early, so my internal alarm clock tends to go off even on Saturdays," Di said as she poured a carafe full of water into the coffeemaker.

"No, I'm fine. I actually slept pretty well. Maybe you can catch a nap later on."

"I'll probably just make it an early night. At least I don't have to work today."

Di started the coffeemaker then left to shower. While she got cleaned up I made us some scrambled eggs and biscuits from a can.

"I wonder if Dave found out anything from Ray last night," I said as Di walked into the room, still massaging her damp hair with a towel.

"I doubt it," Di said. "He seems like the kind of guy who's had a lot of experience with lying. Speaking of lying, just how much do you plan to tell Larry Joe? Everything or just the bit about the security tapes?"

"I think the part about me stealing the tapes and Ralph breaking into the house to steal them is probably about all he can handle at one time."

"That's probably wise," she said. "If you told him about breaking into Ray's camper—twice—and getting caught by the sheriff, I don't think any jury in the state would convict him for strangling you."

After Di and I had finished breakfast I left for the hospital and drove through a fast-food place to pick up coffees for Larry Joe and myself. It suddenly occurred to me that I should phone my mother-in-law and tell her I had picked up the truck, so she wouldn't think it had been stolen. Luckily, she had yet to look out the front window when I called, so no harm had been done.

The coffee helped wash down the lump in my throat as I pulled into the hospital parking lot and thought about confessing my recent crimes—or at least some of them—to my husband.

Larry Joe was a bit surprised to see me. Thankfully, it had been an uneventful night for him and Daddy Wayne, and they were both in good spirits. I started to suggest we go to the diner for breakfast, since I thought it unlikely that Larry Joe would kill me in front of witnesses. But I decided it wouldn't be fair to subject our friends and neighbors to the sight of Larry Joe's head exploding. Instead, when we walked out of the hospital, I jumped in my car and said I'd see him at the house in a few minutes.

I drove quickly to make sure I arrived at the house ahead of my husband, and waited for him in the driveway. He seemed a bit confused when I headed toward the front door, instead of going through the garage, where we usually enter. But he followed me to the front steps.

As I opened the door, I glanced over my shoulder

at Larry Joe. "Honey, don't get freaked out when you see the house. I'll explain everything."

"Did you have another little ceiling mishap?" he asked gently, putting his hand on the small of my back as we stepped into the living room. "Looks the same to me," he said, surveying the room.

"You won't think so when you see the kitchen and den."

He followed me into the kitchen, which looked even worse, since Ted had left behind a chalky film on the cabinets and counters when he dusted for fingerprints.

Larry Joe looked around the room, his mouth agape. "What the hell?"

"The short answer is that we were robbed. Someone took our computer, but the sheriff has already recovered it, and it appears to be undamaged. Let's go sit on the sofa, and I'll fill you in on the details."

We went back into the living room and sat on our drop cloth–covered furniture. I asked Larry Joe not to interrupt until I had told him the whole story; then I proceeded to tell him all about Ralph and the security tapes and last night's break-in. The words came out rapid fire, as if I were trying to say it all in one breath. By the time I finished, Larry Joe's face and ears were bright red. His face turns red when he's mad, but usually his ears redden only when he's embarrassed. Since I didn't think he was blushing, I feared the red ears signaled a level of rage I had heretofore not witnessed. I instinctively grabbed a pillow and clasped it against my body as some kind of emotional defense. Not that I believed my husband would ever actually hit me, but I felt emotionally exposed and vulnerable.

Larry Joe said nothing. He stood, walked out the front door, slamming it behind him. In a moment, I heard the truck door slam and the tires squeal as he peeled out of the driveway.

I hurled myself face-first onto the sofa and had a really good cry.

I'd known Larry Joe, literally, all my life. Our parents were friends; we went to the same church and the same school, although he was a grade ahead of me. Growing up, I never fantasized about being Mrs. Larry Joe McKay, although by the time we were in high school, I did acknowledge that he was pretty cute. I guess I just assumed that I would end up marrying a man from some more exotic place—an *exotic place* being defined as anywhere other than Dixie, Tennessee.

When we ended up at Middle Tennessee State University at the same time, Larry Joe and I seemed to gravitate naturally toward each other. As romance began to blossom between us, it dawned on me that we were already friends, that I'd always had feelings for him, however latent, and I suddenly just knew for certain he was the right one for me. His current behavior, however, might cause me to entertain doubts.

Chapter 24

After I was all cried out, I went in the bathroom and washed my face. The image in the mirror was as appetizing as warmed-over chitlins. Since I looked my absolute worst, naturally, the doorbell rang. It was Dave.

"You okay?" he asked, eyeing me with a look of genuine concern.

"I've had better days. If you're looking for Larry Joe, he's not here, and I don't know where he is. You can try his cell phone. He's not talking to me, but he might answer the phone for you."

"Sometimes it's better not to say anything when we're upset," he said encouragingly. "I'm sure Larry Joe will come around."

I decided I just couldn't think about that right now, so I asked Dave if he had turned up anything when talking to Ray Franklin.

"He backed up Ralph's alibi, as expected. But when I asked where he and Ralph had first met, without missing a beat, he said Darrell Farrell had introduced them. Remember how jumpy Ralph got when I asked him the same question?"

"Yeah, I do. But what does that mean?"

"It confirms, for me at least, that Ralph was lying—and he's not very good at it. I'm on my way back to the station to have a go at Ralph again before his lawyer shows up. Maybe I can make him nervous enough that he'll slip and say something he doesn't mean to. And I just finished interviewing your neighbor, Mrs. Cleats. She took a Valium last night and didn't see or hear anything."

Figures. The one time I wanted her to be nosy, she wasn't on the job.

"Dave, when you do talk to Larry Joe, for the record, I told him about taking the tapes, about handing them over to you, about Ray and Bobo appearing on the tape, and about Ralph's veiled threats. I did not tell him about breaking into Ray's camper. I didn't think he could handle all that at once—or maybe I couldn't handle it. Whatever, there it is."

After Dave left, I just couldn't bring myself to shower in the tub that had served as my hidey-hole the night before. I tossed a few things in a tote bag, drove back to Di's place. Di wasn't home, so I let myself in with the spare key.

After a hot shower and another cup of coffee I'd reheated in the microwave, I tried to decide what to do with myself. I didn't want to go into the office, since I felt as if I might burst into tears at any moment. That might not make the best impression on clients. Thank God, I didn't have an event today. But I didn't want to be just sitting around the house if and when Larry Joe turned up. My quandary was resolved when I checked my cell phone messages and saw that I'd received a voice mail from my mother while I was in the shower.

"Olivia Louise, call me or come by the house as soon as you get this message." *Click.*

Whenever my mom addresses me by my first and middle name, I know she's piqued about something. It was a safe bet that she'd already heard about the break-in at my house from someone other than me.

I slapped on some makeup and drove over to Mama's. I might as well get it over with. I figured, if I was lucky, I'd get a little sympathy and maybe even some cake or pie out of the visit.

I tapped on her side door as I opened it, then walked into the kitchen. I spied more than half a chocolate cake calling to me from the kitchen counter, as well as half a pot of coffee. I called out to let my mother know I was there, as I retrieved a mug and a plate from the cabinet.

Mama hurried in, wearing a housecoat of many colors that would probably best be described as a muumuu. She grabbed me by the shoulders and looked me over, as if expecting to see bruises. "Are you okay? Why in the world didn't you call me?"

"I'm unharmed, just tired and a little shaken up. I was up half the night, talking to the police."

"You've changed your hair. I like it. It gives you some height. Now, darlin', you sit down and let me pour you some coffee. Would you like me to scramble you some eggs?"

"I'd rather have cake," I said, with what I hoped was a pitiable expression on my face. She gave me a slightly disapproving look but put a slice of cake on my plate, nonetheless. After she had poured herself a cup of coffee, she sat down at the table across from me. I knew she was waiting for details.

"How did you hear about the break-in so early this morning?"

"Sylvia called. She had talked to Edna Cleats."

Damn that woman. Was it juvenile for me to fantasize about egging my neighbor's house?

I decided the best way to placate Mama would be to let her know a few details that the sheriff probably hadn't revealed to Mrs. Cleats.

"The sheriff has arrested Ralph Harvey. They found our computer in his truck."

My mother was momentarily speechless, so I savored a bite of moist chocolate cake. It was definitely the highlight of my day so far.

"Did Larry Joe catch Ralph in the house?"

"Larry Joe wasn't at home. He was spending the night at the hospital with his dad. I thought I heard someone coming in, so I hid behind the shower curtain until I heard them leave, and then I contacted the sheriff."

"Oh, my heavens. You could have been killed," she said, reaching across to hold my hand. I sat there, waiting for her to release my hand so I could continue eating cake. "How did the sheriff get onto Ralph?"

"I recognized his voice. He had someone else with him, whose voice I couldn't identify. Dave went to Ralph's house and found the computer sitting in plain sight in Ralph's truck."

"Surely you didn't spend the rest of the night in that house by yourself?"

I had no choice but to drop the other shoe. "No. I stayed over at Di's."

"Why in the world would you call her instead of calling your own mother, for heaven's sake?"

I felt the tide of my mother's sympathy quickly ebbing away from me.

"For the same reason I didn't tell Larry Joe about it until this morning. I didn't want to wake you up or worry you."

"Well, I suppose," she said dubiously. "How did Larry Joe react to Ralph's arrest?"

"He's mad enough to spit nails," I said, which was true, although I wasn't sure whether the preponderance of his anger was aimed at Ralph or at me. Just thinking about the way Larry Joe had left the house, unable to speak or even look at me, made tears well up in my eyes again.

Her maternal sympathy again flowed generously in my direction. Mama scooted her chair beside mine and put an arm around me. She smooshed my head to her bosom, and I let the tears fall.

When I pulled up to the house, I noticed Larry Joe's car in the driveway. The garage door was open, and he was fiddling with something at the back of the garage. My first instinct was to go straight into the house, avoiding him altogether. But I decided to risk a confrontation.

"Hey, honey. Whatcha doing?" I said, keeping my distance.

"I'm installing a dead bolt on this door into the backyard. Dave said the intruders made easy work of getting in through this spring lock," he said, without looking my way.

"That's a good idea. It'll make me feel safer." I lingered for a moment in the awkward silence, then turned toward the house.

"There's doughnuts on the kitchen table," Larry Joe said as I opened the door.

His voice was still gruff, and he wasn't looking at me, but he was making a peace offering of doughnuts. That had to be a good sign, right? I peeked inside the doughnut box and noticed he had picked a variety of my favorites. Definitely a very good sign.

After wiping a damp cloth over the cabinets and counters to eliminate most of the chalky residue Ted had left behind when he dusted for prints, I made some fresh coffee and sat down at the kitchen table, facing the door into the garage. I was hoping that this way, Larry Joe wouldn't be able to avoid looking at me when he came in. Even his yelling at me would be better than the current state of affairs.

I waited, one eye on the door. Staring at the door through which intruders had entered last night brought back the feeling of dread I'd felt while hiding as they rifled through my home. I sipped on coffee, still feeling dull, even though I had already had way more than my usual dose of caffeine for the day. The events of the past week, especially the past twelve hours, had left me physically, mentally, and emotionally weary.

Larry Joe walked in, head down, and glanced up at me briefly before stepping over to the sink to wash his hands.

"There's fresh coffee," I offered as an invitation to join me at the table.

My husband took a mug out of the cupboard,

poured himself some coffee, and sat down at the table.

"Larry Joe, I just—"

"Wait, Liv. Before you say anything, just let me get this off my chest."

I nodded and waited for brimstone.

"I'm so mad at Ralph Harvey right now, I think I could kill him with my bare hands. That he would use McKay's as a vehicle to run drugs, or that he might even be mixed up with killing those two kids, I can't even . . . But that he would have the nerve to break into this house—for whatever reason—and with you here by yourself . . .

"But most of all that you could put yourself in harm's way, taking those tapes, getting mixed up in a murder investigation . . . I know your heart was in the right place, and you were trying to clear any suspicions about me or Dad. But, damn it, Liv, you could have been . . . You have to promise me here and now that you'll stay out of this and let Dave do his job. If anything ever happened to you, I don't know what I'd . . ." His voice trailed off, as he was choked up with emotion.

Despite his ramblings, I knew exactly what Larry Joe was trying to say. That he loves me. The new dead bolt and the doughnuts said as much. I knelt beside his chair and wrapped my arms around his shoulders. He put his hands to my waist and picked me up as he arose from the chair. After a nice long bear hug and a flurry of kisses, he leaned forward and let my feet touch the floor.

"You should eat those doughnuts before they get stale," he said, with that lopsided grin that still makes my heart race.

I really didn't need to add doughnuts on top of chocolate cake. But I couldn't hurt his feelings, could I?

I savored a jelly-filled doughnut and made conversation about noninflammatory topics for a few minutes.

"Hon, I'd love to stay home today, but I've got to go into McKay's. I've been away from work so much lately with Dad, and now this whole mess with Ralph . . ."

"It's fine, honey. I should put in some time at the office myself."

He kissed me and turned for the door.

"Larry Joe, if you should run into Ralph, please don't do anything crazy."

"Crazier than him breaking into our house?" His face turned red at the mere thought of it. He took a deep breath and continued, "Don't worry. I don't expect to run into Ralph. Charlene's packing up the stuff in his office and writing out a check for two weeks' severance pay as we speak, and our attorney is going to deliver both to Ralph's attorney, as well as a notice that Ralph will be arrested for trespassing if he steps foot on company property.

"By the way, here's the new key to the back door," he said, taking a key from his pocket and placing it on the counter. "And be sure to keep the kitchen door locked—even when the garage door is closed, okay? I'll be home before dark."

Chapter 25

The new lock on the back door, as well as Larry Joe's fiercely protective streak, did make me feel better. That, plus the fact that Larry Joe was now actually speaking to me. I decided to follow my husband's cue and go to the office. Keeping busy just now was probably the best thing for both of us. Besides, I had a bridesmaids' tea to put on tomorrow and needed to touch base with my assistant, Holly, and the baker.

I stepped into Sweet Deal Realty before heading upstairs to my office.

"My phone's been ringing off the hook the past hour or so, with folks wanting to know the scoop on your home invasion," Winette said as I walked through the front door. "Word on the street is Ralph Harvey broke into your house, and you bashed him over the head with a cast-iron skillet, tied him up, and held him until the police arrived. Any truth to that?"

"Some," I said as I laid my purse on her desk and sat down. "Ralph Harvey and some unknown person did break into the house and steal our computer. I didn't apprehend him, but the sheriff arrested him a short time later and found the computer in his truck."

"Why in the world would he do a fool thing like that? Seems like folks in this town have just lost their minds. Were you and Larry Joe in the house when he broke in?"

"Larry Joe was at the hospital with his dad. I was hiding behind the shower curtain."

"Girl, a shower curtain's no good hiding place. Didn't you ever see that movie *Psycho*?"

Fortunately, the image of Janet Leigh getting stabbed repeatedly in the shower had not occurred to me last night, while I was cowering behind the shower curtain.

"Winette, if anyone asks, please do me a favor and don't tell them I'm in the office. I'm going to work at my desk, organizing and getting invoices in order. I don't feel much like talking to anyone, and I really don't care to keep reliving the events of last night."

"Will do. Why are you even here today, after such a distressing night?"

"I'm hoping staying busy with work will keep my mind on the safe side of sanity."

After I checked in with the bakery and confirmed with Holly the schedule to set up for the bridesmaids' tea, I actually did manage to finish up some odds and ends. I was leaving the office at about 5:00 p.m. when I got a text from Di, telling me to call ASAP.

"What's up?"

"Can you come over in a few minutes? Dave's on

his way over with Chinese takeout, and he says he has some news about Rudy and Ralph."

"Sure. I can come by, but I don't want to intrude on your dinner with Dave. Would you rather just call me later?"

"You're not intruding. Despite whatever lurid fantasies you may have, we're only having dinner."

Dave was going in through Di's front door when I pulled up to her trailer. I dawdled, digging around in my purse and putting on lipstick, before getting out of the car. I wanted to give Di and Dave time for a kiss or two, should they be so inclined.

Di was putting plates on the table and Dave was opening paper cartons and releasing the intoxicating aroma of garlic, ginger, and soy sauce.

"We've got more than enough. Help yourself to some moo goo gai pan or General Tso's chicken," Di said.

"No thanks. I plan to eat dinner with Larry Joe in a while. I will have a Diet Coke, though," I said, opening the fridge and helping myself. "Di said you had some news about Rudy and Ralph?"

"Yep," Dave said as he sat and scooted his chair up to the table. "Andy, the cop friend I told you was at the concert in Nashville last night, decided to keep an eye on Rudy after the show. He caught him smoking pot in the parking lot and found enough marijuana on his person to arrest him for possession with intent to sell."

"I thought it was heroin, not marijuana, that they found being smuggled on the trucks," Di said.

"It was. Rudy was just falling back into old habits. But the FBI seized the opportunity to have Rudy remanded to federal custody as a person of interest in an ongoing drug-smuggling investigation. Andy said the federal boys had picked Rudy up within an hour of his being booked at the downtown precinct."

"Which must mean they were keeping tabs on Rudy, too," I said.

"No doubt. But the real kicker is, since Rudy had been arrested on a couple of minor drug charges before, although one was as a minor, the Feds were able to use the threat of potential prison time to get Rudy to talk."

The General Tso's proved too great a temptation. I grabbed one of the plastic forks and speared a bite from Di's plate.

"What did he say?" Di and I asked, almost in unison.

"I don't know all the details yet. But, apparently, Rudy implicated Ralph in a big way. It seems Rudy came late to the party. He says, anyway, that he didn't know anything about the drugs operation until after the Farrells had been killed. He claims it was at that point that Ralph recruited him to take over Darrell's part of the operation on the trucks."

"Wow," I said. We all fell silent, and I forked another piece of chicken into my mouth.

"What happens now?" Di said.

"Well, the FBI wants to take Ralph into custody so they can work him over about his role in the smuggling operation, now that Rudy is willing to testify against him. I told them this afternoon that I'd like to hang on to Ralph since he has a possible connection to two homicides. But I've got squat to go on for the murders at this point, and if I don't hand Ralph over to the Feds by the morning, they'll just get a court order to have him remanded to their custody, anyway.

"Dooley, the agent in charge, says he'll share the transcript of Ralph's interrogation and let me question Ralph again in a couple of days, after they've wrapped up with him. I might as well try to foster good will with Dooley so he'll keep me in the loop."

Dave's walkie-talkie screeched.

"This is Dave, over."

"Sheriff, Ted just called in a four-fifty-nine and a possible one-eighty-seven at the mini storage, over."

"Ten-four, I'm on my way."

Dave stood up and put on his hat.

"What do all those numbers mean? Is it serious?" Di asked.

"Yeah, it's serious. We've got a dead body at the storage place."

Chapter 26

Dave hurried out the door as Di and I sat in a stunned and confused silence.

"I wonder if somebody discovered a dead and decomposing body in one of the storage units?" I said.

"If it was decomposing, I hope it was dead," Di said in her trademark deadpan manner.

"Thanks again for being there for me last night. I guess I should head home."

"If you're in a hurry to go home, does that mean things are okay with you and Larry Joe?"

"I think so. Keep your fingers crossed."

I ran by the grocery and picked up a salad bag, a bag of frozen broccoli and cauliflower, and a couple of boneless chicken breasts. At home I panfried the chicken and topped it with some store-bought marinara sauce before popping it in the oven to melt a bit of mozzarella cheese on top. It wasn't exactly gourmet, but it was the best I could pull together on short notice. Besides, Larry Joe likes pretty much anything covered with marinara sauce.

When I heard the garage door opening, I quickly lit candles and placed them in the center of the table.

Larry Joe had a grocery store–variety bouquet of flowers clutched against his heart. "It's not much, but I wanted to get you something," he said sheepishly.

"They're beautiful."

He handed me the flowers, wrapped his arms around me, and swept me off the floor with a passionate embrace. After I relished a flurry of kisses across my face from my sweet husband, my feet finally touched the floor, both literally and figuratively.

"Dinner smells good, honey."

I placed the flowers in a vase and sat them on the table, alongside the candles. Larry Joe uncorked a bottle of red wine and retrieved some goblets from a cabinet shelf.

"I guess I'll have to limit myself to one glass of wine. I'm awful sorry, hon, but I'm going to have to go back to work after dinner. I should be home shortly after the three-to-eleven shift is over. With Ralph gone, it's a little chaotic in the shop. And, as if we weren't already shorthanded on mechanics, Rudy's mom called this morning and said Rudy wouldn't be at work today because he was 'indisposed.'"

"He's indisposed, all right," I said. "He's in jail."

I filled Larry Joe in on Rudy getting arrested in Nashville, getting picked up by the Feds, and squealing on Ralph to save his own sorry patootie.

"That's the best news I've had all day," Larry Joe said. "Not that I'm losing another mechanic, but that Ralph will be doing some time. His lawyer had the nerve to tell our lawyer that Ralph may sue if we fire him before he's been found guilty in a court of law. It's a good thing that lawyer talked to Bill Scott instead of me. I think I would have wrung his scrawny little neck. Bill handled it, though. He told him Ralph was just suspended without pay until after his trial. And even after we gave him the box of stuff Charlene packed up from Ralph's office, he kept trying to insist that Ralph had a right to come on the property, with an escort, to check for his belongings. Bill held the line and told him he would not be allowed on the property for any reason, pending his trial."

"Hmm. Honey, maybe you should call and tell Dave that Ralph seems all hot to go back to McKay's and look around. If he left something there connected to the drug trafficking, Ralph—or somebody who isn't locked up right now—may try to break in late at night to retrieve whatever it is. Dave may want to keep an eye on things there."

"Maybe I should take along my shotgun and keep an eye on things myself tonight."

"No, you shouldn't," I said emphatically. "Besides, I am not ready to spend the night alone in this house just yet. Not after last night. And I was kind of looking forward to having you sleep next to me tonight, too."

"Okay," he said, his pursed lips relaxing into a weak smile. "I don't really want to kill anybody, anyway. I wouldn't mind beating the crap out of Ralph Harvey, though." Larry Joe walked over and kissed the top of my head. "Keep your motor running. I'll be home by eleven thirty. Please keep your cell phone with you tonight. And, just in case, you'd better think up a new hiding place—everybody in town knows about that shower curtain by now."

Larry Joe left for work, and I cleared away the dishes. I couldn't help but worry about my stressed-out, overworked husband. With Ralph, Rudy, Duane, and Darrell gone, and his dad still in the hospital, he was struggling to keep everything going with a skeleton crew.

I gathered supplies to paint my neglected finger-nails and flipped on the TV in the den—the old nineteen-inch television from my mom's sewing room, which she insisted we use until we got a new set. I was only half listening to the news when a breaking bulletin caught my attention, prompting me to punch up the plus sign on the volume button.

"This just in. A man was found dead at the Lock-Ur-Stock Mini Storage near Dixie, Tennessee, this evening. Unconfirmed reports indicate the dead man was the manager of the storage facility and may have interrupted a burglar in one of the units. Sheriff Eulyse 'Dave' Davidson declined comment on the reports, saying that the investigation was in the early stages and that the man's identity is not being released pending notification of the next of kin."

I clicked off the TV, and my cell phone rang.

"Did you see the news?" Di asked.

"Yeah, just now. Have you talked to Dave?"

"No, and I doubt I'll hear from him tonight if he's got a fresh homicide on his hands—to add to the two unsolved murders he's already working on."

"I hope the TV news is wrong about the manager being the victim. Tim Morgan and his wife go to our church. They're a sweet couple."

* * *

About 10:00 p.m. I called my mother-in-law to make sure she had made it home safely from the hospital and to get an update on Larry Joe's dad. She was both excited that the doctor might let Daddy Wayne come home on Monday and worried that it might be too soon.

Still feeling uneasy after the break-in, and feeling creeped out by a new murder at the storage place, I waited up for Larry Joe. True to his word, he was home before 11:30 p.m. We went straight to bed.

Since we woke up the next morning in the same position in which we had fallen asleep—curled up together spoon-style—I could only assume that we had slept so soundly that neither of us had moved a muscle all night. We slept too late to make it to the early church service, and I had to start setting up for the bridesmaids' tea around 11:00 a.m. And although I could definitely use the prayers, I was honestly too tired to make the extra effort to make it to the early service, anyway. I did put forth the effort to whip up some waffles for breakfast.

"By the way, honey, I was so tired, I forgot to tell you I talked to your mom. She said the doctor might let your dad go home tomorrow."

"I hope it's not too soon."

"That's just what your mama said."

Larry Joe retrieved a couple of plates from the cabinet, and I plated up breakfast.

"I phoned Dave last night and told him about Ralph seeming anxious to go on company property for some reason and what you said about him or one of his accomplices maybe trying to slip in at night. He said they'd try to keep an eye on things. But honestly, he's got his hands full now with Tim Morgan's murder."

"Oh, no. So it really was Tim? I sure do hate that."

"Me too. He was a good guy." Larry Joe took a big swig of coffee and doused his waffles with sorghum molasses. "And another thing, Dave said it was Darrell Farrell's storage unit that was broken into. Whoever it was hauled off just about everything and killed Tim in the process."

"Oh, Lord, will this never end?"

I hadn't even entertained the possibility that the murder at the storage place could be connected with the other murders, but the robbery of the Civil War artifacts made it seem likely.

After breakfast, we sprawled on the sofa in the den and divided up the Sunday newspaper from Memphis. I perused the sales circulars, while Larry Joe read the comics aloud. A little after 10:00 a.m., Larry Joe headed out to check on his mom and dad and to find out if there were any definite plans to release Daddy Wayne from the hospital tomorrow.

After he left, I took a quick shower and dressed. As soon as I was in the car, I gave Di a call on my cell. She had heard the news report confirming Tim Morgan as the murder victim, and she really didn't know anything new about the case. I relayed the news that my father-in-law might get to come home from the hospital tomorrow. Mostly, we commiserated about the duress Dave and Larry Joe both were dealing with at present.

"I'm really worried about Dave with all the stress he's under—and all the stress he heaps on himself.

He actually feels responsible, at least partly, for Tim Morgan's murder."

"How can he believe that?" I asked.

"Well, it seems Tim's widow lashed out at Dave when he went to talk to her, saying how Tim wouldn't have been in harm's way if Dave had hauled off all the expensive Civil War artifacts in Darrell's storage unit instead of leaving them there. But you and I both know there's not enough room in the tiny evidence room at the sheriff's office for all that stuff and the FBI wouldn't take it."

"Dave's been in law enforcement long enough to know that the grieving widow was just trying to make sense of a senseless crime and lashed out at him because he was handy," I said.

"I know. But since it seems pretty certain that this murder is linked somehow to the Farrells' murders, Dave thinks if he had caught their murderer by now, Tim would still be alive. Though I don't know what more he thinks he could do. He's working day and night, trying to solve this case."

"Of course. And as much as I hate what happened to Tim, he knew better than to confront a thief like that. If he had just called the sheriff, maybe the Farrells' killer would be in jail right now—and Tim would still be alive."

Although I'd spent more time lately thinking about hospitals and suspects and murders, today I had to pull myself together and concentrate on work. I had a bridesmaids' tea to put on this afternoon.

After a quick stop at the bakery to pick up the raspberry-lemon bars, mini cupcakes, and petits fours I'd ordered, I drove to Meemaw Carter's house, a Victorian much like my own home—minus the scaffolding and drop cloths.

I tapped on the screen door as I entered.

"It's Liv McKay."

"Come on back, darlin'. I'm in the kitchen."

Meemaw was assembling finger sandwiches, which she had opted to make herself. On the counter, I also spied wax paper lined with strawberries that had been dipped in chocolate. I arranged the desserts on cake pedestals and placed the chocolate-covered strawberries on a platter.

"That's probably Holly," I said after hearing a car pull up in the driveway. "We'll start setting up in the backyard."

I left Meemaw to arrange the homemade sandwiches on a multitiered plate stand, which held a variety of her best china plates. There were chicken salad with pecan sandwiches and sandwiches spread with pimento cheese, sometimes referred to as Southern caviar. Meanwhile, I went out to meet Holly, and the two of us unloaded tables and decorations from her van and my SUV.

We set up a round-topped table in the backyard, beside a gazebo, and draped it with gauzy lavender tablecloths. Two giant red maples provided pleasing shade for both the screened gazebo and the table next to it. Holly set out Meemaw's best china dinner plates and tucked a pink rose beside each. We arranged antique costume jewelry, foraged from Meemaw's personal collection, around a centerpiece of light pink roses and dark pink peonies. The jewelry added just the right touch. A wrapped package containing a mirrored compact on which the recipient's name was engraved—the bride's gift to her bridesmaids—was placed in front of each plate.

The table was circled by a charming assortment of mismatched chairs from Meemaw's kitchen, living room, and parlor. An antique-style picture frame sporting each bridesmaid's initials on parchment paper was hung from the back of each chair with lavender satin ribbon. Inside the gazebo, the sandwiches and desserts and pitchers of lemon and mint-infused iced tea were placed on a cloth-draped table adorned with pots of trailing ivy and a centerpiece of Verbascum spikes with blooms in shades of buff, rose, and lavender.

Holly and I stepped back to admire our work. Meemaw came out and joined us.

"Liv, darlin', this is beautiful. Exactly what I wanted—simple Southern elegance," she said. "I wish you were planning the wedding. You wouldn't believe some of the tacky decorations Andrea's mother has dreamed up for the reception. She's not from here, you know. But I try to keep my mouth shut. My sweet girl will make a beautiful bride, anyhow. And thank the Lord, she's marrying a local boy."

Clearly, Andrea's mother is related to Meemaw only by marriage, and I'm sure Meemaw never lets her forget it.

The bride and her friends began arriving in their pretty party dresses. Holly snapped several group and candid shots of the young women and uploaded them to the bride and groom's photo-sharing site on the Web.

After hugs all around, Meemaw fastened a corsage

to her granddaughter's dress with an antique hat pin and gave her a peck on the cheek.

"Aren't you joining us, Meemaw?" Andrea asked as she paused at the back door.

"Naw, sugar. You go and visit with your friends. I got things to do."

I switched on the speakers and hit PLAY on an iPod holding a mix of tunes put together by the bride. Then I wrapped my arm around Meemaw, who had tears spilling over her lower lashes.

"You're a sweet granny, Meemaw Carter," I said, giving her a gentle squeeze.

Maybe not such a prize as a mother-in-law, I thought to myself, *but a sweet granny*.

"Oh, don't go getting all sappy on me," Meemaw said before wandering back into the kitchen.

I left Holly to keep an eye on things, and to keep Meemaw company, and arranged to meet her later in the afternoon to break down the tables and load the van.

As I drove home, the last thing on my mind was another party, especially an unplanned, spur-of-the-moment kind of party. But we never know what the day may hold.

I had just kicked off my shoes and plopped down at the kitchen table with a glass of iced tea when the phone rang. It was Di, and she was still fretting over Dave carrying the weight of the world on his shoulders.

"I'm not sure Dave will be able to cope if these murders go unsolved," Di said. "I mean, he was a homicide detective in Nashville for six years, and while he had a good record, some murders just don't get solved. Of course, in a city the size of Nashville there was always a big case to move on to, something to take his mind off the one who got away, but here . . ."

"Yeah. It's been at least five or six years since we had a murder here in Dixie—and that was a clear-cut case of domestic violence. They knew who the killer was," I said.

"Dave doesn't have the same resources that Nashville does, either. And the Feds are no help. They're really only interested in the drug trafficking, not the murders. And if the murders were committed by professionals hired by some drug lord, how will Dave ever be able to track them down?"

"I don't know about Tim's killer, but I don't think the Farrell brothers were killed by a pro. I mean, they weren't shot in the head. They each had a big hole in their chest. And I don't think a pro would have dumped them in that garage." I paused. "Wait a minute," I said excitedly. "What about all those security cameras at the mini storage? Maybe they got some pictures of the murderer."

"The cameras at the gate and facing the storage unit were bashed in, but they're checking the surveillance footage to see if any images of him were captured, and they're also checking the keypad at the gate to see what code was entered."

"We'll just have to keep our fingers crossed," I said.

We both fell silent for a long moment.

"Liv, could you maybe get Larry Joe to talk Dave into playing some golf or going fishing—anything to take his mind off work for a while?"

"I can't even talk Larry Joe into taking a break, with everything that's going on at McKay's and with his dad."

"You could invite Dave and me over tonight to watch a movie."

"On our fabulous nineteen-inch television? You know we haven't bought a new TV since Ralph smashed the old one."

"Oh, yeah."

"I could invite you and Dave over for a fancy dinner. I really would like to do something nice for Dave. The way he rushed over here after the break-in and all. Of course, I'm running short on time to pull together a fancy dinner for tonight."

"Who says it has to be fancy? We could have a backyard barbecue. I'll help fix the stuff to go with it," Di said.

"That's a good idea. I'll get Larry Joe to throw some steaks on the grill, and I can pick up some potato salad from the grocery store deli."

"I'll toss a green salad and ice down a watermelon."

"Put some beer on ice with that watermelon and I think we're set. Are you sure you can drag Dave away from work?"

"He'll be there, I promise. I mean, the man has to eat, anyway, right?"

"Good. Shall we say about seven o'clock?"

I called Larry Joe, and he was amenable to having Dave and Di for dinner. He was also more than amenable to the idea of a fat, juicy steak.

I went back to Meemaw Carter's to help Holly pack up.

"How'd the party go?"

"It was lovely," Holly said. "After taking some pictures and pouring iced tea for the girls, I kept Meemaw company in the kitchen and helped wash up the dishes. Meemaw told me sweet stories about Andrea when she was growing up. It's obvious she worships that child. I have to admit, I think pretty highly of Andrea and her friends after today. The girls were so sweet. After they finished lunch, they all descended on the kitchen, bringing a plate of desserts to Meemaw and wearing her costume jewelry, which they oohed and aahed over, saying how it made them feel so glamorous. And Andrea started telling stories about Meemaw. It just made her grandmother's day."

"Oh, that's wonderful," I said. "Holly, I'm so glad you had the idea to put out the jewelry as a table decoration. I think we can mark this bridal tea down as a smashing success."

As a party planner, I provide the sets and the props, but the real magic happens when the hosts and the guests take the stage and create the kind of special moments that can't be planned.

After we unloaded and stowed the tables and other gear in the office storage area, I ran by the grocery store to get the potato salad and, most importantly, some thick T-bone steaks.

After everything was chilled and marinating, I freshened up my make-up and changed into a cute shorts set that I'd worn only once or twice all summer. By the time I was dressed and had advised Larry Joe to put on a clean shirt, it was nearly time for our guests.

Di tapped on the kitchen door as she entered, with a wrapped salad bowl in hand. Dave went straight through to the backyard with an ice cooler packed with beers and a small seedless watermelon.

"Dave insists he can't stay too long, even though he's not officially on duty. But I'm hoping we can get him to stop looking at his watch, at least for a while."

"Don't worry. Just firing up the grill seemed to improve Larry Joe's frame of mind. Once Dave's had a couple of beers and inhaled the aroma of that Grade A beef, he'll relax a bit."

"The scent of charcoal and lighter fluid does seem to put men in a good mood," Di noted.

The guys were talking baseball when we joined them on the patio. Di and I didn't interrupt but exchanged knowing smiles. Larry Joe put the steaks on the grill, and he and Dave started philosophizing about the perfectly cooked steak, somewhere between still mooing and not quite medium rare.

"You ladies sure are being quiet," Larry Joe said. "It worries me when they go quiet," he added, turning to Dave.

"Oh, we're just enjoying the nice weather," I said.

The temperature was still in the low eighties, but it was shady, with a faint breeze.

"Yeah, in another month the leaves will be changing colors," Di said.

I requested that Larry Joe make my steak a little less "perfect" and a little more done than his. Di concurred. Larry Joe laid a sizzling steak with a smoky aroma and perfectly seared grill marks on each of our plates. We helped ourselves to the side dishes and gathered around the patio table. An umbrella shaded the table; the scalloped material rimming it flapped gently in the breeze.

"So, Larry Joe, are they going to let your dad come home tomorrow?" Di asked.

"Doc Chase has ordered some tests in the morning. If he likes the look of things, he plans to cut Dad loose tomorrow afternoon."

"That's great news," Di said. "Do you reckon he'll think about retirement now?"

"I don't think it's on his mind, but it's on mine and Mama's. I doubt we can talk him into a full retirement just yet, but I'm damn sure going to make him cut back his hours."

"I just may put in for retirement if there's one more murder in this town," Dave said. "Although, it might not be up to me. The voters may decide to put me out to pasture when the next election rolls around."

"Dave, not one single person in town has said a word about getting rid of you," I said. "My mama's a main branch on the grapevine. If she hasn't heard about it, it hasn't been said."

"I think folks around here know we're lucky to have someone with your experience on the job," Larry Joe added.

"I appreciate the vote of confidence," Dave said.

"Have you had any luck with the footage from the security cameras at the storage place?" Di asked.

"Not yet. Not only did the killer bash in the cameras, but he went in the office and smashed the hard drive, too. I sent the hard drive and the cameras to the state crime lab. They looked them over and say they might be able to retrieve something useful. We should know something in a few days."

"At least you can eliminate some suspects from

the list for Tim's murder," I said. "Since we know Ralph and Rudy and Bobo were locked up."

"Ralph and Rudy were locked up. Still are," Dave said. "But Bobo was released before the murder. A couple of top-tier attorneys—way above his pay grade—got him out on bail. Somebody with deep pockets is looking out for him."

"So Bobo's back on the list," Di said.

"And don't forget Ray Franklin. He was Ralph's alibi for our break-in, and I just don't trust him," I said.

"They're both on my list," Dave said. "Unfortunately, it's a long list. That Carl Adams—the one who broke into the storage unit last week—was supposed to be quietly checking around with some collectors who've been robbed to see if they could identify any of the goods in Darrell's storage room. Any one of those collectors could have broken in, or hired someone to break in, to retrieve their stuff. I'm driving up to Nashville tomorrow to question Adams and find out who all he's shown the photographs to."

I hated to see Dave so down. He looked like a kid who woke up Christmas morning to find that Santa had passed him by.

We never got around to slicing open the watermelon, but I talked Dave into having some ice cream with chocolate syrup and chopped pecans. If I'd had a candy cane, I'd have given him that, too.

After arguing about who should keep the uncut watermelon, Di carried it into the house and plopped it on the bottom shelf of our fridge. She and Dave said their good-byes to us and left together in Dave's truck.

Larry Joe and I started clearing the patio table.

"Is it getting serious with those two?" he asked.

"Your guess is as good as mine," I said. "Di won't talk about it."

"When a woman won't talk about something, it's serious."

Larry Joe's chauvinist remark rankled me a little. At the same time, I couldn't help wondering if he was right.

Chapter 27

Since it was Monday, I decided to start the week off right by trying to get back into a normal routine. I had breakfast with Larry Joe and got to the office before 8:30 a.m. To my surprise, it didn't look like early risers Winette and Mr. Sweet had made it in when I arrived, which is anything but normal.

At little before lunchtime, I made a trip downstairs to use the facilities. I mentioned to Winette that I had noticed they weren't in the office as early as usual for them. Apparently, Mr. Sweet had had some unpleasant plumbing issues at home that had required immediate attention. Winette said she had had a breakfast meeting with some nervous clients.

"They're a cute little couple looking to buy their first house," Winette said. "They've been preapproved by the bank for a loan, and they're trying to buy a house that costs less than they're approved for—which I completely support. I'd never try to push people into buying a house they can't afford. But now they've decided that their three-year-old little girl is intellectually gifted, and they want to make sure they'll be able to afford tuition for a private school. Lord, after spending two hours around that child, I can tell you she's just a cute but very average toddler. Of course, I couldn't say that to her parents."

"Whoa. That's a minefield. How did you handle it?"

"I suggested that they set up a savings account for little Isabella and put a few dollars a month in it for her future. I told them that settling into a place of their own, where they could establish a sense of belonging, would be very healthy for the child. And I also advised them to check out the optional programs at the local public schools to see what they have to offer," Winette said.

"You're a genius, Winette," I said with sincerity. "But I think all three-year-olds seem gifted. I know my niece, Lulu, does. Maybe that's just the age when their personalities really start to shine."

"That's also the age when they start asserting their little attitudes, as I remember from my own son and was reminded of this morning by Miss Isabella. Her parents worship the ground she stomps her tiny feet on. But they're young. They'll learn."

"Really? Are you trying to convince me that you don't worship the ground Marcus walks on anymore?"

"Clearly, my child is exceptional. He's making straight As in college, and he inherited his mama's good looks." Winette let loose a laugh track–worthy guffaw, punctuated by a sigh. "So when is Auntie Winette going to get to spoil little Miss Lulu again?"

"I think my sister and her family are coming to

Mama's for Thanksgiving. And by that time, Lulu should have a new little brother or sister, too."

"Oh, my goodness," Winette said. "I didn't realize your sister was so far along."

A little before noon, my cell phone rang, and it was Larry Joe, telling me that the doctor would be releasing Daddy Wayne from the hospital this afternoon.

"I'm going to the hospital to fetch Daddy. Could you go to the house and help Mama? She's all in a dither, saying she needs to get things ready before he comes home. I don't think there's really anything that needs to be done, but some hand-holding might calm her down."

"Sure, honey. Have they fed your dad lunch?"

"No. I think he'll need to eat when he gets home."

"Okay. I'll help your mom fix lunch. That should keep her occupied, and then we can all sit down at the table and eat with your dad. Maybe that'll help him feel like things are getting back to normal. See you two in a bit," I said before hanging up.

"Did I hear you say Mr. McKay is coming home today?"

"Yes, finally."

"Well, praise Jesus. That is good news."

I phoned my mother-in-law to set the plan in motion. Larry Joe was right; she was beside herself, trying to decide whether to set up Daddy Wayne in the downstairs bedroom or in his recliner, which of his pajamas would be most comfortable, if there was a clear path for his walker, and so on. I could tell right away I needed to get her focused on lunch.

"Oh, my goodness," she said. "It didn't even occur to me that they wouldn't serve him lunch at the hospital. I've been thinking only about what to make for supper, and I'm not sure what I have—"

I interrupted. "Miss Betty, I think we should just keep it simple for lunch. How about tomato soup and grilled cheese sandwiches? Larry Joe and I will join you two for lunch, and I think Daddy Wayne will be happy just to sit down at the table with his family and eat something other than hospital food."

She was quiet for a moment. "I suppose you're right, dear. I guess soup is okay, but do you think grilled cheese is healthy? We're going to have to watch his diet closely from now on, you know."

"You're right. Tell you what, you brew some fresh iced tea, unsweetened, and I'll run by the grocery store and pick up some whole-wheat bread and low-fat cheese—and low-sodium tomato soup, just for good measure."

She was pleased with the menu and asked me to purchase a few other groceries, as well. At the store, I also picked up some salt substitute, which Dr. Chase had suggested. I figured we could replace the salt in the shaker with it and hope my father-in-law wouldn't notice the difference.

After lunch, I cleared up the dishes, while Larry Joe helped his dad get settled in. Daddy Wayne decided it would be easier to get up and down from the recliner, since his leg was still paining him. Miss Betty tucked a sheet around the recliner seat and back so he wouldn't get too hot against the leather. I walked into the den just in time to hear my father-in-law pumping Larry Joe for information about work.

"I know you've been keeping me mostly in the dark about this murder and drug-smuggling business, and honestly, I couldn't think about much of anything with that blasted heart monitor constantly beeping at me. But now I need you to bring me up to speed on things, son. I need to know what's going on in my own company, damn it. I'm not a child. It's more stressful for me not knowing."

"Okay, Dad. Tomorrow I'll come by and fill you in on everything. But today I just want you to rest. Plus, I need to go to the office and take care of some business. I already spent half the day hauling your carcass home, you know."

"All right, go on. Get out of here."

We left as my mother-in-law smothered Daddy Wayne with attention, and he complained with a smile on his face.

Larry Joe and I held hands as we walked down his parents' driveway. He kissed me before I climbed into the SUV and he walked to his truck, parked by the curb.

"Are you really going to tell your dad *everything*?" I asked doubtfully.

"Everything he needs to know."

I had planned to head straight to the office. But I glanced at my watch and noted that Di was probably getting home from work about now. I decided to drop by and visit for a few minutes, let her know the good news about Daddy Wayne coming home.

She was standing on her front deck, just unlocking the front door, when I pulled up. She turned and waved at me to come on in.

"I'm glad Larry Joe's dad finally got to come home," she said, pouring us a couple of glasses of iced tea. "Maybe now he and Miss Betty can get some rest. Nobody ever gets a decent night's sleep at the hospital, with machines beeping and nurses coming in and out all the time."

"I hope so. The old coot really gave us a scare," I said. "You should have seen Miss Betty fussing over him—and him loving every minute of it, complaining all the while."

Di kicked off her shoes and joined me at the dining table next to the front window. She pulled back the tinfoil covering the plate between us, which I'd had my eye on. Underneath were a half dozen chocolate-chip cookies that a lady at the post office had sent home with her. I helped myself to one. Savoring a moist, chewy bite, I looked out through the blinds and spotted a car parked across from Di's trailer.

I didn't recognize the driver. Taking a closer look, I noted that both the driver and the passenger were wearing dress shirts, unbuttoned at the throat, and black sunglasses and were sitting in a nondescript American-made sedan. I could feel the heat of flames rising up my face.

"The nerve of those, those . . . FBI agents," I blurted out.

"What?" Di said. She peered out the blinds and added, "Yeah, they look like some kind of cops, all right."

"After all they've put us through," I said, still steamed. "Hauling Larry Joe and his dad in for questioning, stressing Daddy Wayne into a heart attack. Now they've got the nerve to put me and my best friend under surveillance. I'll not have it, not on the very day Daddy Wayne finally got to come home from the hospital."

I jumped up and stormed out the door. Di tried

to tell me to wait a minute, but I was filled with a righteous wrath.

They averted their eyes as I walked toward the car. The passenger even held up a newspaper to pretend he was reading.

I tapped on the car window. The driver rolled it down slightly and said, "Go away, lady. We're working here."

"I know you're working, Mr. FBI man. You're working overtime at harassing my family, and I'm fed up with it. Why don't you try tracking down some real criminals for a change, instead of persecuting innocent people—"

The driver interrupted me, saying that they weren't interested in me or my family and that I should get lost before I blew their cover.

"I'll blow your cover, all right. I'm calling the sheriff right now and filing a complaint."

The driver started the engine and said, "You just do that, lady. We'll call him, too. I'm going to circle the block. And when I get back, you'd better be gone."

He drove off.

"I'm not going anywhere," I said, shaking my fist at his taillights.

I went back into Di's, still shaking, and started digging around in my purse, looking for my phone. As soon as I pulled it out, it buzzed. It was Dave.

"Dave, I was just about to call you," I said, oblivious to the obvious irony of his calling at that precise moment.

He dressed me down in his bad-cop voice, without letting me get a word in.

"They were running surveillance, but they were not watching you."

"Dave, they were parked directly in front of Di's. Who else could they have been watching?"

"If they were watching Di's, they would not have been parked right in front of her place," he said in a condescending tone, which didn't sit well with me. "They're staking out her neighbor three doors down. Bobo has been known to spend time with the woman who lives there."

After a stunned silence, I quietly said, "Oh." Then my anger flared up again. "Well, you could have told us about her."

"I didn't tell you, because I didn't want you two to go in and try to question her yourselves. Now, stay away from the neighbor and stay the hell away from the FBI agents, or so help me, I'll throw you in a cell. And you better hope and pray that the neighbor was too busy to overhear your little snit. If you've blown their cover, I won't intervene when the FBI takes you into custody for interfering with a criminal investigation," Dave snarled before hanging up.

I collapsed onto the dining chair and looked at Di with the humiliated eyes of a puppy that had just gotten spanked with a rolled-up newspaper. "Since Dave wasn't exactly whispering, I assume you heard what he said."

"Most of it."

"So Bobo's girlfriend lives just a few doors down from you," I said. "Do you think she knows what kind of man he is, what he's mixed up in?"

"I'm not sure she cares as long as he pays cash," Di said nonchalantly.

"Are you saying there's a hooker living just a few doors away from you?"

"Everybody has to live somewhere," Di said. "Anyway, it's not like it's a full-time gig. She also works at a strip club."

"And you never told me this?"

"I only know her to speak to. We don't hang out or anything," Di said. "Besides, I wasn't really sure she was hooking until recently, when I saw Jake Robbins leaving her place with a smile on his face. I knew there was no way anybody would make out with Jake unless there was money involved."

I mulled that over as I crammed half a cookie into my big mouth.

Chapter 28

This week had pretty much been a blur for me—but that's been a good thing. Holly and I had been crazy busy putting together a plan to present to the Dodds for their daughter's engagement party and getting ready for the Erdmans' party, including talking to a nervous Mrs. Erdman at least three times a day. And Larry Joe had been just as busy at work, getting caught up, as well as interviewing candidates for supervisor and mechanic jobs.

But it was a really good kind of busy. We had no reason to visit the hospital, and I scarcely had time to think about the murders all week. Plus, Mrs. Erdman had the deep freezer in her garage removed as soon as the sheriff was finished with it, and she promptly had it replaced with a new, even bigger freezer, which was even now keeping our ice sculptures icy.

It was Friday night—time for the Erdmans' party. I had invested so much time in this party, I was determined that it would go off without a hitch, and that Mrs. Erdman would be impressed, in spite of her cranky self.

The guests were set to arrive at 7:00 p.m. I had been on the go since 7:00 a.m.

At three o'clock, I had done a preliminary check of the house and yard. Earlier in the day their gardener had wrapped twinkle lights around the trunk and branches of a small magnolia tree in the backyard, as well as weaving lights through a wisteria-covered arbor. *Check*.

Kenny had installed a small stage for the Dixieland band, and Holly had attached small foam collars to fresh magnolia blooms to keep them afloat in the swimming pool. While the chrysanthemums and marigolds in the Erdmans' backyard were natural deterrents for mosquitoes, we had added a few citronella torches for extra protection. *Check*.

Around 3:30 p.m., the florist had arrived and placed arrangements in the living room, dining room, and entry hall, and on the screened porch, at my direction. His assistant had wrapped the banister with greenery, accentuated by magnolia blossoms every few feet. *Check*.

At four o'clock, the catering team had arrived. I suddenly realized Mrs. Erdman, who had been trailing me like a bloodhound, had disappeared from the scene. While I was grateful for the break, I was also worried about what she might be up to. Mr. Erdman passed through, so I asked about his wife.

"She's holed up in her bathroom, trying to make herself beautiful. It should take a while," he said with his usual charm.

"By the way, Mr. Erdman, you can certainly drink

whatever you choose in your own home, but I'm not sure the bartender will be comfortable with actually serving the bootleg whiskey."

"That's fine. I'll keep Vern's private stock in my study, and discriminating drinkers can help themselves. Oh, and before I forget, here's your payment," he said, handing me a folded piece of paper. *Big fat check.*

At five o'clock, the bartenders—we had two for the evening—had set up separate bars for the ladies and the men. The ladies' bar would feature mint juleps and fruity cocktails, while the men's bar would offer whiskeys, a variety of choice liquors, and imported beers.

At 5:45 p.m., the band had arrived, had got set up, and had done a sound check. I had grabbed my bag from the car and had changed into black slacks and a white blouse, similar to the clothes the waitstaff was wearing. Some parties I leave once they are under way, but I planned to remain at this one for the duration.

At 6:15 p.m. two guys from the catering crew had carefully lifted the ice sculptures from the freezer and set them on a cart, rolled them into the dining room, and had placed them on the buffet table. I had dimmed some of the overhead lights and had made adjustments to the brightness of a spotlight directed at the center of the table to highlight the sculptures. I had to admit, they looked pretty impressive.

At 6:30 p.m. I had phoned the limo drivers to make sure they were en route to the hotel to pick up the guests. Even the ones who lived in Memphis were staying overnight, since the alcohol would be flowing freely.

At 6:55 p.m. Mrs. Erdman appeared at the top of the stairs just as the doorbell rang. It was show time. I gestured to see if she wanted me to open the door. She nodded regally. I welcomed the guests and allowed the hostess to make her grand entrance.

It was a surreal sight, the women wearing elaborate floor-length gowns lined with starched petticoats. Two of the women were wearing actual hoopskirts. They cut a wide swath through the house, and the waiters performed some nimble moves to avoid getting mowed down by the formidable frocks.

While the women were feeling glamorous, the men were feeling comfortable in baggy overalls and tattered shirts. One rather hairy man was shirtless inside his overalls. Although Mrs. Erdman must have insisted that Walter shave, most of the men, as well as one of the women, were sporting stubble.

The guys piled their plates high with food and hit the bar. The ladies milled around the buffet table, chatting and nibbling daintily. Waiters brought platters and plates over to one woman, who appeared to be lodged in the sofa, disabled by her hoopskirt.

The women ambled out onto the screened porch and sat on chairs lining the patio, near the band, which was playing some mellow Dixieland tunes. An hour or so into the party, Mr. Erdman walked over and extended his hand, asking his wife to dance, keeping his word without having to be prodded— at least not publicly. The other husbands followed his cue, although a couple of them didn't look very happy about it. After a couple of dances, most of the men wandered back into the house to smoke cigars in Mr. Erdman's study, and the women strolled back and forth from the garden to the buffet table and bar.

The festivities continued in this genteel manner until about 10:30 p.m. I wasn't aware of it at the time, but at some point during the evening, the men had replaced the contents of the refined bottles of bourbon the bartender was using to make mint juleps with some of Vern's moonshine. Mr. Erdman had told me the moonshine was more than 180 proof. After witnessing its effects, I don't doubt it for a minute.

I first noticed that some of the ladies were beginning to talk and laugh quite loudly. One woman was guffawing and slapping the knee of the woman next to her, while another lady was punctuating her laughs with a series of piggy snorts. But my first clue that something was seriously amiss came when an exceptionally endowed woman's boobs tumbled out of her plunging neckline, and she just giggled as she flashed the band.

I searched the group for Mrs. Erdman, fearing she wouldn't react well to this impropriety. She was holding her stomach and leaning over her knees. I held my breath, fearing the worst, until I realized she was doubled over with laughter.

While everyone was laughing, one of the hoop-skirted women knocked over a citronella torch and set another guest's dress on fire. One of the men gallantly threw her into the swimming pool. When the shirtless man stripped down to his Skivvies and joined her, I silently hoped he was her own husband and not someone else's.

The woman with the emancipated bosom finally

pulled herself together and tucked things back in place until her cleavage was contained—just barely—by her dress. The band had stopped playing, dumbstruck by the spectacle, so I waved my arms for them to start playing again. They struck up "When the Saints Go Marching In," and couples started marching and dancing around the yard.

Things continued along this course for the next few hours. I basically kept watch to make sure no one drowned or set anyone else on fire.

The dancing and aquatic exercises helped sober them up a bit. A little before 2:00 a.m. things started to quiet down. The bandleader, Wilson Washington, came over and sat down next to me.

"Ms. McKay, you know these folks very well?"

"Way better than I ever wanted to."

"I can understand that," he said, looking around. "Let me ask you something. The fat man who lives here tipped me a hundred bucks. Then, a bit later, he slipped me another hundred. I guess he forgot he'd already tipped me. I don't want to take advantage of folks when they've been drinking. Should I give him back a hundred?"

"Keep it. I think you've earned it."

"Yes, ma'am. Whatever they's paying you, I doubt it's enough. Can I ask you something else?"

"Sure, Mr. Washington. Shoot."

"I don't want to look unprofessional, 'cause I'd be happy to book another gig with you sometime. But the host told us we could help ourselves to some of his whiskey. Would you mind if we sipped a bit while we're packing up?"

"As long as you promise me you have a designated

driver. I'm certainly not letting any of these people get behind the wheel of a car."

"That's not a problem, ma'am. Calvin, our drummer, is a teetotaler. He made a vow to his mama."

"Then, by all means, enjoy."

"I like you, Mrs. McKay. You can hire us for one of your parties anytime."

Chapter 29

After the limo drivers and I had managed to get all the guests to the hotel and up to their rooms, I went back to the house and, with help from the bartenders, managed to put the Erdmans to bed. I got home and fell into bed myself about 4:30 a.m.

Larry Joe didn't stir, and he didn't wake me when he got up. I finally woke up about noon. And, despite the fact that I'd had only one shot of whiskey to steel my nerves the night before, I felt hung over.

Larry Joe was in the kitchen, making himself a sandwich, when I came downstairs.

"Tell me there's coffee," I said blearily.

"There is. I'll heat you up a cup in the microwave."

I downed a mug of coffee in three gulps.

"Whoa, lady," Larry Joe said before taking my cup and giving me a refill. "Rough night, huh?"

"Have you ever heard of one-hundred-eighty-proof whiskey?"

"Yeah. I think my granddaddy used it to strip paint."

"Let's just say things got a little out of hand after

everyone at the party had way, way too much to drink."

"Wow. I can't imagine the Erdmans getting liquored up and rowdy."

"You're lucky. I had to put them to bed, so I've now seen both of them nearly naked," I said, dropping my face into my hands.

"Hon, I think you're gonna need more than coffee to recover from that kind of trauma."

Larry Joe's cell phone buzzed, and he took the call.

"All right. I'll be there as soon as I can," he said. "Look, Liv, I hadn't planned to go in to work today, but there's a freight mix-up, and I have to go straighten it out."

"That's okay. I'll be fine. I don't plan to do anything more strenuous than get dressed, if that."

"The thing is, you can't stay here. Or, at least, I don't want you to stay here on your own."

"What are you talking about? Why?"

"Our attorney called this morning and told me Ralph has been released on bond. I don't think he'd be crazy enough to come to the house to talk to me about his job, but I don't want you here by yourself, just the same."

"You know, I'm eventually going to have to be in this house when you're not home, and Ralph's trial may not start for months. We're bound to run into him around town."

"I know, I know. Just humor me for now. It's still chaos at McKay's, and I can't deal with business and worry about your safety at the same time. Go shopping or go to your mama's. Whatever, please. I'll wrap things up at the garage as soon as I can. I'll call you when I'm heading home, okay?"

"Oh, okay. Just let me put on a bra."

I can't believe I agreed, but I knew I'd given him plenty of reason to worry about me recently. Besides, something about those dimples gets me every time.

He gave me a big hug and a kiss before he climbed into his truck and I got into the SUV. It was sweet of Larry Joe to worry over me—sweet, but inconvenient. I really didn't feel like shopping. I felt even less like listening to my mother for two hours. Plus, she'd want to hear all about the Erdmans' party, and I just didn't have the strength or the stomach to relive that just yet.

I drove down the street. Then I pulled over and texted Di to see if I could hang out at her place. She texted back in a moment. She was out but said I was welcome to make myself at home.

I flopped down in Di's recliner. After a few minutes I noticed there were some dishes in the sink. I figured the least I could do was wash up, considering how much time I'd been spending at Di's and what a high-maintenance friend I'd been lately.

After I had dried the last dish and put it away, I opened the refrigerator door and leaned in, searching for a Diet Coke. Suddenly, I was startled by a man's voice.

"Hey, babe. I picked up the groceries you asked for," Dave said, carrying two bags and kicking the front door closed behind him.

I stood up quickly, conking my head on the refrigerator ceiling in the process. I think it was an even bigger kick in the head for Dave when he realized it was me, not Di, he'd been talking to through the fridge door.

"Ah, Liv. Hi," he stammered. "I just picked up a few things at the grocery store for Di." He sat the grocery bags on the dining table. "I have her spare key . . . for emergencies," he said, tucking a key on its own little key ring into his pants pocket.

"Of course," I said, trying hard not to let the smile in my mind spread across my face. We both stood in awkward silence for a moment.

"Here. I'll put those groceries away," I said, thankful for something to do.

Dave muttered something like, "Well, then," and started to go.

"Dave, since you're here, can I ask you something?"

He looked nervous. I supposed he expected a question of a personal nature. He looked visibly relieved when I asked about Ralph and what would happen next.

Dave sat down at the table, and I took a seat on the sofa. He confirmed my concerns that it would likely be months before Ralph's trial began. Dave filled me in briefly on his trip to Nashville.

"I talked to Carl Adams. Fortunately for me, but unfortunately for him, Adams spent one day in the hospital and a couple of days laid up at home with a kidney stone last week. He had talked only to a couple of collectors about the possibly stolen goods in the storage unit. The Nashville police are going to interview the two guys he had talked to."

"Why is that fortunate for you?"

"It cuts down on the number of suspects for Tim Morgan's murder, in theory, anyway. In reality, the two collectors Adams talked to could have shared that information with several other people. And even if they both have alibis for the time of the murder, that doesn't mean they couldn't have hired someone to break into the storage place, who then panicked when Tim confronted him."

"I hate to bring it up, but did the FBI ever catch up to Bobo when he was visiting Di's neighbor?"

He glowered at me for only a moment.

"Yeah, you lucked out on that one. Apparently, the neighbor was busy entertaining when you raised the ruckus with the agents."

"Good," I said sheepishly.

Di came through the front door, momentarily interrupting the conversation.

"Hey, you two."

She didn't seem in the least unnerved to find her best friend and her boyfriend chatting at her place in her absence. She took a seat on the sofa beside me.

"I guess you picked up those groceries," she said, nodding to Dave. Then turning to me, she asked, "Why exactly are you hiding out here?"

"Ralph was released from custody today, and Larry Joe didn't feel comfortable with me being at the house by myself. Ralph's been warned that he's not permitted on-site at McKay's, pending the trial. Larry Joe's worried he might come to the house, trying to get his job back—which would be a huge waste of time. Larry Joe said he'd call me when he's headed home."

"So, how did the Erdmans' party go last night?" Di asked.

"I'll tell you about it one day—when I'm strong enough."

"*Okay*," Di said. "Dave, tell us about your trip."

Dave brought her up to speed on what happened in Nashville.

"What about the damaged hard drive from the storage place? Have they had any luck getting video off of it?" Di asked.

"No word yet," he said.

"Dave," I said, "assuming the person who murdered Tim is the same person who killed the Farrells, I don't think it likely that it's someone from Nashville or a professional brought in by some drug lord. I mean, the Farrells were both shot in the chest, not in the head, like a hit man might do. And I don't believe a hit man, or any out-of-towner, would have dumped the bodies at the Erdmans' house, would they?"

"In the first place, we can't assume it's the same killer. There's nothing in the evidence to make that case. Secondly, a hit man isn't necessarily a professional, in the sense of being experienced. It's just someone who's willing to kill for a certain amount of money."

"But if it was the same killer, that would rule out Ralph and Rudy, who were in custody at the time," I said, undeterred by Dave's line of reasoning. "So wouldn't that seem to make Bobo a likely suspect?"

"I don't think so," Dave said, promptly bursting my bubble without remorse. "Agent Dooley told me, unofficially, that while they haven't had Bobo under continuous surveillance, it was unlikely, based on their intel, that he was at the mini storage at the time of the murder. Which I interpret to mean they probably have some sort of tracking device on his car," Dave said.

"Did you ever get a chance to check out that Brad guy, Candy's insanely jealous boyfriend?" Di asked.

"No alibi for the likely time of the murders—although with one body in a deep freezer and the other one sweltering in an un-air-conditioned garage, the medical examiner could give us only an approximate time frame. And Brad has been arrested a few times for public drunkenness and assault," Dave said. "But I don't really like him for the murders. He has a black belt in karate and seems to like beating up on people with his bare hands. If he was going to kill Darrell, I think he'd want the satisfaction of beating the crap out of him first. And neither Darrell nor Duane had any injuries consistent with that."

"That has to make Ray Franklin the favorite suspect among the locals," Di asserted.

"He may be a generally suspicious character, and I don't like him any more than you do," Dave said. "In fact, if I had the manpower, I'd keep a closer eye on him. But he has an alibi for the time of Tim's murder. It's not necessarily bulletproof. A friend of his says they were at a movie together, and Ray has a ticket stub with the showtime on it. But without something to go on, that's enough to prevent me from arresting him or getting a search warrant. I checked with the theater. It's one of those second-run places, and they don't have any security cameras."

Sensing that Dave's morale was in a downward

spiral, Di quickly spoke up and offered us snacks and beverages.

"No, thanks. I should be going," Dave said, putting on his hat and rising to his feet. "I still need to run by and talk to Mrs. Donavan over on West Street, who insists she's the victim of a Peeping Tom."

"Are you referring to old Mrs. Donavan, who was the school librarian for ages?" I asked.

"That's the one. She phones the station at least every other week, and either Ted or I go by to talk to her probably once a month about her peeper."

"Do you think anybody's actually trying to sneak a peek at her wrinkly, dried-up self?" Di asked.

"I don't see how. I've never seen so much as a footprint or a broken twig along the side of the house. Besides which, she has a thorn bush growing right under her bedroom window. Nobody could get close to it without getting scratched up. I've bled myself more than once just walking past it."

"How long has this been going on?" I asked.

"At least twenty years, according to the sheriff's office files," Dave said.

After Dave left, Di freed her hair from the ponytail that was holding it in place and grabbed a Coke from the fridge.

"I feel sorry for Dave," I said, "having to investigate crimes both real and imagined."

"It's the real ones that he's losing sleep over—that all of us are losing sleep over," Di said. "Hey, I've got an idea. . . ." Di paused, staring into space.

"Let's hear it."

"Well, it scares me, because it sounds like something you'd dream up. But you know how Dave was just saying he'd keep tabs on Ray Franklin if he had more manpower?"

"Yeah."

"We could provide the manpower, kind of."

"What do you mean?" I said, leaning forward, feeling intrigued.

"There's only one road in and out of the trailer park, and Ray has to drive right past my place to come and go from his camper, right?"

"Right."

"So why couldn't we set up surveillance and keep an eye on him from my front window? We wouldn't try to follow him or anything crazy. But we could call Dave or Ted and let them know whenever he leaves. If they're available, they can track him for a bit. At the very least, we'd have some record of when he was home and when he wasn't, you know, in case anything else happens."

"I'm certainly game, but I don't know how helpful surveillance will be if it's not twenty-four-seven."

"Then let's make it twenty-four-seven—for a couple of days, anyway," Di said. "Hopefully, by that time, Dave will have something from the crime lab on those broken security cameras or something new from the Feds. I'm off today and tomorrow, and I can get someone to fill in for me at work on Monday."

"I don't have an event tomorrow, and I can certainly make a few phone calls from here to follow up with clients."

"And maybe Larry Joe could even help keep watch, too," Di said. "I really do think you should tell him what we're up to, with all you two have been through lately."

Di got on the phone to Dave, and I called Larry Joe to fill him in on our surveillance plan.

Dave reluctantly agreed to the plan, with the stipulation that under no circumstances would we follow Ray on our own. Larry Joe was surprisingly supportive. I think he liked the idea of knowing exactly where I'd be.

Di went out and walked far enough around the circle to Ray's place to spot his truck. He appeared to be at home. She changed clothes and set up her station by the window with a drink and snacks and told me to go on home and have supper with Larry Joe.

"Don't be too late getting back to relieve me, and I really do mean to relieve me," she said. "There's one flaw with our surveillance post, and it's that the bathroom window doesn't look out onto the road."

"Right. We're definitely going to need two people here to make the surveillance work," I said. "Call me if you need to leave your post by the window, and I'll come right over."

After supper, Larry Joe came with me to Di's place, and the three of us sat at the kitchen table, chatting, with one of us peering through the blinds at all times.

"You know, Di, it's probably not a bad idea for me to spend some time around here tonight," Larry Joe said with a grin. "With Liv spending the whole night here a couple of times lately, your neighbor might get the idea that you two are more just than friends."

"If Jake Robbins thought for one minute there was any girl-on-girl action happening over here, Dave would be arresting him as a Peeping Tom," Di said.

At about ten o'clock, Larry Joe suggested that Di

go on to bed to get some sleep and that I stretch out on the sofa and take a nap, while he manned surveillance for a couple of hours. I offered to make some coffee for him, but he was afraid it would keep him up later. Since he couldn't take time off from work just now—even on the weekend—we had decided he would take the first shift and then would go home and get a few hours' sleep before he left for the office.

Larry Joe awakened me at about 1:00 a.m. I went to the bedroom and woke up Di before he headed home, and took my post as the sentry by the window. Di and I swapped places a couple of times during the night. At about 6:00 a.m. Di put on a pot of coffee and made us some French toast. We took turns using the shower, and I put on the change of clothes I'd brought from home.

Ray finally came out of his lair and drove past at about 9:30 a.m. Di called Dave, who was driving an unmarked car for the day. A couple of hours later we saw Ray drive past. Ted, who had taken over surveillance duty from Dave, called to tell us he'd just seen Ray turn into the trailer park. Ray had gone to have breakfast at the diner, had gotten his hair cut at the barbershop, and had gone to the post office to check his P.O. box. Di relayed Ted's report, and we looked at each other, wondering if we could stand the excitement.

"He got a haircut," I said hopefully. "Maybe that means he's planning to meet someone or go somewhere more exciting than the diner later on."

At about half past noon Larry Joe phoned. He said he had planned to come by and see me at lunchtime, but felt like he should go by and check on his mom and dad.

"And the old coot's convinced we're hiding things from him about the business," Larry Joe said. "I'm worried he'll have another heart attack if I don't go and calm him down."

"Of course, honey. I'm sure Daddy Wayne is driving your mom crazy. She could do with some reinforcements."

As the afternoon dragged on, our surveillance detail started to feel like high school detention. We both lost the energy to carry on a conversation.

Di was dealing another hand of gin rummy when I spotted Ray's truck.

"Our quarry is on the move," I said.

Di phoned Dave, who simply said, "Thanks. I'll tell Ted," before hanging up.

"Let's hope Ted catches Ray doing something more interesting than getting his hair cut," I said just before laying down my cards and calling gin.

"Yeah, something as exciting as when Dave caught us in Ray's camper would be nice."

"That was a rough night. But I can't help wondering if there was something helpful in that diary that we missed."

"Surely, you're not suggesting that we steal it again?"

"No, of course not. I've already read it from cover to cover, anyway," I said, sounding as cranky as someone who'd lost sleep and been cooped up all day. "I know the DNA shows Ray is not Darrell and Duane's dad. Still, I don't think everything in the diary is make-believe. I mean, it's most likely a mix of fact and fiction, telling a story through Duane's childlike eyes."

"So, you think if we could sift fact from fiction, maybe we'd find clues."

"Exactly. Some things just don't add up. Like, remember how Duane wrote in his diary that Ray had to hide when their mom dropped by the apartment?"

"Yeah. So?"

"I've been thinking about it, and I don't believe that part was fiction," I said. "I mean, in his fantasy world, Duane had turned Ray into his long-lost dad. So wouldn't that fantasy world also include his mom and dad getting back together and all of them being one big happy family?"

"I suppose."

"I don't remember his exact words, but Duane wrote something like he thought his mom had a right to know, but Ray and Darrell didn't want to get her involved with what was going on. But that doesn't make any sense. If she thought Ray was just one of their reenactment friends, he wouldn't need to hide. She'd have no way of guessing they were mixed up in dealing drugs just because she saw Ray in their apartment."

"I don't follow," Di said.

"We know from the DNA that Ray isn't their real dad, but what if he had actually convinced Duane and Darrell that he *was* their real father? Then he could tell them he had to hide because their mom would immediately recognize him, and they shouldn't put her in danger because of their drug involvement, and whatever it was that had kept him in hiding all these years while they thought that he was dead."

"Only he knew that she wouldn't recognize him, because he's not who he was pretending to be," Di mused.

"Exactly!"

"I want to be as excited about this as you are, but I still don't get it," Di said.

"Don't you see? If he had scammed the boys into believing he was their real dad, he couldn't risk being seen by Tonya. Not because she would recognize him, but precisely because she *wouldn't*."

"Oh, yeah, I get it. He told them that she would recognize him and that he wanted to protect her. But the truth is, he knew she wouldn't recognize him, and it would blow his cover and mess up the scam he was running on the Farrell brothers."

"Right. If he bore any passing resemblance to their real father, that would be enough for the boys. They were just little kids when their dad went off to war. They knew what he looked like only through vague memories and maybe some faded photographs. But Tonya's a different story. She was a grown woman who was married to the man. She'd have known instantly that he wasn't their long-lost daddy."

"I get that. But what would Ray get out of trying to make them believe that he was their father?"

"Making them believe he was their father and had been on the run for years—God knows what kind of story he made up to explain that—would have given him huge leverage to manipulate them," I explained. "Here you have two guys who thought their daddy died more than a dozen years ago. Then, suddenly, he shows up, asking for their help. I imagine they would have done pretty much anything for him, and he used that to get them to smuggle drugs, and Lord knows what else, for him. He probably met them through reenacting and figured out how gullible they were, especially Duane, so he used that to his advantage. What I don't understand is why, after hiding from Tonya at the apartment, he would go to see her at her house that day I followed him."

"Why not?" Di said, leaping up from her chair and pacing with excitement. "Assuming Duane and Darrell never told her about their back-from-the-dead father, he could just show up at her door as Ray Franklin, friend and mentor to her late sons. He must have some angle, though. I mean, if he was low enough to scam those boys into believing he was their daddy, he isn't going to call on their mama just to express condolences."

"Oh, my God, Di, you're right. He may be afraid she knows something or that she'll figure out something when she sorts through her sons' belongings. We need to call Tonya and warn her about Ray. If we're on the right track about any of this diary stuff, she could be in real danger."

I looked up the number for Rascal's Bar and Grill and gave them a call. The waitress who answered said Tonya was scheduled to be at work, but she hadn't shown up. She said she had been calling Tonya's cell but couldn't get through.

"That don't mean much," the waitress said. "Cell phone reception is pretty bad out around her place. Still, it's not like her, not showing up for work."

After she hung up I told Di, "I remember not being able to get my cell phone to work that day I was at Tonya's. We'd better drive out there and warn her about Ray while we have Ted keeping an eye on him. I have a feeling that we'll all be ready to drop this surveillance job by tomorrow morning, anyway. You should probably call Dave to let him know where we we'll be."

The call to Dave went straight to voice mail, so Di called the dispatcher and left a message for the sheriff concerning our whereabouts. We jumped in Di's car and headed out of town.

"Oh my God, Di! 'One lie too many,'" I said as Di stomped her foot on the accelerator. "That was the last entry in Duane's diary. Maybe Darrell found out that Ray was a phony. Maybe that was the lie. And maybe Ray killed them because of it."

Chapter 30

Di and I barely talked during the drive out to Tonya's place, both of us preoccupied with thoughts of Ray. I did blurt out some profanities a couple of times as Di less than expertly negotiated the pothole-studded back roads of Delbert County at high speeds, bouncing us off our seats.

Di pulled into the driveway and slammed on the brakes. Tonya emerged from the house just as the two of us jumped out of the car with panicked looks on our faces.

"Tonya, thank God! Have you seen Ray Franklin recently?" I said.

"No," she said with a puzzled look. "Why would I?"

"It's a long story, but you may be in danger."

"From Ray?"

Di broke in, saying emphatically, "Tonya, do you have a friend you could stay with for a day or two? It really may not be safe for you to keep staying here on your own."

"I suppose so," Tonya said slowly. "Why don't

you two come in the house and tell me what's going on while I throw a few clothes in a bag?"

We stepped inside the house and then followed Tonya into her bedroom and talked as she thumbed through her closet.

"So, are you saying the sheriff thinks Ray Franklin killed my boys?"

"He's definitely a suspect," I said. "We're pretty sure Ray Franklin is not who he pretended to be. He may have deceived your sons into believing that he was their daddy, that their father wasn't really killed in Iraq."

"We have reason to believe Darrell found out that Ray was lying—and Ray killed both of the boys because of it," Di added.

"This is so hard to believe," Tonya said. "I don't really know Ray, but both my boys spoke highly of him. What kind of evidence does the sheriff have?"

"Duane's diary indicates that the boys thought Ray was their father," I said. "However, DNA tests prove Ray definitely is not their biological father. We think he scammed the boys into smuggling drugs for him through the trucking company with the ruse that they were helping their long-lost dad."

"It's also possible that he was even involved in the murder at the storage facility," Di added.

Tonya finished stuffing some clothes and toiletries into a small suitcase.

"We really should get going. We may not have a lot of time, and it's not safe here," Di said.

Tonya picked up the suitcase, and we all turned toward the bedroom door, just in time to see Ray

Franklin step out of the shadows in the hall and into the doorway, with a gun in his hand.

"That's a real in'eresting story, ladies. Unfortunately, sticking your noses where they don't belong can be real bad for your health. Let's step outside," he said, stepping back and motioning us into the hallway with the gun.

When we got to the back door, he shoved me into Di, forcing us into the backyard. He told us to keep walking, and I could see the bed of his truck sticking out from behind a shed.

"You can't get away with this!" I said. "The sheriff knows we're here."

"You really expect me to believe he'd let you two come out here if he thought there was any danger? Now, climb up into the back of the truck," he growled.

Di and I both froze.

"Move it!" he shouted.

We looked at each other and slowly climbed up into the bed of the truck. When we turned to face him, we could see Tonya tiptoeing up behind Ray with an extended rifle in her hands.

"Okay, ladies . . . ," Ray said with a sneer.

He started to say something else but was interrupted by a rifle blast to the back. His eyes went glassy and blood gurgled from a the corner of his mouth before he fell limply to the ground.

Horrified, but relieved, Di and I jumped down from the truck bed. But as we started walking toward Tonya, our relief quickly turned to dread when she raised the rifle and pointed the barrel squarely at us.

"You were right, girls. It's not safe here," Tonya said with a wicked smile.

"I—I don't understand . . . how," I stammered.

"I understand," Di said. "You helped Ray convince Darrell and Duane he was their long-lost daddy. Of course! The sheriff said Ray didn't even serve with their dad. He couldn't have pulled off the deception without your help. You gave him the photo of them as kids and the postcard they had written to their dad—everything he needed to persuade two gullible boys their father was still alive."

"How could you do that to your own sons?" I said, still reeling with disbelief.

"What do you know about it!" Tonya shouted, her eyes wide with rage. "I was seventeen when I got pregnant with Darrell. Bobby joined the army to support us. It was tight early on, but he made it through training, got promoted. Then he got sent to Iraq. We figured once he finished his tour, he'd get another promotion and we'd get stationed somewhere—maybe even get to see some of the world. Instead, I was a widow at twenty-three." Tears streaked her cheeks, but Tonya's face was still twisted in anger.

"That must've been real hard on you, being left to raise two little boys by yourself at such a young age," Di said, sounding sympathetic. I surmised that she was trying to keep Tonya talking, trying to keep her calm—hoping to keep her from pulling that trigger.

"You have no idea what it was like," Tonya said in a shrill voice. "I went from having a future to having nothing. I worked day and night to put food on the table and had to move in here with my grandmother. The price of keeping a roof over our heads was me being her slave. I not only worked at the bar, but I had to do the laundry and the cooking and the cleaning around here. I would have run off with just about any man to get away from her. But do you think any guy would take on a widow with two kids? Not for anything more than a one-night stand, I can tell you that."

My head told me I should follow Di's lead and try to humor Tonya, but my big mouth impulsively blurted out, "But your sons. It wasn't their fault." I immediately knew I'd made a big mistake.

Tonya steadied the rifle and walked toward us with slow, deliberate steps. We both froze. When she got to within inches of us, she suddenly lifted the rifle, pivoted the barrel over her shoulder, and slammed the rifle stock into the side of Di's head, knocking her to the ground. I looked down at Di, and before I could blink, Tonya had the rifle against my head. I could feel the edge of the cold metal pressing against my temple. A sudden wave of nausea washed over me, and I thought for a moment my knees would buckle.

"You don't have kids, do you?" she said, pushing the rifle hard against my skull.

I moved my lips, but no sound came out. I shook my head slightly.

"They worshipped their grandmother, who bad-mouthed me to them nonstop. And they whined about missing their daddy. How could they miss somebody they could barely remember? They treated me like the maid. The last time either one of them cared enough to give me a card for Mother's Day was when Duane brought one home for me that he'd made at school.

"The past two years things began to look up for me. First, that old biddy finally died and left me this house. Next, Darrell got a job, and I told him to move out and take his half-witted brother with him. Then I met Ray. Me and Ray had a chance to be happy together, if we could just get some money. He was doing some thieving and some penny-ante drug stuff and said he could parlay that into some big money if I could get my boys to move drugs through the trucking company. I knew they wouldn't do shit for me. But they'd do anything for their dead daddy."

"I understand," I said mildly, following Di's lead to try to calm Tonya down. "You were just trying to make some money. You never meant for anyone to get killed."

"Move," she said, jerking the gun to the right. "Just inside that shed, there's some rope. Pick it up and toss it over to me."

I did just as she told me.

"It's too bad the sheriff caught on to Ray. I guess I'll just have to figure out a way to spend all that money by myself. Now, grab Ray by the legs, drag him into the shed, and shut the door."

It took every ounce of my strength, fueled by a will to survive, to drag Ray's dead weight across the rutted dirt and into the shed.

"Now, take this rope and tie your friend up real tight."

"But I—I—I . . ."

"If you don't tie her up, I'll have no choice but to put a bullet through her head."

Fortunately, I could feel that Di was still breathing as I tied her up. Then I grabbed her under the arms and pulled her onto the back floorboard of Tonya's car, as Tonya instructed me to do. She tossed me the keys and told me to get into the driver's seat, while she climbed into the backseat.

"Now, you drive real careful exactly where I tell you. I've got this rifle barrel right up against your friend's head. You try anything stupid, and I'll blow her brains out."

As the sun sank into darkness, we snaked our way along back roads for over an hour. I was desperately trying to think of some way to get out of this alive. I decided if I saw a police vehicle of any kind, I was going to lay on the horn and swerve into the side of the car. Of course, you can never find a cop when you need one. In fact, we passed only two or three cars during the whole trip. I thought about running the car into one of them, but I figured I'd just end up getting some other innocent person killed.

The silence was maddening.

"Tonya, what happened?"

"I don't think I owe you any explanations. If you two had minded your own business, you wouldn't be in this situation."

I figured she wouldn't shoot me while I was driving, so I pressed my luck.

"Look, you plan to kill us, anyway. How did Darrell and Duane end up dead? I'm sure that wasn't the way you planned for things to turn out."

"No. Nobody had to die. But the boys started to get nervous when that idiot Bobo kept ramping up the delivery schedule. Darrell, who was never better than a C student, started to figure things out. He came by the house to ask me some questions and heard someone slipping out the kitchen door. He ran after him and discovered Ray. Darrell told him he was going to the cops. They started fighting. I panicked. I just grabbed the rifle and shot Darrell without thinking. After I fired the shot, I dropped to my knees, crying, and Ray lifted the gun from my hands.

"I didn't know Darrell had left Duane waiting in the car. But when he heard the shot, he came running around the side of the house, wearing that ridiculous uniform, still playing soldier, like a little kid. When Duane saw Ray standing over me with the gun, he yelled, 'Don't you hurt my mama!' and started running toward us. Ray raised the rifle and put a bullet through him. I couldn't believe that slow-witted fool actually tried to defend me. . . ." She sniffled as her voice trailed off.

I continued to drive, half dazed, with no idea where we were at or where we were going. When Tonya instructed me to turn onto Highway 22, I finally figured out where we were. We were near the Shiloh park and battlefield.

Please, God, let there be a park ranger out on patrol, I prayed silently.

We drove slowly along the winding park roads until Tonya instructed me to pull down a dirt road that disappeared into the woods, which were devoid of light but were filled with the sounds of owls and cicadas and crickets and unknown animals snapping twigs and crunching leaves as they moved through the forest. Still, I would have felt safer with anything in those dark woods than I did with Tonya. And I would have taken my chances and made a run for it if Tonya didn't have that rifle pressed against Di's head.

If I had any muscles, I would have tried to wrestle the rifle away from Tonya. I wished I had joined a gym. I wished I'd taken a karate class. I wished I could see Larry Joe just one more time.

Di moaned a little as I pulled her from the car. At least I knew for sure she was still alive. Tonya told me to drag Di over a rise into a small moonlit clearing. I complied and she followed us, keeping a tight grip on the rifle.

When the ground flattened out, Tonya said, "That's far enough."

"Tonya," I said hoarsely. "You don't have to do this."

"Shut up. You're done talking. You ladies are standing on hallowed ground. You may remember, if you ever took a school field trip to Shiloh, that this right here is the area known as the Hornet's Nest. About six thousand Union soldiers fought desperately to defend a line here. There were heavy casualties, and the Confederate troops eventually captured the Hornet's Nest, taking more than two thousand Yankees prisoner. You two are about to become part of history.

"I know this place looks pretty deserted. But starting tomorrow afternoon, trucks and vans filled with pretend soldiers will descend on Shiloh and start setting up camp. And on Saturday even more cars and trucks will show up, with people coming to watch. And when those fake bullets start flying and Union soldiers start retreating over that hill, they'll find you two here, plugged with very real bullets."

Chapter 31

Tonya raised the rifle and aimed it squarely at me. My head was swimming. I was sure I'd faint before she could shoot me. I hoped that meant I wouldn't feel the bullet rip through my flesh.

Suddenly I heard a rustling in the woods just beyond us and saw a flash of light, followed by what sounded like a stampede. Tonya swung around toward the noise. But before she could do anything else, two husky men in blue Civil War–era uniforms grabbed her by the arms and lifted her off the ground, knocking the rifle from her grasp. Several other Union soldiers, some of them carrying lanterns, raced in behind them.

The world started spinning under my feet. The next thing I remembered, I was lying on the ground, looking up at a bearded man who was kneeling beside me.

"You and your friend will be okay now, ma'am. We've called for the police and an ambulance. Good thing Ricky always has his friggin' cell phone on him, even though he's not supposed to when he's in uniform."

I felt my lips part in a faint smile as I grasped the man's calloused hand. "I've never been so glad to see a bunch of damn Yankees in all my life."

"Happy to oblige, ma'am," the bearded man said. "There actually isn't a battle scheduled this weekend. We're just setting up a period camp and doing some cannon-firing demonstrations. Certainly never expected to capture a rebel brandishing a rifle. If you want to see the Battle of Shiloh, you'll have to come back in early April," he said, giving me a smile and squeezing my hand.

"And the lady with the gun didn't quite finish that story she was telling," he said, casting a stolid glance toward Tonya, who was still struggling against her captors. "Federal forces went on to win the Battle of Shiloh."

Dave and Larry Joe and I were standing at her bedside when Di started to come to. She blinked and looked up at us blearily.

"Is that you there, Liv?"

"Yes, sweetie. I'm right here." I reached out and took her hand.

"Come closer," she said softly. "So I can kill you," she said a little less softly, tugging at my hand.

"Sounds like she's going to be just fine," Larry Joe said from the opposite side of her bed.

"That's right, Di," Dave said. "The doctor says you have a pretty nasty bump on your head. They had to put in a couple of stitches, and they're going to keep you here overnight for observation. But they did a brain scan and said everything looks good—which was a complete surprise to me. I figured both of you must have brain damage, going after Ray Franklin like you did."

"We thought Ted was keeping an eye on Ray. Besides, I called your voice mail and your dispatcher before we left," Di said, trying to sit up before plopping her head back onto the pillow with a moan.

"Whoa, there. Settle down," Dave said. "The doc doesn't want you trying to raise your head just yet."

"We had just gotten word from the crime lab that they had retrieved a bit of footage from the security cameras that clearly identified Ray. I was tied up on the phone with the state police, then the FBI, and didn't even see I had a voice mail from you," Dave said. "When you called Terry and left a message that you had gone to Tonya's, you didn't explain to her what that meant. She didn't realize it was a message of any urgency. So I didn't get the message until I called dispatch to check in. I hightailed it over to Tonya's house the minute I heard, but you were gone by then. If only Ray had left his place ten or fifteen minutes later, we would have had him in custody, and none of this would have happened to you."

"And Ray would be locked up, but still very much alive," I said.

"I called Dave when I got to Di's place and saw that you two were gone," Larry Joe said. "When he told me he'd found Di's car and Ray's body at Tonya's, but no sign of either of you . . ." Larry Joe started to get choked up, imagining what might have happened. I walked over and slipped my arm around his waist.

"Since there was no sign of Tonya, either, I had to

assume she was involved," Dave said. "I put out a BOLO in four states for all three of you, and we called in volunteers to comb the woods around Tonya's farm. Then, when Terry relayed the nine-one-one report that two women had been rescued at Shiloh by some Civil War reenactors and were being transported to the hospital, something told me I'd find you two here."

Dave sniffled and cleared his throat, trying to act like it was merely allergies that were making his eyes turn red. "I've never been so relieved to see somebody who drives me crazy as I was when I walked into the emergency room and saw you on that stretcher," he said, looking down at Di, his eyes all dewy.

"You were relieved," Di said incredulously. "I opened my eyes and saw this blinding light. For a minute I thought I must be dead—until I realized the light was fluorescent." Di ran her hand across the top of her head. "Oh, great. I have a bald spot. I'm going to look like a mangy dog."

"That's just where they had to put in the stitches. It's barely noticeable, really," Dave said unconvincingly.

The doctor came in to examine Di, along with a nurse, who shooed all of us out of the room.

"Dave," I said once we were out in the hallway, "Tonya told us most of the story leading up to her and Ray killing Darrell and Duane. If she decides to clam up and wait for her attorney, I can give you most of the details."

"Oh, she's been talking nonstop. Started the minute the reenactors nabbed her. I think she's trying to line up an insanity defense. I don't know. Maybe she's got a case. She seems pretty crazy to me."

"I see how the drug smuggling came into play, but how do all the stolen Confederate artifacts fit in?" I asked.

"Ray was part of a burglary ring connected with organized crime. That's how he first met Bobo and the drug end of the business. Ray was stealing expensive Confederate collectibles from shops and some individual collectors who were insured for the goods. They'd collect the insurance money and then resell the stuff on the black market. But the gear had to be stowed out of sight for a while, until things cooled off. Ray was getting a cut but figured out an angle to make even more money for himself by selling the artifacts to Darrell and Duane before he had to turn them back over to their fences."

"Why would Darrell and Duane go for that?" Larry Joe asked.

"They didn't know the goods were stolen. Ray convinced them that the collectibles were a good investment, that they could buy this stuff below market value, hang on to it for a year or so, and then resell it for a handsome profit. This scam served a dual purpose, because it helped keep Duane and Darrell from blowing too much of their cut of the drug-smuggling money and it funneled it directly into Ray's pockets," Dave said.

"Does that mean the collector from Nashville you caught at the storage unit was part of the theft ring?" I asked.

"No, he wasn't. He came into the picture when Darrell innocently sold a few items to him, not knowing they had been stolen. The ironic part is that they used the money from the stolen goods Darrell sold to Adams to buy a really nice sword for Ray as a Christmas present—the one Adams took from the storage unit. They sold the stuff without telling Ray because Darrell and Duane wanted the gift to be a surprise for him."

The doctor came out of Di's room and joined us in the hallway.

"I rechecked her pupils, and we're going to give her something for nausea. Things are looking pretty good, but I still want to monitor her overnight and do an MRI in the morning to be on the safe side."

"Is it okay for me to sit with her tonight?" Dave said.

"That's fine. Try not to let her get upset, and if you notice she seems confused or is slurring her words, call the nurses' station at once." The doctor looked over the chart on his clipboard and headed off down the hall.

"All right, then, Larry Joe. I'll stand watch with this lunatic, and you keep your eyes on that one," Dave said as he opened the door. He stepped back into Di's room, leaving Larry Joe and me alone in an empty hallway that smelled of disinfectant.

"I'm sure you've got a lecture in store for me, and maybe I even deserve it, but can you please save it for the morning?"

Larry Joe leaned over and planted a kiss on my forehead. "You're alive. You're safe. That's enough for me," he said. "For now, at least."

He took my hand, and we started walking toward the elevators.

Epilogue

After recuperating at home for a couple of days at Larry Joe's insistence, I was back at work. I had walked over to the real estate office and was chatting with Mr. Sweet when Winette fluttered through the front door with a big smile on her face.

"I sold a house yesterday. I've got a closing tomorrow. And I'm on my way to show a house to some prospects who are just itching to buy." She hurriedly grabbed some papers from her desk drawer. "Wish me luck. I'm going for a trifecta," Winette said, giving us a wink before exiting as quickly as she'd entered.

Mr. Sweet looked over at me with his typical deadpan expression. "I'm glad at least one of us is having some good luck."

"Dead people showed up at a meeting with my last clients," I said. "I figure it can only get better from there."

"I dunno," Mr. Sweet said. "Been my experience that dead people are less trouble than living ones."

My cell phone began to buzz. It was Mrs. Erdman, thanking me for planning the perfect anniversary party, telling me that everyone said they'd had such a wonderful time and that she and Mr. Erdman had decided to go on a second honeymoon, only this time to Italy instead of Alabama. She went on to say she wanted to book me for a New Year's Eve celebration and launched into a long monologue about all the wonderful ideas she had for the party, including having a large lighted orb descend from the top of a tree in their backyard. "It'll be just like Times Square," she gushed.

As I listened to her rattle on, a big smile involuntarily crept across my face. Things really were back to normal.

I love my job.

Tips for Hosting
Your Own Moonshine and
Magnolias Party

(Or alternately, for evening outdoor festivities, perhaps with less emphasis on alcoholic beverages, call it a Moonlight and Magnolias Party)

FASHION

Choosing from breezy summer dresses in pastels and florals to floor-length gowns and hoopskirts, you can decide what kind of Southern belle you want to be.

For the guys, jeans are a practical alternative to overalls. For men who want to go a bit dressier, light khakis and short-sleeved dress shirts are classic. If you add suspenders, all the better!

FOOD

You'd be hard-pressed to find a Southern buffet that doesn't have deviled eggs and cheese straws on it. Include them for authenticity. Fried chicken and waffles are a soul-food classic. Gussy it up a bit by cutting the waffles into cookie-size rounds, topping them with fried chicken tenders and a drizzle of molasses, and securing them with wooden skewers.

Add a Southern twist to standard party fare. For example, make your favorite spinach dip but substitute turnip greens for the spinach. Add a dash of hot sauce, and you're good to go.

DRINKS

It's hard to go wrong with whiskey. If you don't happen to have a cousin with a still, you can create the moonshine vibe by serving whiskey in mason jars. Be sure to plan for sleepover accommodations and designated drivers or taxis. Never let guests drink and drive.

Mint Julep
Yield: 1 serving

4 fresh mint sprigs, plus 1 sprig for garnish
1 teaspoon powdered sugar
2 teaspoons water
Shaved or crushed ice
3 ounces bourbon (or to taste)

Place the 4 mint sprigs, the powdered sugar, and the water in a highball glass and muddle the mint. Next, fill the glass partway with shaved or crushed ice and add the bourbon. Top with additional ice and garnish with the remaining mint sprig. Serve the mint julep at once with a straw.

Note: Bourbon, a type of whiskey, is a little sweeter than other whiskeys and is a traditional ingredient in mint juleps. Other bourbons may also be used, but Kentucky bourbon is the most authentic. Traditional recipes call for 1½ to 3 ounces of bourbon.

Note: For teetotaler friends—especially those who have made a vow to their mamas—offer a nonalcoholic version of the mint julep by substituting ginger ale or lemonade for the bourbon.

DECORATIONS

Scents and Sparkle

Floating magnolia blossoms and candles add a romantic ambience to any outdoor party.

Magnolia blossoms will float. But to keep them floating for longer periods of time, cut Styrofoam into thin pieces just smaller than the blooms and insert one stem into each piece of Styrofoam. If the magnolia blossoms are used as decorations in a swimming pool, be sure to turn off the pool filter, or the floating blossoms will all be drawn into it.

If you don't have a swimming pool, buy a plastic kiddie pool and spray paint it a dark color so the magnolia blossoms really pop. Fill the pool with water and place potted plants around the outside perimeter. Gently place the magnolia blossoms in the pool. The addition of floating candles adds sparkle and elegance.

Magnolia blossoms and floating candles can also be placed in water-filled half whiskey barrels and large galvanized tubs as a focal point in the backyard. Or line a walkway with gallon buckets of floating blossoms and candles to greet guests as they arrive.

Ice Sculptures

If you have your heart set on ice sculptures, they can add an impressive accent to your buffet table.

For large or custom ice sculptures, you will need to hire a professional. Ice sculptors can create anything out of ice, from a Plymouth Barracuda to a custom business logo. Prices can range from fifty dollars to five thousand dollars or more. Check out the National Ice Carving Association (Nica.org) to search for an ice sculptor in your area.

For a do-it-yourself approach, you can purchase ice molds from restaurant supply stores and online sources. One-time-use ice molds produce sculptures with fine details. They are also generally more expensive, ranging from sixty-five dollars to one hundred dollars for small standard styles.

Reusable molds run from about twenty dollars to forty-five dollars for popular styles that are twelve to twenty-four inches tall. These molds, also available online, can produce some nice pieces and are a good option for the budget minded or those who will use them over and over. Larger, more elaborate ice molds can also be purchased from specialty suppliers for five hundred dollars or more. Generally, the smaller, more affordable ice sculpture molds come in a limited number of popular designs, such as hearts, swans, bride and groom statues, dolphins, and angels.

Make sure you have enough freezer space to accommodate the ice sculptures, and keep in mind that many of the sculptures take at least forty-eight hours to freeze properly.

A BRIGHT IDEA
FROM THE BRIDAL TEA:
PHOTO SHARING

For the wedding, the bride and groom usually depend on a professional photographer. But for events like the bridal tea, bridal showers, bachelor and bachelorette parties, and the rehearsal dinner, casual snapshots taken with cell phone cameras are an easy and natural way to capture the moment— and share it instantly. Web-based photo storage and sharing sites, such as Shutterfly, Photobucket, and Snapfish, make it easy to share events with guests, friends, and family.

Shutterfly, for instance, enables users to upload, organize, edit, and share photo albums with others. Users set privacy controls, so they can share photos and videos with everyone or with just a small group. Plus, it's easy to sync photos from computer, mobile devices, and Facebook. Android, iOs, and Roku apps are available. And reasonably priced prints and other photo items, such as refrigerator magnets, can be ordered and picked up at stores, including Walgreens and Target.

Don't miss the next book
in the Liv and Di in Dixie series,

It's Your Party, Die If You Want To

On sale October 2016!

Chapter 1

I entered Town Square Diner and spotted Morgan Robison, who despite my druthers was meeting me for lunch. She was strategically positioned in a corner booth licking her chops, peering over the top of her menu at a well-built, younger man seated at the lunch counter. If he was typical of Morgan's usual choice in men, he was also married.

I was seemingly invisible until I cleared my throat and spoke her name.

"Liv McKay," she said, lifting her butt just high enough off the seat to give me a limp shoulder hug. "Sit down. I've been waiting for ages."

"Am I late?" I asked, knowing I wasn't.

"No matter. You're here now, and we have so much to talk about."

Morgan is president of the Professional Women's Alliance of Dixie. The group's unfortunate acronym is commonly pronounced *pee wad*. Our conversation mostly consisted of Morgan giving me marching orders for PWAD's annual retreat, set for the coming weekend.

"You're just a doll for taking care of this for me, Liv," Morgan said, answering the buzz of her cell phone as she leapt up from the table and hurried on her way—leaving me with the bill. But I figured picking up the check was a small price to pay for her to go away.

I strolled back to the office on the opposite side of the square, from which I operate my party-planning business. The October air was crisp and the red maples in front of the courthouse dabbed flames against the sky. Hay bales, gourds and scarecrows decorated several storefronts.

Before going up to my office, which is located above Sweet Deal Realty, I tucked into the real estate office to chat with Winette King, who works there as an agent. The bell on the front door jingled as I entered.

"How was lunch?" Winette said.

"I had lunch with Morgan Robison."

"You have my condolences," she said. "I suppose Morgan issued your assigned duties for the retreat. She e-mailed me my to-do list."

"What's she dumping on you?" I asked.

"Clean-up. I'm sure she thinks my people are well suited to cleaning. I probably remind her of the mammy she had as a child."

"No, she didn't," I said.

"Oh yes, she did."

Since Winette is the only active member of PWAD who's African-American—not to mention that she stands head and shoulders above Morgan in intellect, heart and moral fiber—it really chapped my hide that Morgan would ask her to do the clean-up. I can't say, however, that it came as a complete surprise. Morgan was raised with a silver spoon, the only child of one of the wealthiest families in the county. She's a vice-president of Dixie Savings and Loan. Her major qualification for the job is that her daddy owns the bank.

After standing with my mouth agape for a moment, I said, "I'll help with the cleaning up."

"You bet you will," Winette said, matter-of-factly.

"Better yet if you'd like, I'll swap jobs with you. Morgan wants me to babysit our guest speaker, Lucinda Grable."

"That ghost woman on TV?"

"Yep."

"No, thank-you. I'd just as soon hang onto my broom and dustpan," Winette said.

Unless you count the lady who won a set of luggage on *The Price is Right*, Lucinda Grable is the only television celebrity that the town of Dixie, Tennessee can lay claim to. She hosts a "paranormal reality" series on cable, called P.S. Ghost Encounters. The P stands for psychic and the S stands for scientific. I'm not sure how much of the show qualifies as scientific, or reality, for that matter. But it is entertaining.

Lucinda provides the psychic element as she senses and sometimes even talks to ghosts. She works with a team of investigators who use infrared cameras and other specialty equipment to demonstrate that some otherworldly phenomena are supposedly present.

"This may be a silly question, but is there any practical or sane reason that we're having a psychic as the guest speaker at our professional women's retreat?" Winette asked.

"Lucinda's supposed to tell us how she built her local ghost hunting business into a television empire. But, she's also going to try to make contact with ghosts in that little family cemetery down the hill from the lodge."

"Lord, help us," Winette said.

"Okay, Winette, I'm headed upstairs. Do you know what Mr. Sweet is up to? I haven't seen him at all today, or yesterday for that matter."

Nathan Sweet is my landlord and the "Sweet" of Sweet Deal Realty.

"He's involved in the development of that new shopping center they're building up on the highway. He spends more time investing in new development these days than he does in selling existing properties," she said. "The old coot's probably still got the first dollar he ever made, but he's busy making more money. You'd think at his age he'd want to retire and enjoy spending some of that legal tender before he kicks the bucket."

"Are you kidding? I bet he outlives both of us," I said.

"You're probably right," Winette said, tossing her head back and letting loose a room-filling laugh.

While my office is directly above Sweet Deal Realty, the entrance to the staircase leading up to the office is next door beneath a green awning that displays the name of the business, Liv 4 Fun. I had to choose a short business name, since the width of the glass door comprises the entirety of my street frontage. There's no restroom upstairs, so my rent includes use of the facilities in the real estate office.

Not completely convenient, but the rent's cheap and the location on the square is primo.

I had settled in at my desk and had touched base with a couple of vendors when my cell phone rang. I knew from the ringtone that it was my mother, but I answered anyway.

"Liv, jump in your car and get over here right this minute," she said in a panicked voice.

"Mama," I said. "What's happened? Are you okay?"

I heard some kind of tapping sounds.

"Oh, dear Lord," Mama said in a breathy voice before the phone went dead.

I grabbed my purse and raced down the stairs, hurrying to my car without even taking time to lock the office door.

My mom lives in a neighborhood just east of the town square, so I was in her driveway within four or five minutes of backing out of my parking space.

I rushed in through the kitchen door, which is never locked, and started calling for her. I ran through the house worried I might find her unconscious— or worse.

I finally found my mama, who stands almost six feet and weighs well over two hundred pounds, cowering in the doorway to the back porch, her eyes transfixed. She had one hand clutched to her chest and the other was holding a hoe.

Grab These Cozy Mysteries
from
Kensington Books

Available Wherever Books Are Sold!

All available as e-books, too!

Visit our website at **www.kensingtonbooks.com**